A Becky Hawk Murder Mystery

BLACK LAKE

A Becky Hawk Murder Mystery

By Robbie Lanier

TESSELLATA

Black Lake: A Becky Hawk Murder Mystery

First edition, 2023

TESSELLATA BOOKS

Printed in the United States of America

ISBN 978-1-7369492-7-6
Library of Congress Control Number: 2023917465

TESSELLATA BOOKS
Virginia, USA
editora@tessellata.org

To my mother,
Marie Penry

1

Her seclusion lasted ten days before she left the old house with a folded American flag under her arm. A gust of wind from the water greeted her with a blunt reminder that winter was near. A girl with an unfamiliar face and white ribbons in her hair pressed her nose against the back window of a passing school bus. A small hand waved. Becky returned it and cast a quick smile. She watched the girl keep waving while the bus drove away. Hesitantly, Becky left the porch and walked across the yard toward Dalton Street. She hoped they would be her first steps toward healing. Real healing this time.

Once a train depot, the police station stood between the tracks and waterfront. Rusted clips swung from rotting ropes on a flagpole there. She secured her flag and raised it to half-mast. Headlines blared through dew-covered, plastic sleeves of newspapers accumulated at the door. She knelt and picked up each one.

Inside, the office was as she'd left it. Her thermos sat on the desk. A paper bag containing a now stale peanut butter sandwich lay beside it. She placed the papers on the floor to dry then lifted a photograph of her and her husband. She kissed it. The black and white picture possessed the power to stir a different emotion in her each time she looked at it. She wanted a laugh badly that morning and reflected on the tight-fitting tuxedo he wore. But her spirits wouldn't change at will. She looked at his smile and dark eyes, which seemed to sparkle back at her. She remembered he'd been his happiest then. He'd told her so. She decided this would be her source of comfort for the day.

A tree faller's job brought them to Black Lake. Ed didn't mind the hard work, but something about the chief's position intrigued him when it became available. He applied even though he'd never done the work before. So, an invitation to an interview surprised him. The town council wanted a local man for the job, experience or not. He came home with a badge and smile. Chief Edward Hawk— Becky felt pride in the title even though the town employed just one officer.

The job description was simple: Check business doors at night. Handle the easy calls. Call the sheriff in the event of serious ones. But Ed applied himself more than required. He studied law books and wrote to the State Bureau of Investigation for evidence handling and crime scene preservation manuals. Long workdays preceded a few hours of night patrol. Becky felt happy for him, but missed his being home. Then, Ed somehow convinced the mayor and commissioners to create a second position. Chief's Assistant was the title. Answering the phone and writing reports for a small wage were the duties. For a brief period, Becky delighted in working with her husband. Then he was murdered.

She felt a new wave of depression while adjusting the thermostat and considered going home. Instead, she walked to the back room to make coffee. She was on her second cup when the phone rang. She found her pen and notepad. It made her feel better having something to do.

"Black Lake Police Department. May I help you?"

Kids walking to school were cutting through Pearl Wilson's lawn again, damaging her flower garden and wearing a trail in her grass. Becky had heard the complaint before, but enjoyed talking to the gabby woman that day. It was a distraction she needed. Pearl's voice eventually became gravelly before an extended coughing fit. She then caught her second wind and jumped into more complaints with a fervor before a quick goodbye.

Becky hand-wrote a detailed trespassing report and placed it in the basket for pickup. She realized the sheriff would need to know she'd returned and made a quick call to the county dispatcher before unwrapping the November 23rd edition of the Bolton Record. She read it, feeling guilty for finding some solace that Jackie would also soon spend her first Christmas as a widow. She thought of Officer Tippit too and wondered if he'd been married. The news didn't say. She closed the paper and now seriously considered going home.

Pull it together, dammit. You've still gotta live.

She looked at the picture again. It wasn't the first time she'd heard Ed speak to her since his death. She knew skeptics would say it was her grief riddled mind playing tricks on her. Becky believed differently. "I'm trying," she told him.

Her spirits rose a little when she remembered her standing invitation for free lunch. Black Lake Elementary offered it as a thank you for the mornings she worked the school crossing. Eating in the cafeteria saved her money and provided much needed company and conversation. But it was also where she'd learned just how fragile she'd become after Ed's death. She'd just finished a meal with Wendy Martin and other teachers when Principal Gentry entered with a pale face and walked to the table.

"Kennedy has been shot," he'd blurted out loudly enough to make several nearby kids turn. "They think he's dead."

Wendy's scream silenced the cafeteria.

The shock paralyzed Becky. Some of the kids around her cried. Becky wanted to comfort them, but couldn't. Her world had turned black again.

She spent the following days and nights in front of the television. She had to have the company of it and see others mourn with her. The emotions of Ed's death became raw again. Seeing Oswald shot live made sure of it. Each night, she chose the sofa over the bed then more than less passed out on it with a dangerous amount of sleeping pills in her.

"Well, look who's back." Sheriff Scotland smiled when she looked up. "I was headed this way when dispatch said you were working."

Becky noticed his wrinkled uniform shirt. He appeared tired. "Hello Sheriff." She took a swallow of coffee to clear her raspy voice. "How was Thanksgiving?" She motioned to a chair.

"Working. Just like every other damned day recently. Ate something like turkey and dressing that the jail served up." He sat with a tired gesture. "And drop the Sheriff crap. I've told you it's Pete." He twisted the corner of his mustache while his blue eyes examined her. "Good Lord, you look worse than me," he said. "You shouldn't be here. Let me take you by the clinic. Maybe you can get something to calm your nerves."

Becky scribbled absently on her notepad. "No thank you. I've been holed up and drugged up too long. I want to get back to work."

She looked out the window. Sunlight glinted on the large lake the town took its name from. A morning mist had lifted. It was a clear day. Even Boar Island was visible. The Black Lake Lumber Company's barge passed on its way to another day of harvesting pines and yellow poplars. It churned up a tea-colored wake. Will Bailey's boat bounced through it. She felt happy to see Will had two clients. He was the guide who'd shown Ed and her the good fishing and hunting spots after they moved to town. He was also the first friend they made there. His boat turned away from the barge and sped toward the side of the lake where the best duck hunting was.

"Guess you know what's best for you," Pete said. "Good idea putting a flag half-mast. Didn't vote for Kennedy, but I think he did some good things."

"It's the flag Ed flew at our house."

"Nice gesture. Secret Service should've never allowed him to ride in an open-top car with all those buildings around. Must've been real hell on his wife seeing him get..." Pete stopped and traced a finger around the pearl grips of his .357 Colt Python. "Sorry," he said. "Sometimes I just get diarrhea of the mouth."

"It's Ok, Sheriff. I mean, Pete. You don't have to treat me with kids' gloves. There's a new report for you. Pearl Wilson again."

"What now?"

"Kids walking on her lawn."

Pete scanned the report for ten seconds while he twitched his mustache corner. Becky figured the crude handlebar style was strictly from this habit and not design.

He tossed the report back into the basket. "Well, Pearl will just have to wait. If I go talk to her, I'll never get away. I'm too busy to listen to her ramblings."

Becky took a long drink of coffee. The caffeine wasn't helping her fatigue. She knew her eyes were sunken and dark and that her face was probably pallid, but she didn't care that day. "Please tell me there's something new," she said.

Pete frowned. "Not much. We traced the call to a phone booth in Flat Rock, not far from where Ed was found. No doubt it was a setup. I've scoured this county from one end to the other and talked to all my snitches. He's either far away or has a very good hiding place. I expect he's out of state. Something should've shaken loose by now if he were still around. But I promise you I'll find him."

"Call me when you do," Becky said. "Even if it's late."

"Sure thing."

A fog in Becky's mind since the murder kept the details she'd been told scrambled. But the events that led to it stayed clear.

It was Halloween, a night for pranksters and minor property damage in Black Lake. Ed patrolled extra hours before coming home and watching television in the den. Becky went to bed before him. She'd heard the phone ring and words spoken before Ed walked up the stairs. He dressed and told her he'd return soon. It still haunted her that in those last moments with her husband, she hadn't told him to be careful, especially considering the situation at the time.

Her heart fell when she woke and saw his side of the bed undisturbed. A shotgun Ed left for her protection still leaned against the wall. She remembered some type of commotion in the night-sirens in the distance maybe. In her gown, she'd run out the front door and into her nightmare.

"Is it possible you hit him?" she asked. "Maybe he's holed up somewhere with a bullet in him."

Pete shook his head. "No. Both rounds hit the wall. There was no blood. I'm ashamed to say it, but he took me off guard when I went in. Don't reckon I'd be talking to you now if he didn't drop his gun when we scuffled. By the time I made it out the back he was hightailing it away. I fired my other four rounds at him. Might've hit the back of his car. I feel terrible he got away."

"Are you sure Ed's badge wasn't in that house?"

"Yeah. I looked good. Sorry. I know how much you want it back."

"I still can't believe he was evil enough to tear it off his uniform."

"Just the kind of man we're dealing with," Pete said. "As disgusting as it sounds, he probably kept it as a trophy."

Becky felt her coffee churning in her stomach. She opened the desk drawer in search of a Tums. The bottle was empty. "I've heard he has a girlfriend named Candy Fritz. Have you talked to her?"

"Can't find her all of the sudden. She could be with Jessie, but just doesn't seem the type who's loyal enough to stay on the run with anyone for long. She'll be around town though, just like a stray cat that keeps coming back. Let me know when you see her. Her mugshot is probably in the book."

"It is. Chief Wilkes arrested her three years ago. Intoxicated and disruptive."

Pete studied her with his tired eyes. "Well, I don't blame you for wanting to poke around some. Nothing wrong with pulling out the mugshots. But I'd just keep it at that."

"I only wanted to know what she looks like. I hear there may be a few men at the lumber plant she has regular flings with. You could try there."

"Sounds like you have been snooping."

"Some."

"Be careful, Becky. People in this town talk. Word could easily get back to Jessie if he's around."

"I'm sure he's more worried over the murder charge than my asking questions."

"Probably. But you don't know this guy like me. It could be that Ed's badge isn't the only trophy he wants."

"What do you mean?"

Pete broke eye-contact. "Well, I wasn't going to bring it up, but maybe I should since this guy is still out there. Ed worked Jessie over at the lumber yard for more reasons than a knife pulled on him. He told me later that Jessie threatened to cut this throat then come after you if he didn't back off."

"Why? I've never even met him."

"Just his way. He finds what scares people the most so he can run over them. Still, I'd never take lightly his threats. He's a psycho, but smart enough to know it's only a matter of time before he's caught and probably sent to death row. It wouldn't shock me if he wanted even more revenge on the man who stepped all over his badass reputation, especially if he thinks you're helping look for him."

The stress Becky had felt for over a month sometimes made her light-headed or nauseous. Both symptoms struck her now. She wrapped her brown ponytail around her hand and tugged it, as was her habit when anxiety struck. "Why didn't Ed tell me?"

"Probably didn't want to scare you. I doubt you have anything to worry about. But I suggest you leave the investigating to me."

"If Settle is like you say, why wasn't he locked up before this?"

"I've tried. He intimidates witnesses. Beats the hell out of them if that doesn't work. Just recently, he dragged Candy into an ally in Cypress Cove and worked her over with a lead pipe. It was bad. She'll never testify, though. Jessie had his own little enterprise going there —pimping, drugs, extortion— whatever paid out. Wouldn't doubt if he did Frye's Jewelry Store robbery too. Like I said, he's crazy, but smart enough in his own way to have dodged serious trouble for a long time. But he made the biggest mistake of his life when he killed a law officer in my county."

"Thank you for everything you're doing, Sheriff."

"It's no problem. Hope I didn't scare you too bad. I just thought you needed to know the whole story."

"Glad you told me."

"And, just to let you know, there's a county board meeting tonight. I'm asking them to offer a reward. Maybe that'll loosen some tongues."

He reached into his shirt pocket, unfolded a wanted poster, and laid it on the desk. "Put this one on the board. I'll have more printed with the reward amount on them."

Becky looked at the frontal and profile shots of a smirking Jessie Lee Settle. It appeared he'd tried copying Sal Mineo's hairstyle and failed. Black strands of greasy hair fell around his perpetually wild eyes. He appeared to be peeking through wet vines. "I'll post it now." she said.

"Call me if you need anything. I'll have my guys patrol around your neck of the woods again tonight. Sure you're Ok?"

"I'm fine." Becky smiled, but twisted her ponytail.

She held tight to her tray at the cafeteria when children left their seats to hug her. Friendly waves came from the lunch line. She smiled and bent slightly to receive each child's arms. Wendy Martin wore the biggest smile at the teachers' table as she pulled out the seat beside her.

It took but ten minutes of happy conversation to lift Becky's spirits higher than they'd been since the assassination. She knew the teachers were going out of their way to cheer her up and didn't mind. The children's hugs had softened her. Wendy's jokes clinched it. Becky began laughing. Nothing could've felt better.

"I see you're still going to the same hairstylist," Wendy said, pumping a few more giggles from her audience.

Becky felt happy Wendy wasn't being overly delicate with her. "Yes. She does wonders."

"Dye it red and you have the Pebbles Flintstone look."

A new teacher at the table cast an indignant stare.

"Ease up there, Carol," Wendy said. "She's known I'm a shrew from hell for a while." She gave the ponytail a tug and made a foghorn noise.

Black Lake   Robbie Lanier

Hazel Robbins, a white-haired lady of sixty-five, peered over half-rimmed glasses. "Would you like for me to place her in detention, Becky? I have the seniority to do it."

"Hazel used to teach some of my students' moms," Wendy said. "You know what they say they asked about her then?"

Becky looked at Hazel smile and wink.

"When's Old Lady Robbins going to finally retire?"

"I'll still be here after you retire, sweetheart," said Hazel over the laughs.

Dinah Doby turned to Carol. "Getting to know Wendy is like jumping into a cold swimming pool. Once you get past the first shock it's not as bad."

"Only one normally has the option of diving into a cold pool or not," said Hazel.

Wendy clapped. "So, you've been catching up on Jack Benny, huh?" She looked at Becky then around the table. "You know what's in order, girls? A makeup bash tonight." She slapped the table for emphasis and looked around with an expectant grin.

"Not tonight," Dinah said. "Papers to grade."

"So, you're still selling Avon on the side, huh?" came from Hazel.

"Yes, I'm still selling Avon on the side," Wendy drawled, rocking her head with each word. "How about you Beck? There's a first time for everything. I'd love to see what I could do with your face."

"That bad, huh?"

"No, just too plain. A little rouge and eye shadow would do wonders." Wendy formed a frame with her fingers and thumbs and peered at Becky through it. "Uh, huh. Uh, huh. I'm seeing it. I'm seeing it. High cheekbones and round face that could use some contouring.

16

Maybe add a sweep of green eyeshadow and highlight those brown peepers."

"Oh, stop it, Wendy," Hazel said.

Becky wanted the company. "The grill Ed bought is still in the yard. I'd like to use it once more before I put it away for the winter."

Wendy slapped the table again. "Perfect. Who else is in?"

"It's Monday," Hazel said. "Not a good night for most people."

"Such squares," Wendy said. "What time, Beck? Around five-thirty?"

"That's fine."

"It's set. I can pick up some hamburger on my way over."

"I've got some venison in the freezer that I may be able to unthaw in time," Becky said.

Wendy cringed her nose and pretended to heave into her napkin.

"You mean deer?" Dinah asked.

"Yes. Shot it last season."

Carol cast a dismayed expression. "You shot a deer?"

"Yeah. A six-pointer."

"Venison is good for you," Hazel said.

"Not if you choke on it," replied Wendy. "You see Carol, Becky is actually a time traveler from eighteen hundred. She hasn't learned the concept of buying her food yet. Better get back, Rebecca. Daniel Boone is waiting. I'll bring hamburger and buns."

The bell rang. Trays rattled and chairs grated on the floor.

Becky returned to Dalton Street with a small bag of groceries in her arms that afternoon. She'd ridden waves of various emotions all day. Now, she felt familiar melancholy on her approach to the house. The view was a reminder of things that would've been, like a new boat that Ed had been saving for docked out back. A vegetable garden plot awaited planting in the spring. The rusting tin roof was to have been replaced. Two sides of the house already had a new coat of white paint. The other two, along with the second-floor window dormer did not. They'd rented the house with the option to buy. Owning it one day and growing old together there had been their plan. Finding a cheap apartment now topped the list of Becky's things to do.

"Hello, Becky," Cynthia Billings said from the porch swing.

"Hi, Mrs. Billings. Didn't see you there." Becky stepped onto the porch and sat down.

"Cooking tonight?" Cynthia asked.

"Having a friend over. Thought it might be nice to grill once more before the weather gets too cold."

Cynthia lit a Pall Mall. "A friend?"

"Wendy Martin from the school."

"Glad to hear it. I was going to invite you over for dinner, but we can do it later this week. There's a persimmon pudding for you on the counter. Cleaned up some for you too. Put your mail on the kitchen table."

It never bothered Ed and Becky that the Billings sometimes cleaned and made small repairs in the house in their absence. It was James' old home place. He and Cynthia lived there for the first few years of their marriage, before they built their large house on the hill next door.

Cynthia propped one foot on the swing and rocked herself with the other. She took a pull on her cigarette and sent a stream of smoke into the air. She'd reached her fifties, but still possessed a youthful beauty despite her streaks of gray and eye wrinkles. When she tried, she could be stunning. Today, though, she wore jeans and an old sweater. A scarf held her hair rollers.

Becky felt a special gratitude for the woman. It was Cynthia who met Becky at the door the morning Ed didn't return. The expression that fell over Cynthia's face when she called the sheriff's department told it all. And, even though her own husband had been hospitalized the day before, it was Cynthia who gave soft, sympathetic words that day and a shoulder to weep on.

"Thank you," Becky said. "I'm sorry the place was such a mess. I just haven't felt like doing much recently."

Cynthia waved her hand dismissively. "Totally understood. You just work on getting back to the girl we all know."

"How's Mr. Billings?"

"Not good. It's spread to his pancreas and liver. I don't know when he'll come home. His surgery is next week."

"I'm so sorry."

Cynthia's eyes glistened. "Things happen for a reason. I'll get through it."

"How's Bobby taking it?"

"I've just told him Uncle Jimmy is sick. I haven't told him he's dying. I don't know how he'll deal with it. Hard, I'm afraid."

"Would you like for me to talk to him?"

"Perhaps later. You're dealing with so much of your own. Things like that shouldn't happen in this little town. I think everyone is still in shock. What happened in Dallas certainly didn't help. I'm sorry I gave you more bad news."

"I'm glad you told me," Becky said. "Mr. Billings was very good to Ed. You're good neighbors. I want to help if I can."

"Thank you. Jimmy is a good man. So soft-hearted. I know I'm biased, but I believe he's been the best mayor this town has had. He listens to people and tries to understand their concerns. Ed had that trait too. That's why Jimmy wanted him as chief. Anyway, how are you today? I'm guessing your getting out is a good sign."

"I finally forced myself to go to work. Glad I did now. I had lunch at the school and saw the kids. It was the best day I've had in a while."

"You enjoy your work, don't you Becky?"

"I only write reports, but yes."

Cynthia crushed out her cigarette in an ashtray on her lap. "Just know Jimmy has done his best to keep that position for you. He called each council member from the hospital about it."

"You mean they might cut it?"

"Oh, Becky, I assumed you had been told. Yes, they're considering cutting the police department entirely and contracting with the sheriff. Jimmy is against it, of course. But Frank Frye and Sam Roberts are pushing it, and those two can be very hardheaded once they set their minds to something."

"No, I haven't heard. Why are they doing that?"

"Well, it's certainly no reflection on you or the job Ed did. I think it's more of a money versus practicality thing. Their view is that since the sheriff's department already dispatches our calls and covers when our officer is off duty, why not let them do it all."

Becky looked away.

"Oh, dear, I've upset you. Darling, you know Jimmy and I will take care of you. If Jimmy can't keep the position, then my brother in Wilmington could get you something. He has lots of connections. There could even be something for you in his investment company. I'd hate seeing you move though."

"I'm afraid I wouldn't be able to afford the rent anyway." Becky said, "Even when my widow's benefits start coming."

"Oh, we're not going to even think about that now. I've told you that you don't have to pay rent until you're able. Jimmy and I are going to give you time to get on your feet." She stood. "But you have company coming and groceries to put away. I need to check on Bobby. He was out back, messing with those rocks Ed gave him. He misses your husband so much. Knowing Ed was one of the best things ever to happen to him."

"Ed thought the world of him," Becky said.

Wendy arrived in her bright red Hudson convertible at six o'clock. The twelve-year-old car was her pride and joy. She'd bought it the summer before and quickly ran up the odometer while cruising the twisting lake roads with the radio loud and her blonde hair waving. The cool weather, now, had forced her to put the top up. "Sorry I'm late, hot cake," she said. She carried a grocery bag and Avon case. "Been having to explain to a guy why I'm not going out with him tonight."

"The one who works at the register of deeds office? He seems nice. You should've taken him up on it. I would've understood."

Wendy rolled her eyes. "Believe me, I'd much rather be here eating burgers and chewing the fat with you. Jeremy *is* nice, but about as fun as a hemorrhoid. Besides, we just went out Saturday and... What the hell is that?" Her eyes focused on Becky's holstered .38 revolver beside the grill.

"Just makes me feel better having it close right now," Becky said. She took the grocery bag and picked up the holster. "Let's go make up the burgers. I'm hungry."

"Sure. Just promise you won't get too upset if I mess up your makeup."

Becky smiled. "Let's just eat and chat tonight. You can make me pretty later."

"Party Pooper," Wendy complained.

An hour later they sat on the porch, sipping wine at a card table. They'd put on sweaters.

"Well, Beck," Wendy said, "you sure grill a mean burger. The pudding ain't bad either."

"Plenty left. Want another?"

"No. One is enough. Watching the figure these days."

Becky found the last rare patty and put it on a bun with a smear of mayonnaise and pickles. "I'd rather have another burger. I gave up on curves a long time ago."

"Don't go hard on yourself," Wendy said. "You have a nice figure."

Becky took a bite and looked over the trees. "Maybe a nice full figure. Speaking of full, think we'll ever go there?" She pointed to the moon.

Wendy held her blue glass up and looked through it. "You mean us?"

"You know what I mean. Do you think a man will go there like Kennedy said? I hope it happens, but it seems so impossible."

"Yeah," Wendy said. "I believe there's a bunch of stuff that'll happen that seems impossible now."

"Me too. I see things happening now that most people wouldn't have believed not so long ago. I'm so glad there are people with the courage to dream."

"Well, I guess burgers and a full moon bring out the deep thinker in you. You know what else takes courage? Drinking this wine. Where the hell did you get it?"

Becky took a sip. "Ed and I made it from muscadines," she said with a smirk. "They grow wild behind the house."

"Oh. Well, I meant it takes courage to delve into the sinfully addictive pleasures of this nectar from the gods."

"It's an acquired taste, I guess." A car passed, and Becky looked to her holster on the porch swing.

Wendy noticed. "Good grief, Becky. You can't jump at everything that moves. Why don't you stay with me for a while? My apartment is small, but I have a foldout sofa. We can go half on groceries. I also heard there's a job in the school cafeteria coming open after Christmas break. It's yours if you want it. We'll be a team. I'll give 'em an education and you can give 'em indigestion."

Becky spit her wine back into her glass before laughing. "It sounds good. But I'd rather wait and see if the town keeps my job first. Ed got it for me. Also, it just feels like there's still a part of him here. Leaving just seems to make it all so darned final. Bet that sounds silly."

"Not at all. You and he probably shared big dreams here. People get comfortable in places and become attached to the memories there. I know. My dad was in the Air Force. I grew up moving all over the world and cried every time. But you adjust and have new experiences. You meet new people. Sometimes you even find out some things about yourself that you didn't know. You just need a touch of that courage you were talking about to take the first step. You're not leaving Ed behind. He'll be with you in spirit wherever you go."

"I believe that," Becky said. "I'll think about it." She saw movement at the corner of the house, reached for her gun, then quickly pulled her hand back.

"Who's the kid?" Wendy asked while watching the person turn around on the Billings' driveway and walk back up the hill.

"He's not a kid. It's Bobby Billings, James' nephew."

"What's he doing slinking around?"

"He probably was coming over to visit and saw you. He's scared of people he doesn't know. He has cognitive problems. They believe it's from his mother's drinking and using drugs when she carried him. His growth was stunted by it too. James unofficially adopted him."

They watched Bobby stop on the drive for a few seconds and look back.

"What's he doing?" Wendy asked.

"I'd guess trying to get up the courage to come down here." Becky waved. "Hello, Bobby. It's Ok if you come down."

He turned and walked away, disappearing into the tree line where the driveway turned up the hill.

"Poor guy," Wendy said. "Wish he wasn't scared of me." She poured herself another glass of wine.

"Think nothing of it. He was afraid of Ed and me too at first. He likes me now, but he loved Ed. Thought you didn't care for that stuff."

Wendy swirled her glass under her nose with a fake, snooty expression. "I'm developing a taste for it, my fine lady. The undertones of swamp mud and frog piss are growing on me. It's called getting a buzz."

"Maybe you should sleep here tonight."

"I'm fine." Wendy turned her nose up. "You smell a cigarette?"

"Mrs. Billings was smoking here earlier."

"Weird I just now smelled it. Hell, maybe it's the wine."

Becky sniffed the air and caught the faintest smell of burnt tobacco.

A Bolton County sheriff's car slowly cruised up and swept a spotlight across the porch.

"Well, hello," Wendy yelled with a big wave. "Come join us for some burgers and wine."

The car stopped. "Ya'll Ok?"

"Yes," Becky answered. "Aaron?"

"It's me." He flipped on the interior light for a moment, smiled, and waved.

"Hold me," Wendy blurted out.

"Having a good night so far?" Becky asked.

"Been busy. I'll set up camp in your drive once the calls die down."

"I'm shitfaced and need to stay here tonight," Wendy whispered.

"No need in that," Becky yelled to Aaron. "Everything is fine."

"Shut up," Wendy said. "Yes, you do that, Aaron. We'll have a burger waiting for you."

Aaron smiled. "Be back as soon as I can."

"You got a last name?" Wendy called.

"Powers," he answered before driving away.

"He just graduated from the academy," said Becky. "It's hard to believe he's old enough to be a deputy."

"Aaron Powers." Wendy said it five times, committing it to memory.

The phone in the den rang.

Becky stood. "Leave him alone. What about Jeremy?"

"Hell, we're not married," Wendy said while Becky walked inside.

"Hello?"

Silence.

Becky tried again. "Hello?"

"Beck- Becky?"

"Bobby?"

"Yeah, It's me."

More silence.

"Are you Ok, Bobby? You didn't have to run off. Wendy wanted to meet you. She's a teacher."

"I was- uh- I just wanted to s-show you the arrowhead I made today. B-but I'll show it to you tomorrow."

"Yes, please do. I bet you're good at making them by now."

"It's not as good as the ones Ed made, but it's the b-best- the best one I've made."

"Well, be sure to bring it by tomorrow."

"Becky?"

"Yes, dear."

"Who's that man?"

"The deputy? Aaron Powers. You've met him."

"No. Not him. The one s-smoking cigarettes."

"Where, Bobby?" Becky's voice dropped. She glanced at the windows.

"On the b-back porch. He was there when I walked down. I'm watching him through the window now. Who is he?"

"I'll see you tomorrow, Bobby," Becky said. She hung up and ran toward the back of the house. "Wendy, come inside!"

"Why?"

Becky almost fell over a chair before she got to a window. In the moonlight, she saw the outline of a man walk into the woods near the public boat access drive. He got into a car there and drove with headlights off toward the street. She ran to the front door. "Just get in here."

Wendy came to the door. "What's up?"

The car, lights still off, pulled in front of the house and stopped.

Wendy waved. "Who's this? Another flutter bum bodyguard?"

Becky looked out the door to her revolver on the porch swing.

The car's engine revved. It spun a half donut turn, sending gravel and a dust cloud into the air. The driver's window now faced the house.

"Wendy, move away from the door."

The engine revved again.

Wendy stepped inside but not before extending her middle finger toward the car. "Climb it Tarzan!" she yelled.

The car window rolled down and the barrel of a shotgun came out.

Becky pulled Wendy out of the doorway.

A shot thundered over Dalton Street.

2

Is this what a breakdown is like? It must be, and it's hell. Becky's thoughts made the conversation around her distant. She felt a hand. It was Cynthia's. Becky leaned into her arm.

"It's going to be fine," Cynthia said. She patted Becky's back. "Just try and relax."

"Ready for pancakes, Beck?" Wendy asked from the stove.

Becky blinked her eyes open. "Thanks, but no." She tasted her coffee and found it had turned cold.

Aaron walked in with a large screwdriver. "This should work," he said, going to the hole in the wall.

"What do you think you're doing there, young man?" Cynthia asked.

"Removing the slug."

Cynthia's eyes snapped. "Absolutely not. My husband's father built this house with his own hands. I don't want more damage to the walls than already has been done."

"But it's evidence. We may need it later."

"It'll be right there if you do. Come and eat. You've had a long night like the rest of us."

Aaron stepped away. "Yes, ma'am."

Wendy poured coffee into a mug. "Here ya go, cowboy." She smiled at Aaron when he took it.

"Thank you." He sat down beside Becky and pulled a plastic bag containing cigarette butts from his shirt pocket. "Found these on the back porch. He was there long enough to smoke three Camels."

Becky looked at the bag. She knew the thought of Jessie Settle waiting on the porch for her to be alone might never leave her head.

"And just where were you all that time?" Cynthia asked.

"Don't blame Aaron," Becky said. "He came by when he could."

Cynthia lit a cigarette. "Well, I'll certainly tell the sheriff to post an off-duty deputy here at night. I'll pay for it myself if I must. Just praise be nobody was hurt."

Wendy laid plates and a tray of pancakes and sausage. "Chow down. Take what you want but eat what you take. It is pork sausage, right, Beck?"

Becky nodded.

"It looks great," Aaron said. "Sit down and eat with us."

"Maybe just a sausage patty for the road. I'm running late for work as it is. Guess I'll lose some fashion points by wearing the same dress two straight days." She stepped over and leaned toward Becky. "I'll find a substitute and be back as soon as possible," she said.

"No need in that. Tell the kids I'm sorry I didn't make the crossing again. Let them know I'm thinking about them and not to forget me."

"Oh, those munchkins aren't forgetting their favoritest most ever crossing guard," Wendy said. "You really should eat then sleep some."

"It's been a pleasure meeting you," said Cynthia. "I think you made a friend." She smiled at Bobby coating his pancakes with maple syrup.

"Nice meeting you too, Mrs. Billings. Make sure that guy goes easy with the stuff."

Bobby grinned. "Thanks for breakfast, Wendy."

Wendy took a sausage patty from the tray and took a bite. "You're welcome, big guy," she said. Drop by the Long Branch, Marshal, and I'll buy you a drink," she told Aaron.

Aaron blushed. "Sure thing."

"You know what they say about us teachers." Wendy slapped the back of her hand. "Shut up, Wendy. See you guys."

Becky watched Bobby laugh. During the hectic night, he'd warmed to Wendy and Aaron. Becky noted his relaxed, almost jovial, mood. It was the Bobby she loved most, and wished he was not so often trapped in fear and hesitancy. He was almost thirty and a good man but would always have challenges because of his mother's choices before he entered the world.

"Who's there?" Cynthia called when the front door opened a few minutes later.

Pete Scotland walked in with a rolled piece of paper in his hand and a serious expression. He examined the hole in one wall then the other where the slug lodged. "Well, I'd say it's a damned good thing nobody got in the way of that." He turned to Aaron. "You want some overtime?"

"Sure."

"Then finish your report in the car and wait for me."

"I've already written it."

"Go to the car anyway."

"Yes, sir. Bye everybody."

"Thanks for everything, Aaron," Becky said.

Cynthia gave Pete a hard look. "Things are getting out of hand in this town, Pete. These things cannot happen. It must stop."

Pete poured a cup of coffee and sat down. "I'm doing my best, Cynthia. I only have so much manpower."

"I'll pay for a deputy to stay here until this man is caught."

"Can't spare one. I'm shorthanded as it is. This confirms Settle is still around, so we're going to be busy looking for him." He looked at Becky. "I told you he's dangerous."

Pete's manner and tone gave Becky a bad feeling. She hoped his visit would be short. "I guess it was him," she said. "I didn't get a good look at him." She turned her head. "What's wrong, Bobby?"

He was pale and trembling.

"Are you alright?" Cynthia asked him. "Are you choking?"

Bobby slid his chair back and ran out the kitchen door.

Becky stood to go after him.

Cynthia stopped her. "I'll check on him, dear. He has spells sometimes."

Becky watched through the window as Cynthia hurried up the hill after him. "What got into him?"

"That young man has issues that can't be fixed," Pete said. "Sit back down. We have a few things to go over."

Becky slid back into her chair. "What is it, Pete?"

"Did he try getting into the house last night?"

"No. I don't think so."

"Did you see what kind of car he drove? Color? Model?"

"It was a dark color. Four-door, I think. I don't know a thing about cars. I couldn't begin to give you the model. It looked like a double-barreled shotgun he fired though. Twelve gauge judging by that hole."

Pete unrolled the sheet on the table. "Just so you know, I'm calling in the reserves and deputizing a few volunteers. The board agreed to a three-thousand-dollar reward. We'll start putting the new posters up around town and the rest of the county. It'll be in the paper and on the local news too. Hopefully we can put enough pressure on this guy to get a break."

"I hope so. I just don't think I can deal with all this much longer."

"Will you be here today if I need to contact you?" Pete asked. He slid his chair and the paper close to Becky.

"Yes. May I ask what that is?"

"An insurance investigator working the Frye's Jewelry Store robbery visited me yesterday." He turned the sheet so Becky could see it better. "We started going through everything and found this. Obviously, I should've looked through the file better when you gave it to me. Read it."

Becky saw Ed's handwriting. Each line of the sheet described a piece of jewelry.

"All this was taken from the robbery," Pete said. "Ed received them on October thirtieth from a person listed here as C.I. dash one. That's his signature, right?"

This had the feel of an interrogation. Becky felt her mind spinning. "Yes- yes. It's his."

Pete sat back. "The sheriff's office stores all Black Lake police department's evidence because we have a secured area for it. This evidence never made it there." He gazed at Becky as if he were gauging her reaction. "So now we're faced with the awkward problem of lost evidence."

"I don't understand this," Becky said. "I had no idea Ed collected any evidence from the robbery. What does C.I. dash one mean?"

"Confidential informant number one I'm assuming. Did Ed say anything about having an informant?"

"No."

"Where might this jewelry be?" Pete leaned in close when he asked.

Becky realized she felt guilty for no reason.

Cynthia walked back in. "Bobby is going to be fine. Just too much excitement, I think. Maybe too many pancakes also." She looked at Becky and Pete. "Did I interrupt something?"

"Seems we're missing Frank Frye's jewelry," Pete said. "It appears Ed recovered it after the robbery and, for whatever reason, failed to turn it over to the evidence room." He stared at Cynthia in what appeared to be a contest to establish the upper hand then turned his eyes back to the report.

"So, what are you saying, Sheriff– that Ed stole it?" Cynthia sat down beside Becky.

"No, I'm not. It's just that I have an evidence sheet here listing recovered stolen property and I don't have the property. There's over eight thousand dollars' worth of merchandise listed here. You know how Frank Frye is and what hell he'll raise when he finds out."

Cynthia glanced at the report. "You didn't by chance lose it yourself did you, Sheriff?"

Pete's neck grew red. "We need to find this," he said. "Are you sure it's not at the police department?"

"I don't think so," Becky said. "There's no place to secure evidence there. Ed wouldn't have just left things like that lying around."

"Could it be here?"

"No," Becky said flatly.

Pete leaned in again. "Mind if I look anyway?"

"I mind," Cynthia snapped. "Becky said it's not here, and I won't have you trashing this house over nothing. Maybe you need to better check your own evidence room first."

"I have," Pete said, his voice rising. "It was never turned over to us. I need to find this."

Becky sat rubbing her forehead. Her thoughts seemed as if they were in a blender. She was very glad Cynthia had returned.

"Do you have any idea where Ed may have placed those things, dear?" Cynthia asked.

Becky shook her head.

"Well, then, Sheriff, I suppose you're done here."

The red made it to Pete's face. "You know what a stink this is going to cause, Cynthia."

"I'll deal with Frank. You find Jessie Settle. That should be your priority now. And make sure we don't have another episode here like last night."

Pete snatched the report. "I'm doing the best I can," he said before storming out.

"Thank you," Becky said.

"Don't let this bother you," said Cynthia. "He's under a lot of pressure these days. I think Jessie Settle getting away from him hurt his pride more than a little. You look so tired. Would you like to sleep at my house?"

"Not now, but maybe tonight."

"Well, of course. I'll cook us all a nice dinner and we can watch TV. I think Bobby will need extra support also. I'm taking him to see Jimmy today and don't know how he'll handle it. Sure you'll feel comfortable here by yourself for a while?"

"Sure," Becky lied.

3

After Cynthia left, Becky walked to the two mailboxes at the end of the Billings' driveway. Inside hers was November's power bill with a late notice for October's. She realized she'd also forgotten that month's phone and water bills, along with the payment on a small loan Ed took out.

She walked to the street and studied the tire marks where the car spun around. A rattle from the boat access made her flinch. A duck hunter there loaded decoys from his truck. Becky returned his wave then walked to the approximate place the man entered the woods the night before. Just past the grass of the yard, she found the partial print of a shoe or boot. The hunter motored away from the pier. Becky walked through the woods, looking for more prints. At a muddy spot near the access road, she found two. She knelt to look closer and determined a large boot made them. Ed wore a size ten. These, she guessed, were twelve or thirteen.

She felt a wave of nausea while backtracking the man's route. The lawn hadn't been mowed since Ed's murder. Tall, turned back grass blades made a trail, which she followed to the back porch then around the house. At the back corner of the front porch stood a crape myrtle that Ed mulched with pine needles the previous spring. Becky noticed the needles disturbed in one spot and a few of the lower twigs of the shrub broken. She knelt there and looked up to the porch. A person from that vantage point could've reached out and touched the chair she'd sat in the night before. She was unprepared for the rush that came from her stomach and vomited over the front of her housecoat.

Every window and door were locked when she showered and put on pajamas. She cleaned her mail with a washcloth, walked downstairs, and tossed her housecoat into the washer. The phone on Ed's desk rang. Hesitantly, she answered it. It was Marge Bowers, the town clerk, calling about timesheets.

"No, I worked eight hours yesterday," Becky said. "That's all for this week. Sorry I didn't turn the time in. I've just had so much going on that I forgot."

"No problem," Marge said. "I'll fill one out and sign your name if that's Ok. Guess you're not working today since I didn't get you at the office."

"No. I haven't slept at all after what happened last night."

"Good gracious, what happened last night?"

"I'm not really in the mood to talk much." Becky knew Marge was dying to know but didn't feel physically able to tell the story. She also knew Marge would find out through her connections quickly enough.

"I hope it wasn't anything too bad," Marge said. Then, when Becky didn't respond, "Well, I'll have your check here when you come by. Are you making it in tomorrow?"

"Probably." Becky pondered for a moment. "Marge, I hear the council is planning on cutting the police department. Have you heard anything?"

Marge spoke low after a few moments of silence. "They are discussing it. Ever since James got sick, Frank and Sam have been talking about a lot of changes. You know those two, always looking for ways to save money. Doing away with the police department seems to be their number one priority. Like usual, they just need to persuade one of the three others to vote their way."

"I know."

"I'm very sorry. If worse comes to worse, Mason Fabrics in Cypress Cove is always hiring. It's only a few miles away."

"Thanks, Marge. I'll be by for my check tomorrow."

"Great, we can catch up some. See you then."

She pulled out each drawer of the desk and rummaged through the contents. Ed was the organized type. He'd rubber banded the paid bills and receipts in stacks. Paper clips, pens, and an application form for criminal justice night classes at the community college were also there. In the bottom drawer she found the heavy keyring Ed had used to reset business alarms. A key marked "PW" was there in case emergency entry was ever required for Pearl Wilson's home. It had never been needed, but Pearl had insisted that Ed have it handy. Becky placed the keys on top of the desk with the intention of returning them to town hall.

In the upstairs bedroom, she removed a small key from the nightstand then pulled a chair into the closet and stood on it. Her hand traced over the top shelf until she found the metal box. She sat on the bed and unlocked it while telling herself how senseless her guilt for removing the money was. She found a ring and necklace her mother gave her. Ed's Golden Gloves medal, Bronze Star, and service ribbons were there too, along with a stack of letters from Ed's war buddy, Mike Ledford. Attached with the letters was a photo of Ed, Mike, and two other Marines holding a captured Japanese flag on Okinawa. She remembered that she must write Mike and tell him of Ed's death. She went through the papers and found the contract Ed signed with the town, his and her birth certificates, a copy of their medical insurance, and the envelope for boat money. She opened it then leafed through each document page by page. The money was gone.

It was nearly ten o'clock. She felt exhausted. Insomnia had become a familiar enemy, and she realized immediately she was in for another bout with it when she lay down. She tried switching her mind off, but it whirled out of control with old and new concerns. Stronger than the fear that someone wished her dead was the thought that something had happened in Ed's life she didn't detect. Had his mind been distracted at the end? Would he still be alive if she'd seen whatever he'd been dealing with? These were questions she knew might haunt her forever unless she got answers. But she had to sleep. She rolled over and reached for her bottle of sleeping pills on the nightstand.

It took only a few minutes before the ceiling dimmed. She blinked then closed her eyes. Briefly, she felt comfortable. Scraps of dreams with gunshots and screams then leaked in before images of Ed's face, cringing like Oswald did. She wanted to not see it, but it wouldn't go away. When it did, the Kennedys rode past. They smiled and waved at her just before John's head exploded into a red cloud. Then it was Jessie Settle, smirking and filling Ed with bullets before pointing the gun at her. She felt hands pulling her toward a grave. The images and sounds became sharper when they played over, making her desperate to wake from it, but the pills wouldn't let go. A voice yelled for her. She tried crawling toward it on numbed limbs. The hands tried holding her back. She fought with them.

"Becky!" Wendy's face appeared.

Becky sat up and clutched her. She cried on Wendy's shoulder. It was a fierce weeping, every bit as retching as at Ed's funeral.

"You're Ok. Relax. Relax, Becky."

The weeping eventually reduced to sobs and hiccups. "I'm trying," Becky breathed. "Every time I think I'm getting better, there's more. There's always more. I just keep getting pushed back down. It's breaking me."

"Easy," Wendy said. "Let's talk about it." She held her for another minute then guided her to the edge of the bed. "Good lord, I didn't realize you were like this. Dumb me should've never left you alone."

"I really thought I was going to be fine when you left." The pills made Wendy and the room swimmy.

"Let me get you a tissue." Wendy reached for one on the nightstand and noticed the empty pill bottle. "Becky, did you take all these?"

"It wasn't full."

"How many were in it? How many, Becky?"

"Four. Maybe five."

"Holy crap!"

"I wasn't trying to kill myself if that's what you're thinking."

"But you could have." Wendy placed her hands on Becky's shoulders and examined her eyes. "You're still nodding. I need to call an ambulance."

"No. I'm fine. I just couldn't sleep and felt like I really needed to."

"I'm still calling an ambulance." Wendy stood.

"I said no," Becky yelled. "I'm Ok. I promise. I won't do it again."

"You'd damned well better not. If you're going to be my friend, there are a couple of rules you're going to have to follow. Number one: Don't do dumb things that can hurt you. Number two: Under all circumstances call me when you're having problems, even if I'm at school. Think you can follow that?"

"Yes." Becky tried focusing her eyes on the trees outside her window. "I'm sorry I scared you," she said. "How did you get in?"

"Had to break a window. I heard you screaming all the way from the street."

Becky drug her palm over her face. "No. The hole in the wall last night and now this. Mrs. Billings *is* going to want me out. Did you break it bad?"

Wendy cocked her head. "Is throwing a porch chair through it considered breaking it bad?"

"Wendy, Mrs. Billings has a key."

"I thought you were in trouble. At the time, I really didn't give a damn about the window."

"After last night, did you even think about what you might have been walking into?"

Wendy made a sarcastically thoughtful look. "Nope. I usually don't when I think my pals need help."

Becky raised her head and mustered a smile. "Thank you," she said.

"You're welcome. Now, let's get you a cold shower, then we'll ride to the hardware and see what we need to fix that window. After that, you're going home with me."

"Thanks, but Mrs. Billings has already invited me over."

"Then tell her you're staying with me. I know a good Chinese restaurant. We'll eat there tonight then go to a movie. *It's a Mad Mad Mad Mad World* is playing. I hear it's hilarious, just what we both need."

"That sounds great. But I think Bobby may need the extra company tonight. I think the poor guy may be in for a hard night. He's going to see Mr. Billings today."

Wendy frowned. "I hate that. He was so happy this morning."

"He was until Sheriff Scotland showed up after you left."

Wendy sat back down. "What happened?"

"I really don't know. Bobby was fine and laughing, then ran away like he'd seen a ghost when Pete walked in. I know Bobby has his mood swings, but I've never seen him that scared."

"I probably would've split the scene too when Scotland walked in," Wendy said. "Something about him I don't like."

"Really? What?"

"I don't know. Some people just rub you the wrong way. He's one of them for me."

"He kind of rubbed me the wrong way this morning," Becky said.

"What did he do?"

"After you left, he came by with a report that Ed wrote. Ed apparently recovered some of the things from Frye's Jewelry Store from a confidential informant. The stuff was never turned over to the evidence room, and Pete asked me questions about it."

"Good grief, was he accusing Ed of something?"

"I don't know. But he sure carried a different tune from all the other times I've spoken to him. He was asking who the informant was and wanted to search the house."

"Did you let him?"

"No. Mrs. Billings came in and put a stop to it. But there's nothing here. Ed wouldn't have taken evidence."

"Of course, he wouldn't. Ed was straight as an arrow. Scotland should've known that."

Becky looked down and grasped her hands together. "I know Pete has got to follow up on it, but it was just the way he came across. Then,

I looked in Ed's lock box, just to see if he may have put the things in there, and there's two hundred dollars missing. I've got late bills due now plus funeral costs and it sounds like I'm losing my job. Damned if I know what to do."

Wendy waited until Becky turned her face up. "I won't pretend to know what you're going through," she said. "But I do know there are times when you have to be a fighter. Sometimes life tries to run you over. You have to stand up then and punch it in the nose, just so it'll know who it's messing with. You just have to be a tough bitch sometimes."

Becky snorted. "I'll have to practice. Never tried being that."

"Oh, you are, Dolly. You just don't know it yet. I know a tough bitch when I see her."

Becky now chuckled. "Takes one to know one, huh?"

"Right you are. I spend ten months a year in a small room with fourth graders. It's a requirement. So, welcome to the club. Sure you won't come home with me tonight?"

"Let's do it this weekend. Chinese food and a movie *do* sound good."

"Just don't forget to bring your muscadine wine," said Wendy. "It's the preferred spirit of tough bitches everywhere." She pulled Becky's arm. "Now, let's get you a cold shower."

4

The mood at the Billings' that evening direly needed cheering up. That's why Cynthia served her spaghetti and meatballs on TV trays in the living room. But even one of Red Skelton's Junior skits wasn't improving things. Becky didn't feel much like laughing but did in hopes of producing a smile from Bobby. He watched the television with the same somber expression he'd worn all evening.

Cynthia smiled at Becky from her recliner. "This is Jimmy and Bobby's favorite character." Red skipped across the screen in his child's attire while holding an oversized lollipop.

"I've s-seen this one," Bobby said. "It's a rerun." It was the most words he'd spoken together all evening.

"But it's still funny," Becky said. She forced a laugh when Red used a three-foot match to light Stubby Kaye's loaded cigar. She'd seen the skit too and remembered how she and Ed truly laughed when they watched it. "How about we go fishing this weekend?" she asked. "We can build a fire and cook them over it if we have any luck."

"Excellent idea," said Cynthia. "We haven't had a fish-fry in a while. We can eat beside the firepit."

Bobby shrugged. "We can try. B-but they don't b-bite much this time of year."

"Yes, we can try," Becky said. "And, if they don't bite, we'll cook hotdogs."

Bobby moved his tray aside. "Ok. I'm getting s-sleepy. Think I'll go to my room."

"Good night, Bobby." Becky began to say more, but Cynthia lifted her hand and shook her head while Bobby left.

Cynthia waited until they heard the bedroom door close. "Becky, I just don't know what I'm going to do. That poor boy is going to be lost without Jimmy. He may never get over it."

"I wish I could've helped more. Taking him fishing was the only thing that came to mind."

"It was a nice try. But there's not much that can be done when he gets this way. I wish I had an answer to it." Cynthia moved her tray, walked across the room, and turned off the television. "He was so excited about seeing Jimmy today. I just cannot stand seeing him in this daze." She sat back down and lit a cigarette while extending the footrest of the recliner. "I've seen him this way before. I believe there are things that go on in Bobby's head nobody understands. I believe there are things that torment him."

Becky had considered the same. She felt deep pity for the young man. "Ed had a way with him," she said. "I know I can't replace him or Mr. Billings, but maybe I can do some things with him they did."

Cynthia smiled. "That's very sweet of you. I must admit that the prospect of trying to provide for him emotionally scares me. Jimmy and his first wife were like parents to Bobby. I don't think he's ever seen me in the same light. I know things are hard for you now too, but perhaps spending time together would be good for you both– when you can, of course. I certainly would be thankful."

"I'd be happy to."

The phone beside Cynthia rang.

"Hello." Cynthia looked at Becky with an exasperated expression. "Yes, Sheriff. I should've told you. She's staying with me tonight and probably every other night until you catch this man."

Becky vaguely heard Pete's voice.

"That was an accident," Cynthia said. "Bud sent a man to put the plywood up. They'll be back tomorrow to replace the window."

Pete asked a question.

"Yes, we did look. We found nothing. You need not worry about that, Sheriff. You know as well as I there are other matters far more important now. Thank you for calling. Good night."

"Checking up on me?" Becky asked.

Cynthia nodded and toked her cigarette. "Yes, one of his deputies saw the board over the window and couldn't get you to the door. He radioed Pete and gave him an update. Looks like they're keeping on the ball a little better after last night."

"Sounded like he asked about the jewelry too."

"Pay it no mind. That blasted jewelry will show up, and I can about guarantee there will be egg on the sheriff's face when it does."

"Do you trust him, Cynthia?" The question came out spontaneously. Becky felt a little uncomfortable she'd asked it.

Cynthia flicked her cigarette on the ashtray. "I trust him to do the best job he can in his own way. There's certainly the trait of cordiality missing from his personality that I wish he would obtain. But being gruff and a little intimidating seems to be his natural way of handling business. Would he bend the truth when it serves him? Maybe. Why do you ask?"

Becky hadn't planned for this conversation but decided to now voice her concerns. "Just the jewelry thing. I was thinking about that report Ed wrote. Nothing there shows those things made it to the evidence room. Ed used to talk about chain of custody and how important it is. If he *had* turned it over to the sheriff, I'm pretty sure he would've documented it. If he didn't, then why? What would've been his reason not to?"

"Oh, Becky, you're making too much of this." Cynthia crushed her cigarette, put on her readers, and lifted her needlepoint. "Unfortunately, when a person passes away suddenly there are often matters left unresolved. Sometimes there are questions left unanswered. You can't let your mind suffer from it all."

"You're right. It's just so hard clearing my head of it. Things keep coming to me that don't make sense. I guess I just want everything to fall in order so I can understand it."

Cynthia squinted and aimed her needle at the fabric in her hoop. "Well, you will have to get on with your life at some point. Of course, I have the advantage of being able to prepare myself for Jimmy's passing. I wish I could give you better advice. It's natural for you to want answers. I know Ed cannot be brought back. But that man will be arrested and brought to justice. I'm betting sooner than later. The sheriff has his faults, but he's like a stubborn coon dog when he's on the trail. Just remember that Ed loved you. Fill your mind with all the wonderful times you had together. Those are the gifts your marriage gave you. They never die as long as you cherish them. They're certainly far more important than Frank Frye's second-rate jewelry."

"Yes, we did have wonderful times."

"Tell me about some. Tell me about your anniversary trip last summer." Cynthia put her needlework down and removed her glasses.

Becky pushed her tray aside. "Well, Ed wanted to go to the mountains and rent a cabin near where he proposed. It was a sweet idea, but I'd heard of the Lumina at Wrightsville Beach and thought it would be fun."

"Been there," Cynthia said, tossing an afghan over her lap. "Very nice choice."

"It *was* nice. But I don't believe Ed really liked it. He hated crowds. Also, looking back, I think he saw all the beaches he cared for in the war. But he finally gave in, and we took the bus there. We lay on the beach and went to the movies and bowled. The ballroom was above our room. At night we heard the bands playing. I kept pestering Ed to take me." She chuckled. "You can probably figure out his response to that."

Cynthia laughed. "I'm sorry, but Ed just didn't seem the type you'd see on a ballroom floor."

"I never thought so either. But, on our last day there, I decided to take one more stab at it. I believe he finally understood how much it meant to me."

Cynthia made a happy face.

"We found a place that rented formal wear." Becky coughed and waited for her throat to relax. "I found a red dress. They didn't have a tuxedo just Ed's size, so he got the closest they had. That night we were sitting at our table in the ballroom. I can't remember the name of the band, but they were very good. I enjoyed just listening to them and watching the other couples on the floor. I looked at Ed and could tell he was struggling to ask me out there. He was so darn nervous. It reminded me of our first date. I was beginning to wonder if he would ask. Then, he stood and took my hand."

"Don't tell me he was a good dancer."

"No. Terrible."

They laughed.

"He tried hard. But the poor guy was just too awkward. Those rented shoes had scuffs all over them the next day. I felt sorry for him. So, when the first song ended, I started walking back to our table because I just knew he was done. Instead, he pulled my hand and asked, 'Where are you going?' He pulled me to him and said, 'Let's do this our own way.' So, we just held each other and rocked slowly to the music. It was more a hug than a dance. I swear I felt his heart beating. I don't know how long it lasted. I just remember him holding me while I rested my head on his shoulder. Then the band stopped playing, and I realized just how much I loved the man."

"Such a lovely story," Cynthia said. "That's something you'll never forget."

"Never. Afterwards, we drank a bottle of champaign on the beach and watched the sun rise over the ocean. I knew it would be a one-time thing for us. There were just too many people there for Ed to feel comfortable. Still, I'm so happy we had that one time."

"He was exactly like Jimmy in that sense," said Cynthia. "His favorite place is the Outer Banks. I wanted to go to Miami Beach or Las Vegas for our honeymoon, but Jimmy chose Springer Island. It's beautiful, although I doubt there's a more isolated place in the state. Jimmy has an old school friend who let us stay at his summer house there. There's nothing but marshes, sand dunes, and trees around it. Jimmy fished while I read and swatted mosquitos. We went back for our anniversary once. It was still the same."

"Sounds like he is a lot like Ed."

"Yes. I used to tell Jimmy he was too private a person. You know, Becky, I've found there's a certain gentle and romantic air about men like our husbands. It's not obvious. In fact, it's quite hidden. However, on rare occasions it comes out. And when it does it's something very beautiful and memorable, like the story you told."

Becky nodded and ran a finger under her eye. Her attention fell to a wall of photographs past where Cynthia sat. It was a shrine to the family's history. A particular one caught her eye. It was an old photograph of what must have been the Black Lake Lumber Company in its early days. A group of men with axes and crosscut saws stood around a monstrous log with a hollowed center large enough that two men wearing fedoras sat side by side in it. The man sitting on the right appeared to be James, not much older than twenty. The facial resemblance of the other told her it was his father.

"Would you like me to show you your room?" Cynthia asked. "It's been a long, trying day. I'm a bit tired. You may stay up for as long as you like."

"Yes," said Becky. "I'm ready for bed myself."

Becky had never been past the Billings' living room but saw just how grand the house was when Cynthia led her down the hallway. A dining room featured a chandelier and table large enough to seat a dozen people. They then passed double doors with full length windows and a large deck that overlooked the lake. Next was a billiard room, followed by a study with book covered walls, fireplace, and leather couches.

When they reached the staircase, Cynthia pointed to the closed door on the right and then to the one on the left. "That's Bobby's room and this is mine. Don't think you're bothering us if you need anything in the night." She flicked on an upstairs light, and they began their walk up a royal blue stair tread.

"Your house is beautiful," Becky said.

"Thank you. Jimmy wanted to build on this hill even before his first wife died. He and I drew up the floor plans ourselves. I don't think either of us initially planned on it being this large, but we just couldn't help ourselves once we started. Now that we're older I think we both wish we'd been more conservative."

They reached the top of the stairs and a sitting area with a bookcase. Two ceiling-height arched windows provided a rolling, aerial-like view of the lake and its islands. The moon's reflection on the water illuminated a train crossing a trestle ten miles away.

Becky gasped at the sight.

"My favorite part of the house," Cynthia said. "You should see the view in the fall."

"Amazing," Becky said. "I've never been in a home like this."

"Well, it was Jimmy's father, Collin, who possessed the foresight that made it possible," said Cynthia. "He was a smart investor who moved here before Black Lake was even a town. Land was cheap then, and he bought up thousands of acres. Collin began timbering it in the late eighteen-hundreds then built the lumber company later. He had to rebuild once after it burned, but that was a blessing in disguise, because he made it bigger and better. When Collin died, everything was split between Jimmy and Darlene. I suppose you've heard she's Jimmy's sister and Bobby's mother. She's also as useless as... Well, I won't go into that."

Cynthia entered the first bedroom and turned on the light. "Anyway, Jimmy bought what she inherited. She never would've known what to do with all that land. Lord knows she would've made a mess of the lumber company if she'd had a hand in it. Of course, she squandered the money Jimmy paid her in no time.

"I'm letting you have this one because it has its own bathroom. I got you fresh towels and changed the bed sheets earlier."

Becky looked around the well-kept room. A framed campaign sign hung on the wall. White letters spelled "Tolly for State House" on a blue background. A mounted largemouth bass with plague commemorating the catch and an autographed picture of Gene Autry also hung on the walls.

"As you might have guessed, this is my baby brother's room," Cynthia said. "He left so many of his things in the old house when he moved to Wilmington that I figured I'd just use them to decorate a room. It's better than having them clutter up things. I think it's kind of special to him when he visits–kind of a time capsule of his youth."

Becky walked to a glass cabinet filled with sports trophies. On the top shelf lay a football painted blue and orange. "Black Lake Warriors–1946 State Champions," was written in white letters on the center of the ball. A picture beside it showed Quincy Tolly and Bud Sweeny in uniform. They knelt and smiled while holding the ball between them. Behind them stood two cheerleaders and a strikingly handsome man with a whistle hanging over his Warriors sweatshirt. "Quincy must've been some athlete," Becky said.

Cynthia walked over. "Yes. He played all sports. That was his passion back then. Unfortunately, he had his eye on girls too much to make good grades. But he's always been hard driven when he sets his mind on something. That attitude has done him more in business and politics than high marks ever would have."

"State champions," Becky read aloud. "Very impressive."

Cynthia nodded. "Yes indeed. The same year Jimmy and I married. That was an exciting time here in Black Lake. The stands would be packed. Bud quarterbacked and Quincy played receiver. I've never enjoyed anything more than watching Quincy run past everyone on the field and Bud put the ball right in his hands every time. Nobody could stop them. I'm proud of them. They've been a huge help with the company. Quincy is always sending us new buyers he meets through his own business and legislative sessions. And we couldn't ask for a better floor manager than Bud. Those years quarterbacking really taught him leadership skills."

A more recent photograph of Quincy also stood in the cabinet. He and other newly elected state legislatures took their oaths of office. Cynthia stood there also, smiling at Quincy while holding his bible.

Becky remembered a story Ed told her once about the brother and sister. When Quincy was three, the family was returning from a shopping trip. Cynthia sat in the backseat while Quincy slept in his mother's arms in the front. An oncoming car tried passing another on a hillcrest. The other driver and both parents died. Their mother had just enough time to drop Quincy on the floorboard and cover him with her body. Her final act saved him, yet he still lingered near death for weeks before requiring months of extensive rehabilitation. Cynthia worked with him every day of it, and eventually helped him regain full use of his legs. The age difference between them was great enough that Cynthia was awarded custody of him after she graduated high school.

"I expect he'll be visiting soon," Cynthia said. "I'll invite you to dinner when he does. Maybe we can talk to him about a job for you."

"Thank you. And thank you for dinner and a nice evening. I hope Bobby has a better day tomorrow."

"It's a hard time for us all," Cynthia said. "But we'll pull through it if we stick together. So, feel comfortable and sleep well. You're safe and loved here." She gave a soft hug. "Remember, wake me if you need anything."

For a moment, Becky considered asking if she had sleeping pills. "Good night, Mrs. Billings," she said instead.

Becky did sleep well for the first few hours. The bed was soft, the room comfortably warm and free of draft, much different than hers in the old house. It was a calming sleep she enjoyed. She dreamed of her home in the Smoky Mountains. She was there gardening and canning vegetables with her mother. They then sat beside the fireplace at night while her mother wove a basket and Becky shelled peas.

"When is Ed asking you to marry him?" her mother asked.

"I think soon," Becky replied. "I believe he's trying to get the courage."

"He will," her mother said. "I can tell his love for you is greater than his shyness." She paused with her basket. "I pray your union will be warm and glowing with love in your hearts." It was words she'd spoken at Ed and Becky's wedding.

This dream faded into another. Becky heard waves washing ashore. She lay on sand the early morning after she and Ed had danced, drunk champaign, and made love on the beach. She reached for him, but he was gone. She ran down the empty beach, calling his name. She saw his footprints and followed them to the Lumina. She stood on the dance floor with the couples, asking them if they'd seen him. They only danced and smiled at one another. She asked the band members, but they kept playing. One last look around told her he was gone. She walked outside, leaned against a balcony railing, and looked out at the ocean. Her leg went over the top rail.

She woke to primal fear. She knew it had been a dream, but it was a dream that tapped into something tucked away from her consciousness. It was that final solution to her pain that existed just below the surface of her thought. In the moment it took her brain to fully wake and regain its defenses, the solution surfaced, and its very existence horrified her. She remembered she was at the Billings', took a deep breath, and rolled over. *Relax and sleep*, she thought. But the fear still held her. In the corner of the bedroom window, she saw the flickering glow of a fire.

She walked downstairs in her slippers and bathrobe and looked out the double doors. The fire burned in a pit at the bottom of the hill, near the Billings' pier and houseboat. Becky knew it was Bobby sitting there. She unlocked the doors and stepped into the chill.

Bobby and Ed built the firepit with rocks the previous summer. This was Bobby's refuge. Many nights Becky and Ed saw the fire burning. Ed went there when he felt Bobby needed company more than solitude. They fished and talked, sometimes late into the night. Ed showed Bobby how to make spearheads and arrowheads from flint and quartz. It was a skill he'd learned as a child. His work bore a rugged beauty that amazed Bobby. Stone chips now covered the area from the hours Bobby had spent grasping the rudimentary principles of flint knapping.

He sat hunched over the fire and held his flake in a scrap of buckskin while shaping the edges with the point of a deer antler. Becky approached and tried not to startle him.

"Bobby," she said just loud enough for him to hear.

He tensed then folded the buckskin over his work.

Becky sat down in an old chair Ed had kept there. "Osiyo," she said.

The fire highlighted tear trails on Bobby's cheeks. "Osiyo," he whispered.

Becky leaned into the warmth. "It's getting winter fast."

Bobby nodded.

"Were you surprised by how Uncle Jimmy looked today?"

"He—He's dying. I know it. I s-see it."

Becky slid the chair close to him. She started to speak three times. "I know it's hard," she said finally.

"Why does it have to be like this? Why does God let it happen? First Ed, now Uncle Jimmy. Why?"

It was a question Becky recently asked herself. "I don't know. I wish I could tell you. Maybe there is no reason. Maybe there are some things even God can't change." She stirred the fire with a stick, more to break eye contact with him than anything, then tossed another piece of wood into the pit. The flames jumped and illuminated more of the surroundings. "What I mean is, maybe there are things God isn't supposed to change." She saw confusion on Bobby's face. "Let me see what you're working on."

He opened his hand and unfolded the buckskin. Though crude, the shape was noticeably an arrowhead.

"That's very good." She took it from his hand and looked at it. "I think it's your best yet. Quartz too. That's not easy to work. You've learned so fast. Ed would be proud."

"It's too thick," he said. "It'll never attach to a s-shaft. I'll never be good like Ed was." He took it back and began chipping it again.

"I think you will. You're just learning like Ed learned from his father, and his father learned from his grandfather."

"B-but I'm not Cherokee."

"It doesn't matter. The old ways are there to be learned by anyone who wishes."

"Are you?"

"My mother was."

"Your daddy wasn't?"

"No. But I barely knew him. My mother raised me." She remembered the conversations she and her mother had around the fireplace on cold nights. It was after Becky's father had left that her mother told her more about her heritage. Things came to mind that Becky hadn't thought of in years.

"Is s-she still alive?"

"No. She died a few years after Ed and I married."

"Is your daddy?"

"I don't know."

"Was your daddy like my mama? You know–not-not-"

"Yes. He left us when I was five. I saw him only once after that." She remembered clearly her father coming to the door drunk. He'd needed money. Her mother refused him, and he beat her. Becky jumped between them and got pushed to the floor hard enough to split her head and require stitches. When her father saw what he'd done he ran away. Her mother sent word to him that she would kill him on sight if he ever came back.

"I'm sorry," Bobby said. "I know that makes you s-sad." He inspected his arrowhead. He placed it on his knee and pressed the antler against it. The arrowhead snapped in half. Bobby let out a cry of frustration and threw both halves into the water.

"It's Ok," Becky said.

"No. No, it's not." Bobby's face covered in rage. He kicked the firepit rocks and sent sparks sailing. "Dammit," he yelled at the lake. "Dammit!"

Becky recoiled.

Bobby threw the antler down then silently stared at the ground.

"It's fine. I know that can be frustrating. Ed used to get mad too when he broke one."

Bobby shook his head and trembled. "I never saw him b-break one. Not one. Ed was good. I'm not. Now he's not here to teach me. I wanted to be good like him. It's always somebody. Everybody I like goes away. They all go away!" His voice carried over the lake.

Becky wanted to say something to calm him, but sensed anything she'd say would only worsen matters.

Bobby stood and picked up a large stick. He slammed it into the fire. A cascade of sparks in the air forced Becky to jump up. "Shannon! Ed! Uncle Jimmy!" He struck the fire and surrounded himself in sparks each time he screeched a name.

Becky moved away while she watched. Bobby seemed to have forgotten she was there. He walked with stick in hand, mumbling to himself and intermittently screaming a profanity with another strike against the fire. Becky decided to get Cynthia and was stepping away when Bobby threw his stick into the lake and sat back down. He looked around. "Beck- B-Becky?" he yelled with desperation.

She walked back and sat down. "Right here." She managed to keep her voice soft.

Bobby looked up with eyes that hadn't settled. The muscles in his sweaty arms twitched. His jacket bore small burn marks. He kept his eyes on Becky then raked his hands through his hair. "I-I'm sorry," he said. "I'm sorry."

Becky patted his shoulder. "It's Ok," she said, but worried. She'd never seen Bobby act that way, nothing close. She understood his despair over Ed and his uncle, but wondered if there were more. She remembered the episode from that morning. "I'm afraid there are things that torment him," she remembered Cynthia saying. Becky also wondered who Shannon was, but knew it wasn't the time to ask.

He dragged his fingers through his hair again. "I can't explain it," he said with a heavy voice. "It just... They all go away. Uncle Jimmy s-said today that I have to be b-brave. But I'm not brave. What do you do when you're not brave? What do you do?" He watched Becky as if he were waiting for an answer. "I wish–I wish I could be like Ed. He was b-brave. He made me feel s-safe, like Uncle Jimmy does. I can't describe it. Things just feel different when they're around. I feel happy. I feel normal."

Becky struggled for something to say. Then, she thought of something. She looked at the fire and tried remembering her mother's voice tell it when Becky once felt as Bobby probably did now.

"There's something you should know about the Cherokee," she said. "We believe that the Creator blessed every person and everything with a spirit. And all the spirits that live or have lived on this earth are joined as a whole. Every spirit has something meant to be added to that whole. Every spirit has a purpose. You are who you are because the Creator blessed you with something he knew was meaningful. It's inside you. But you must look with a clear and strong mind to find it and accept it. When you do, you will have power from the Creator, and you'll surprise yourself."

Bobby looked at her silently. His face calmed.

"It's very late," Becky said. She stood. "I need to sleep. You should as well."

"I'll be up soon," Bobby said. "Thank you, Becky."

"Just remember it." She started toward the house.

"Becky?"

She turned.

"What do you say for goodbye?"

"The Cherokee language has no word for goodbye," she said.

She slept soundly until the alarm clock rang, then removed her pajamas and looked out at the vague, orange glow of sunrise over the lake. She slipped on her robe and left the house through the deck door. Frozen grass crunched under her slippers. She felt she must do what she planned and prepared herself. Coals smoldered where Bobby's fire had been. A new piece of worked quartz lay on the stump.

She stepped to the water's edge, looked across the lake, and removed her slippers and robe. She huffed breaths while wading into the biting cold water, sliding her feet over sand and rough stones. When the water was just below her shoulders, she turned and looked at the sunrise. Her body trembled. In the darkness, the lake appeared as a black void between the banks. She'd calmed some from the initial shock when a soft breeze ruffled the surface, and a ray of sunlight shined over the trees. An egret landed in the shallows nearby. It made a bobbing wade while searching for its breakfast. Becky closed her eyes and slipped under. She came up with a gasp then sank again. Seven times she did it. The egret flew away with a fish in its beak when she waded back to shore. She wrung her hair then wrapped her robe tightly around her.

The Cherokee tradition of going to water is a cleansing of the spirit. Bad thoughts are washed away. The mind and body are purified and made ready to begin anew.

5

As with all weekdays, downtown Black Lake became busy early that morning. Lights in a village of little homes near the lumber plant came on before sunrise. Smoke from rekindled fireplaces and woodstoves drifted over the lake. Some plant workers grabbed a quick breakfast at Jabber's Grill while others stood on the street corners, enjoying cigarettes and conversation before the workday began. That morning there was much to talk about.

A heavy law enforcement presence had come to Black Lake. Jessie Settle had been spotted. While quail hunting, Will Bailey saw a black Mercury stop at Vick Dempsey's home, close enough for Will to see Vick walk from the house and pass a bag of groceries to Jessie. Also spreading was news of the discovery of a possible murder scene. The evening before, a woman's purse with its contents spilled was found along a creek bed near a walking trail at Simpson Park. Gossip had it, there were signs of a struggle with fresh blood and drag marks trailing to the creek. A woman's shoe was stuck in the sand. Jessie quickly became the primary suspect among the workers.

The lumber barge pulled away from the dock. It made logs in the water beside the plant bobble. These logs would be the first of the day to be pulled onto a conveyor belt and debarked before being cut, dressed, and loaded into the kiln at the other side of the building. Flatcars stood ready for the cured lumber. The barge blasted its horn twice to warn other boats and signal the beginning of the workday. The workers converged upon the plant.

A waft of diesel fumes swept past Becky. She stood near the dock in her toboggan and coat. Her eyes scanned the workers who walked toward the debarking area. The one she looked for passed. He carried a paper lunch bag and made quick strides with his long legs.

"Whitey," Becky called. "Are you Whitey Gallimore?"

The lanky man turned. His freckled face and greased down hair gave him a comical look. Becky decided he could be Alfalfa's double if the hair was darkened.

"Can I talk to you for a moment?"

"Gotta get to work," Whitey said. "I'm late as it is."

She went into a trot beside him. "It won't take but a minute."

"About what?"

"About what happened between Jessie Settle and my husband. I heard you saw it."

Whitey's jaws tightened. "I ain't testifying. Don't try making me." He led Becky to the foot of a ramp, where the logs were loaded onto the conveyor belt.

"I don't want you to testify. I just want to know what happened that day."

Whitey stopped and looked at her. "You're Chief Hawk's wife?"

"Yes. I hear Jessie was trying to cut you when Ed showed up."

"Danged if he tried. He did." Whitey pulled back his coat sleeve and displayed an angry, curving scar from wrist to his elbow. "He cut me in other places too that I ain't showing you. But I ain't getting cut up no more if I can help it. So don't be asking me questions about Jessie."

"Well, what brings Becky Hawk here today?" Bud Sweeney stood smiling at the top of the ramp. Even in work clothes he looked dashing. He wiped a brown curl of bangs from his eyes while walking down. "Good morning," he said.

Becky took his extended hand. "Good morning, Bud. I just needed a minute with Mr. Gallimore. I promise I won't keep him long."

"I'm getting to work right now, Mr. Sweeny," Whitey said. "Sorry I'm a little late today." He began a trot up the ramp.

"Hold on Whitey. Mrs. Hawk said she needs to talk with you. Her husband saved your ass, so I think you can spare her a minute." He looked at Becky and winked. "Whitey isn't very talkative. Take all the time you need with him. I'll have that window replaced for you today."

"Thank you, Bud."

Bud gave her another smile and a thumbs-up as he walked back up the ramp.

Whitey took a tube of snuff from his overalls. His eyes darted everywhere except to Becky. He poured some powdered tobacco into his lip. "What do you want?" he asked, eyes still scanning.

"I'll make it quick. That day Jessie cut you, what was said between him and my husband?"

Whitey spit brown juice to the ground and smirked. "Said? Wasn't much said at all. Jessie pulled a knife, and the chief whupped his ass. That's about the size of it."

The machinery inside fired up. There came a bang. The conveyor belt shook then moved. Logs were hooked and drug onto it.

"I need to get to work," Whitey said.

Black Lake   Chapter 5

Becky blocked him. "Just a second. What kind of threat did Jessie make about killing me?"

Whitey scowled then grinned a little. "Why, he never said shit about killing you. Why the hell would he? You weren't here."

"Why did Ed beat him like he did then?"

"Because Jessie wouldn't let go the knife. Chief told him to. Jessie said he'd cut his throat. I expected Chief to shoot him. Kind'a wish he'd had. But he decided to use his fists instead." Whitey laughed, displaying a mouth of decaying teeth. "It was the damnedest thing I've ever seen. Chief would knock him down and Jessie would just hop right back up and come at him again. It was like something you'd see in a funny show on television. Chief's fist sounded like an axe hitting a tree. Jessie just wouldn't let go his knife. Made my face hurt watching it. I guess it was about the sixth or seventh lick when Jessie went down for good. Never thought I'd see Jessie Settle get the mule shit kicked out of him like that. Damn your husband could fight."

"And that was it? No other threats were made?"

"Nope. None I heard." Whitey spit once more and walked up the ramp. "Sorry about your husband," he called back. "Wish I didn't have to drop the charges, but I don't want Jessie after me again."

"What did you owe him money for?" Becky asked.

Whitey chuckled and shrugged.

She made the crossing ten minutes before the school bell rang. She was glad she did. The short time with the kids helped calm her mind and allowed her to think. She decided she would need to stride carefully to get answers, but also realized there could be times to throw caution to the wind. She hoped she would be wise enough to know when these times were. She also hoped the big stories around town would overshadow any talk about her visit to the lumber plant.

She'd just returned the heavy key ring to town hall when a deputy's car passed her on the street. It stopped and backed up.

"Need a ride?" Aaron asked.

Becky got in. "Good morning. Hear you guys are busy today."

"Very. This is the most I've seen happening in this county since I was hired."

Becky saw the excitement on his face. "Anything new on Jessie?"

"He's around. We've had more sightings of his car. He probably doesn't trust whoever's been hiding him now that there's a reward. The sheriff has Vick Dempsey in his office now. Sure wouldn't want to be Vick."

"I heard you're also looking for a body."

Aaron nodded. "Headed that way now to relieve the man on the scene. The rescue squad's been dragging that part of the creek since last night. The water moves fast there though—empties out to one of the deepest parts of the lake. We have our work cut out for us on this case."

"Who do you think it is?" Becky asked, purposely adding drama to her voice.

"Keep it to yourself, but we found Candy Fritz' driver's license there."

This confirmed Becky's suspicion. "I suppose Jessie is the suspect."

"Probably a good guess. Candy was the closest person to Jessie. But I can imagine a three-thousand-dollar reward looked pretty good to her. Unfortunately, Jessie probably knew it too."

"I hope you find her," Becky said. "And I hope you find him. Will you please keep me up with what's going on?"

They stopped in front of the police department.

"Sure will. Is- uh- Is Wendy going to be at your house tonight?" Aaron's voice tightened halfway through the question.

Becky stepped out of the car with a grin. "No, but I'll be seeing her. Why are you asking?"

He blushed. "Just asking. Thought I might call her sometime. Do you think she might want to go out with me?"

"I know she would. Be sure to give her a call."

"Sorry about inside," said Aaron. "We didn't have time to straighten things back up before we got busy yesterday."

Becky looked back at him driving away then pushed the door open and stepped inside. Desk drawers stood half open with the contents piled on top. Books on the shelves sat haphazardly. In the back room she found cleaning and office supplies removed from a closet and placed on the floor outside it. A filing cabinet stood open with all the reports removed. Becky jerked open the other cabinets to find them empty as well.

She walked to the desk and checked the things left piled there. Her anniversary photo sat in the same place but with a crack in the glass. She began placing the items back in the drawers then discovered Ed's phone number and address book missing. This clinched it. She reached for the phone, but it rang.

"Black Lake Police Department." Becky repeated it in a less sharp tone.

"Becky, this is Vivian at dispatch. Are you alright? You sound upset."

"Sorry, Vivian. I am a little. Can you put me through on the sheriff's line?"

"He's busy in his office. He's got Vick Dempsey in there. Have you heard what's going on?"

"I heard."

"I'll have him call you when he comes out. It could be a while though."

"Never mind," Becky said. "I'm sure I'll see him soon. Thanks a lot."

"Wait. Don't hang up. I called you. Remember?" Vivian giggled. "I just want to go over something with you. You're liable to get calls out the wazoo today. Ever since the reward was posted, every Tom, Dick, and Harry are calling when they see a black car or some shady character. Got paper and a pen? I need to go over our procedures for taking information."

Once Becky cooled down, she was glad the sheriff had been busy. A calm approach, she decided, was best. She'd spoken to two callers who provided possible information about Jessie. The first gave his name and the other wished to remain anonymous. The information provided by both was shaky, but Becky recorded it in detail. As Vivian had instructed, she gave the second caller a number, which could be redeemed at the bank for the reward if his information led to an arrest.

She took advantage of the lull afterwards to ponder an idea. She'd never been good at lying and felt nervous while silently rehearsing her line and paging through the phonebook. She wondered if her personality would fit the ruse and decided to borrow Wendy's. She dialed the phone.

"Bolton County Clerk of Court's Office, criminal division. How may I help you?" The girl would've sounded robotic if not for her gum smacking.

"Hi, hotcake," Becky blurted out. She cringed immediately.

"What?"

"Very sorry," Becky said in a more reserved tone. "I was talking to somebody else in the office when you answered."

Only gum smacking followed.

"This is Susie with the Wilmington Beacon." Becky began sweating. "I'm doing a story on the excitement you all have going on there."

"Ok." More gum smacking.

Becky guessed she would've gotten the same response if she'd told her she was Liz Taylor. She banged on a typewriter she never used a few times.

"What may I help you with?"

"The Jessie Settle case. Yes, just wondering if you could give me a little information. He was arrested in your county, I think, sometime in late October."

"Give me a minute."

It took a lot more than a minute before the girl came back. Then: "Jessie Lee Settle. Arrested ten twenty-eight, sixty-three. Charged with assault with a deadly weapon inflicting serious bodily injury, resisting arrest, and assault on a law enforcement officer. E.W. Hawk arresting officer." The girl said it all in one breath.

Becky felt she needed to reply fast before the girl hung up. "Thank you. But there's a little more information I need. Can you tell me how much his bail was?" She heard the girl smack her gum louder, probably in annoyance, while pages turned.

"Bond was set at five hundred dollars and posted on ten thirty."

"And who posted it?"

"We don't give out that."

"But it's public information," said Becky, "Most clerks I speak with know that." She was winging it and hoped the girl wanted to get her off the line as much as she sounded.

"I'm not familiar with that."

"Well, good heavens," Becky declared with fake astonishment. "I guess I'll need to speak with your supervisor then. Give me your name please." She hit the typewriter keys again.

More sounds of leafing and gum smacks came. The girls' voice was low when she spoke again. "The receipt copy says the bond was posted by a Phyllis Underwood. Don't dare tell anyone I gave you that."

"Thanks, darling," Becky said. "Don't worry. I don't even know your name."

She grabbed the phonebook and turned to the U's. The phone rang. She decided to let it go. The only Underwood in the book was Max B. with an address of route four, box seventy-six. The phone rang four times. After a short interval, it rang again. The person calling apparently knew the call rolled over at five rings and wanted to speak directly to the police department. Becky snatched the receiver up and forced a professional greeting.

"Well, I was beginning to wonder if you'd closed down entirely." Pearl Wilson's voice had a bite to it. "I've been calling since yesterday. Those children are still cutting across my yard. They've worn a trail in my grass and trampled my winter irises. I yelled at them yesterday morning and one of the little devils said something horrible to me then kicked my angel statue into the fishpond. Now, something must be done. Nobody has come out here yet. Didn't you tell anyone when I talked to you before?" Pearl huffed for breath.

"I'm sorry, Miss Wilson. I wasn't here yesterday. You can let the phone keep ringing and the sheriff's office will answer."

"No. I want to speak with someone here. I pay city taxes and expect city services. Those other people don't give a hoot about me. All they do is ask a few questions then say they'll pass it along. Their passing along hasn't done a thing to keep my property from being destroyed.

Now, I want a solution to this today." Her huffing increased. "Just a second," she said. "I need to sit down."

Becky realized this could easily go on for an hour if she let it. She waited until she heard Pearl's breathing again. "Miss Wilson, I'm very sorry about all this." She didn't care if her voice sounded gruff now. "I did tell the sheriff about your problems. That's all I can do. But they have been very busy. I'm also very busy today. I'm sure you've..."

"Well, what am I paying taxes for? Am I supposed to go without police services whenever you or the sheriff get busy? Maybe I should tell these kids who are ruining everything of mine to stop until you and the sheriff are no longer busy." She sighed. "Chief Hawk stayed busy too, but he had time for me. Oh, how I wish he were still around."

Becky's annoyance with the old lady melted into guilt. "I bet he did," she said. "He was a good man." Her eyes turned to the anniversary picture.

"You'd bet right. I didn't have to call the police department then. He'd check on me often–sit down and talk with me like he really cared. You have no idea what that means to an old woman who lives alone." Her voice broke. "I guess it's wishful thinking to expect others to be like him."

Becky realized she'd never introduced herself to Pearl. She'd only been a voice on the phone.

"But since you all are so blasted busy. I won't bother you with my problems. Seems I have no other choice than to let those children destroy the yard and gardens I've toiled over for the past fifty years. Apparently, it's not important anymore." A click followed.

Becky considered calling back with a heartfelt apology before thinking of something else. But it would have to wait for now. She made another call instead.

"Bolton County Sheriff's Office," Vivian answered.

"Vivian, Becky again. I just had a tip that I believe I should pass on right away. It was anonymous. He said we should check route four, box seventy-six. It's a Max Underwood address, and there's a chance Jessie has been staying there."

"It's been checked out," Vivian said. "We've had a lot of calls about that one. I should've told you. Max and Phyllis Underwood are Jessie's only kin around here. Uncle and aunt, I think. The sheriff knows them well. They've promised they'll call if they see or hear anything."

Becky began writing notes. "Where is that address?" she asked.

"Highway 9 near Flat Rock. As a matter of fact, they own the old house Jessie was in when he got away from the sheriff. The guys are watching it pretty good, but Jessie's not dumb enough to go back there."

"Sounds good. Thanks a lot Vivian." She underlined the names and address she'd written.

The search for Candy Fritz lasted two days more then abandoned. It was decided she'd been washed to the deep part of the lake where the dark water, full of rotting vegetation, would hide her until she floated. Searching for bodies was nothing new for the Bolton County Rescue Squad. Nearly every year fishermen and swimmers disappeared beneath the surface. Only with luck were they found quickly. The big lake contained strong currents. Bodies usually moved miles from the original location before being found with only shards of clothing on the bones and whatever decaying flesh the snapping turtles and alligators had left. Sometimes the remains were pulled deep into the swampy areas. Bleached bones extending from the water there were not an unusual find.

But finding the man presumed responsible for Candy's disappearance was the primary focus of the sheriff's office. Tips poured in. The sheriff finally persuaded Vick Dempsey to admit Jessie stayed with him several nights and that he'd been providing Jessie with provisions. Jessie, Vick said, moved mostly at night and never stayed at one place more than a few days. Jessie wanted to leave the state but didn't have the funds and was running out of options. He was receiving less handouts from friends and running out of gas for his vehicle. Since he hadn't heard from Candy, he'd become convinced she'd turned on him. For this information, Vick was awarded a charge of harboring a fugitive and placed in the county jail with more than a few bruises on his body. The sheriff believed the arrest would serve as an example to others assisting Jessie and turn up the heat on him even more.

Becky kept atop these details through Vivian, who seemed to have as much inside information as anyone. Becky called her often and learned the best ways to pump out information.

James Billings' surgery was moved up to Friday, with hope fading. The aggressive tumors ravaged him. Becky stayed the nights preceding it at the Billings', providing what comfort she could. Friday morning, she found Bobby dressed and waiting in the living room while Cynthia prepared herself for the trip to the hospital. Becky waited with him and talked.

"I hope you never go away," he told her.

Later that morning, she caught the school crossing then walked to the police department with an overnight bag. Wendy was to pick her up after work for a night on the town then a sleepover. The phone was ringing when Becky walked into the office. She answered it then was interrupted by four more calls before she finished her first report. This continued throughout the day. In between reports, she took information concerning Jessie. She worked through her lunch and didn't leave the office all day. It was five before five when she finished with a sore hand and rumbling stomach. She'd just called Vivian to tell her she was leaving for the weekend with a stack of reports ready for pickup when Frank Frye walked in. Becky knew from his face the visit wouldn't be pleasant.

"Hello, Becky," he said before sitting in front of the desk and straightening his tie.

Becky placed her last report into the basket. "Hello, Frank."

Frank kept his eyes down while he adjusted a geometrically shaped, gold colored tie tack. Becky had seen him wear it before but had yet to determine if it was a bird or animal engraved on it. "I hear that your husband collected a good bit of my merchandise awhile back." His eyes met hers. "Where might those things be now?"

The unwarranted guilt Becky had felt during her conversation with Sheriff Scotland returned. "I have no idea, Frank. I told Pete that."

Frank's fingers drummed the desktop. "Well, they didn't just disappear. Nothing was returned to me. The sheriff doesn't have them. We must get to the bottom of this."

Becky felt her face burn. "I would love to get to the bottom of it. Tell me how."

Frank chuckled. "Listen, Becky, I'm not here to cause you trouble. I know you're going through a hell of a time right now. Your husband was a hard worker. For the most part, he provided a good service to this town. He did the best he could with his lack of experience in the job. I respect that. So, here's what we're going to do." He leaned forward. "You're going to get my things back to me by Monday. I don't care how. Leave them on my doorsteps. Put them in my mailbox. If the things have been sold, get them back. Nothing else will be said after that happens."

Becky pushed back her anger. "I have no idea what you're talking about," she said. "It sounds like you're saying..."

Frank held up his hand. "I don't want to hear anything else. If this whole thing is an unfortunate misunderstanding, fine. I don't really care how it happened. I'm not in the mood for stories and excuses. I just want my jewelry back."

Wendy opened the door. "You ready, hotcake?" The smile dropped from her face.

"One minute," Becky said.

Wendy looked then balled her fist when Frank turned back around. Tough bitch, she mouthed silently. "I'll be waiting in the car," she said.

"Tell you what," Becky said, "how about I do a missing property report for you, and we have the sheriff investigate this thoroughly."

"I'm considering that. Except you won't be the one writing the report. I just wanted to try the easy way first."

"So, the easy way is getting me to confess to something I know nothing about?"

"Don't even think about getting sarcastic with me." Frank's voice rose. "I'm not playing around here. Property missing from police custody is something I won't take lightly. I understand the sheriff told you about this several days ago, and you never said a word to me about it. You could've easily called or just walked over to town hall and told me. That itself makes me suspicious. I'm not saying this is your fault, but I believe you know something about it. This is a small town. Robberies don't happen every day here. I just cannot believe your husband recovered something of this value and never told you anything about it."

Becky stood and put on her coat. "Don't know what else to tell you then," she said.

"Sit down," Frank said. "I'm the acting mayor and you're a town employee. Show me some respect dammit."

Becky slid on her toboggan and buttoned her coat. "My workweek is over, Frank. I don't know why the sheriff didn't receive your things. But I do know my husband was as honest as the day is long. If Ed didn't turn it over to Pete, I know there was a good reason. I wish I could give you that reason. But I won't sit her and take your backhanded accusations against my husband and me. I don't give a damn if you're the acting mayor or not."

"Watch your tone with me, woman."

"I have a friend waiting outside. We can discuss this more Monday if you wish."

"Then I think it best you leave your key with me," Frank said. "You're on leave until Monday night. The only thing to be discussed then will be at the town council meeting to decide if your services are needed any longer. There's a question of trust now."

Becky lifted her bag and removed the photograph from the desk. She dropped her key in Frank's lap. "There sure is," she said.

"How was your day?" Wendy asked when Becky got into the car.

"Got fired."

Wendy turned the key. "Cool. Let's shake rattle and roll." She cranked the radio up, peeled out, and waved at Frank when he walked from the office.

6

The wait was half an hour at The Dragon's Wok, enough time for Wendy to finish a Singapore sling at the bar. She drank her second at the table while struggling with her chopsticks and spicy wontons. It didn't help that she and Becky shook with laughter.

"It shan't escape me," Wendy said, this time stabbing the wonton with one of the sticks before popping it into her mouth.

Becky chuckled over a bite of lo mein. "Use your fork, for heaven's sake."

"That takes all the fun out of it." Wendy carefully lifted another, but it fell to her plate. "Slippery sucker," she said. She used an overhand stab this time. A string of juice from the wonton struck a hanging lantern over the table. It made a rain on canvas sound. Wendy looked up in amazement. "Wow. This one sure is a squirter."

This was the finisher for Becky. She pressed her napkin over her face but couldn't block her screeching laughter. Seeing this started it for Wendy. They both fell into hysterics. Becky propped her head between her hands and hung over her plate. She farted loudly, which took everything to a different level. Wendy screamed and flopped against the wall. She slammed her hand on the table three times, making the plates and silverware jump. Becky fell over in her booth and convulsed. The restaurant manager stood at the table when she was able to rise. Becky felt glad he was smiling.

"Happy you're enjoying The Dragon's Wok so much," he said. "But, please, go easy on the furniture and keep the noise down." He placed the ticket and fortune cookies on the table. "Thank you for coming. Hope to see you back soon."

"Thank you," Becky snorted. She unfolded her napkin and wiped her entire face with it before another fit of laughter hit her.

Wendy waved at the manager walking away. "We enjoyed it." She wiped her eyes then looked at the other diners, some of whom had begun chuckling themselves. "Can't take her anywhere," she said. The chuckles became laughs.

"Let's get out of here," said Becky.

A line had formed for the late movie when they exited the theater. The mild weather had brought more people out than normal for that time of year. Becky and Wendy shared the remainder of their popcorn while they walked to the car.

"That was fun," Becky said. "Hadn't seen a movie since my anniversary. Can't remember the last time I ate Chinese food."

"Welcome to the thriving metropolis of Deaton and its many cultural pleasures," Wendy said. She unlocked her door then slid across the seat and opened Becky's. "How'd ya' like the movie?"

"Loved it. I only wish there had been more than one scene with Don Knotts."

"Guess they had to be sparing with all those other funny people in it," Wendy said. "But none of them made me laugh harder than I did over our squirting wonton, fart ripping episode."

Another five minutes of laughing and commentary of the incident followed before Wendy asked, "Where to now? The night is young."

Becky stopped laughing and turned to Wendy. "Would you mind driving me to Flat Rock?"

Wendy blew a sigh. "Why, Becky? That's just going to depress you all over."

"It would mean a lot to me if you did."

The drive from Deaton to Flat Rock was twenty minutes. Becky removed the revolver from her pocketbook and used the illumination of passing streetlights to check her rounds.

"Good grief, it's like driving Bonnie Parker around," Wendy said. "This was supposed to be a fun night, Becky."

They left the Deaton town limits, and the road darkened.

"It's still a fun night. Just look at it as a late-night drive through the country." Becky smiled while waiting for Wendy's reaction to that one.

"Well, I'm glad you came armed for all the badassed deer and opossums we're going to meet on our relaxing, late-night, drive. Now, tell me what you're up to."

Becky slipped the revolver back inside her pocketbook. "It's only for protection. This is the first night I've felt like I have the guts to go to where it happened. Your being with me makes it easier. I don't mean to ruin your night, but this is something I really think I should do and get behind me while I'm up to it."

"You're not ruining a damned thing," Wendy said.

The only services the residents of Flat Rock weren't required to make the three-mile drive to Black Lake for were a post office and general store. Those stood at the corner of Highway 9 and Floyd's Ferry Road. Becky took note of a phone booth at the post office. "Slow down," she said.

"We need to make a turn?"

"In about another mile I think. Ed would've made a left back there at the crossroads when he came here."

Wendy slowed to about thirty. "So, what are we looking for?"

"Just drive slow." They passed one of the few houses in the area, and she read the address on the mailbox. "Slow down more. Can you see the name and address on that next mailbox coming up?"

Wendy crept up to it. "Route four, box something. It's hard to read. Underwood is the name. The house must be up that drive."

Becky looked up the dirt driveway that led into the woods.

"What's with that?" Wendy asked.

"I'll tell you later. Just go on to the recreational area. I think it's down here on the right."

Wendy made the turn and drove a tenth of a mile on a graveled road. The road ended at a parking lot about an acre wide. The launch consisted of two boat ramps and a dock. A small row of picnic tables stood at the back of the lot. The place stayed packed on summer days, but rarely was used after Labor Day.

They passed a wadded ball of crime scene tape in the ditch.

"You sure you're up to this, Beck?" Wendy asked. "I'm getting jittery."

Becky nodded. She'd never been there but knew enough details of Ed's murder to know where to go. "Drive to the end of the lot," she said. "The back corner."

Wendy did then turned off the engine and lights. "So, this is where it happened?"

"Yes," Becky said. "A couple came here to neck and found him facedown, about ten feet from his car." She clutched her mouth. "I think I need to get out." She shoved open the door and spit a mouthful of saliva onto the gravel.

Wendy hurried around. "Are you Ok?"

Becky gained control of her stomach. "Yeah. Yeah, I'm fine. Let's just walk around some. I need fresh air."

The lot darkened as the moon over the lake faded behind clouds.

"You got a flashlight?" Becky asked.

"Don't think so. I can turn on the headlights"

Becky kept her eyes on the gravel while she walked. "Please do," she said.

Wendy started her car and turned it so the headlight beam spread over the corner of the lot. "Are we looking for anything particular?" she asked when she walked back.

"Nothing particular." Becky kicked an empty soda can. There were also bottlecaps and an empty bait container. She dug a lug nut from the gravel with her shoe. "Just looking."

"I don't mean to add to your questions," said Wendy, "but what was Ed doing out here that night?"

"The call to our house had something to do with it." Becky knew they stood close to where Ed's body was found. She turned a slow, complete circle and scanned every angle. "I wish I knew more about it. My mind just overloaded after it happened. I never asked all the questions I should've. Haven't wanted to know all the details really–not until now."

Wendy placed a hand on her shoulder. "Be careful what you're letting go through your mind. You've come too far to fall back now."

"I'm fine. Just help me out here. Ed was shot twice at close range in the back of the head. How does that happen to him here?"

"Not following you."

"This is an open area. Nobody is going to catch him by surprise here. Nobody is going to walk up and shoot him from behind. If Jessie had been parked here, Ed would've been careful. He surely wouldn't have turned his back on him."

"Maybe Jessie left his car here and shot Ed while he was checking it out."

Becky considered it. "It's possible. But Ed would've been on his guard. Footsteps can be heard on this gravel. I can't believe Jessie just walked up and shot him."

"I understand your wanting to know, Becky," Wendy said. "Any wife would be the same way. But some of these questions just may never be answered. You may have to accept that and move on."

Becky gave her an agreeing, sad smile. "I know. I may never know. Cynthia said the same thing. But it will kill me if I don't try."

"Take as long as you need. I'll wait for you in the car."

Becky walked to a picnic table and sat atop it. She watched the moon slip out of the clouds and restore a light glow to the lake and parking lot. Since Ed's death, she was certain she'd felt his spirit several times. She wished she could then. A feeling like claustrophobia hit her. She knew she would be unable to stay there long. She looked over the lot and let her mind offer several scenarios of her husband's murder. None were believable—none that included Jessie Settle alone anyway.

"Ready to head back to Deaton?" Wendy asked when Becky returned to the car.

"I know you're never going to want to go out with me again," Becky said, "but I have one more stop I'd like to make."

Wendy turned off the radio. "And I'll bet it has something to do with that mailbox we passed coming here."

Becky nodded. "I just want you to drop me off there. Drive around for about fifteen or twenty minutes then come back and get me."

"Oh, you're going to have to tell me a whole heck of lot more before I agree to that."

Becky knew she couldn't think of a believable lie. "That's where Jessie Settle's aunt and uncle live," she said. "I think the old house he was staying in before he shot Ed is down there too."

"You want me to just drop you off there and drive around awhile? Are you loco? There's no way."

"I doubt he's there now."

"And you know that for sure? So, what's the purpose of going?"

"I guess I want to see if things are like Pete says they are. I want to see if bullet holes really are in the wall."

"You think he's lying about it?"

"Somethings just aren't adding up," Becky said. "Pete's story of what happened that night is all I have. I can't have doubts about it, or I may never get out of this hell."

Wendy took a deep breath. "I understand. But what if Jessie is there?"

Becky removed the revolver from her purse.

Wendy shook her head. "All I wanted was dinner and a movie," she huffed.

Wendy drove past the Underwoods' mailbox then backed into a small clearing in the wooded area before turning off the headlights. The moon, now unhindered by clouds, lit a dirt driveway that led up a hill. To the left of the car, sections of a tin roof showed through trees.

"Is that the old house you were talking about?" Wendy whispered.

"I think so. You don't have to whisper. There's nobody around."

"I know. This just feels like a whispering kind of deal. It don't feel right either. You sure you want to do this? You sure you want to go up there to the house where Jessie Settle could be. Do you happen to recall that little stunt he pulled earlier this week? Why don't you be smart and ask Aaron to bring you out here during the day?"

"Because then Pete would find out and know I'm suspicious."

"Let's cut to the chase, Becky." Wendy stopped whispering. "Do you think the sheriff had something to do with Ed's murder?"

"I don't know. It never entered my head until I found out Ed didn't turn that jewelry in to him. There already are some things I know Pete lied to me about."

"Like what?"

"Like telling me that Jessie threatened to kill me when Ed arrested him."

"Why would he make up something like that?"

"I don't know. I just think there's more to this than has been told."

"Good grief, I hope you're wrong," Wendy said. "So, tell me, what do you do if Jessie is inside snoozing?"

"Ask him if he killed my husband."

"Oh, I'm sure he'll be completely upfront with you about that. Come on, Becky, what will you do?"

Becky thought for a few moments. "I don't know yet. I'll play it by ear."

Dogs barked somewhere in the woods.

"I don't like this at all, baby," Wendy said. "This just feels like a bad scene. Let's go for a drive and talk about it awhile. It doesn't sound like something you can just play by ear if the shit hits the fan."

"Just go drive around. Come back here in fifteen minutes."

"There's no way I'm leaving you here by yourself."

"I don't want a deputy seeing your car parked here and checking it out. Please do what I say, Wendy."

Wendy switched on the car and backed it far enough to be concealed from passing vehicles. "There. Problem solved," she said.

The women kept silent during their walk up the drive. Becky held her revolver by her side with her eyes trained on the roof of the house. The fact that she hadn't thought to bring a flashlight angered her. She took a glance at the sky and was glad there were no clouds threatening to cover the moon. She nudged Wendy and pointed to the woods when more of the house came into view.

Hunting had taught Becky to walk quietly. But Wendy's high heels seemed to find every dry twig along the way. Briars also snagged her dress. Her tugging to free herself tore it. Wendy cursed under her breath.

"Kneel down here," Becky said. "I'm going to move a little closer and try to see if anyone is there." She stayed low, moved forward fifty feet, and crouched at the edge of the woods.

The house had once been white. Just enough scraps of paint remained on the rotting boards to show this. Becky guessed it had been built before the turn of the century. Weeds had taken over the yard and were now closing in on the house from all sides. Poison ivy vines had a foothold on a crumbling chimney. No cars were seen, but Becky guessed the parking place was in the back. She watched the windows for light or movement. As she did, the breeze blew in a smell that told her Max Underwood was a hog farmer. She turned and signaled for Wendy.

"Is he here?" Wendy asked with a stressed voice when she crouched beside Becky.

"I don't see any sign of it. But I need to get to the other side to see if his car is there. Do you want to stay here?"

"Hell no. I'm glad now you have that gun."

"Walk softly," Becky said.

Becky moved slower behind the house than she would've on her own. Wendy's heels continued to be a burden. Becky considered asking her to take them off but knew the thorns and briars there would make quick work of bare feet. She motioned for Wendy to stop before carefully stepping onto the side porch and testing the door. The knob turned but the door was jammed tight. She came down and peeked around the corner of the house.

No car was parked there, but weeds lay back where one had been. Someone had taken the time to clear some of the brush there, probably to make parking and entry to the back door easier. She looked back and waited for Wendy.

"I'm checking that door," Becky whispered. "If it's unlocked, I'm going in. I'd rather you wait here. Those high heels will make too much noise on the floor."

"I can fix that," Wendy said. She removed her shoes. "Let's go."

Becky made sure her finger was off the trigger of her revolver. She remembered tracking a trophy buck once when the tension of the moment had caused her to involuntarily fire the gun. "Stay on this side of the door," she said. She passed the door and looked through a window. Little of the darkened room inside was visible, but she could discern the front door where Sheriff Scotland said he entered the house to confront Jessie. Her eyes adjusted some. She saw a fireplace and a chair. Toward the back of the room, a sofa became barely visible. A blanket appeared to cover someone on it. She felt adrenaline hit her as she walked back to the door and tried the knob. It turned. "Stay right there."

"Is he in there?" Wendy's whisper was tight.

"Maybe." Becky put the revolver in front of her. She pushed open the door despite Wendy's protesting hand motions.

The inside of the old house smelled musty. Becky grasped the revolver with both hands, pointed it at the sofa, and stepped lightly toward it. In the dark, she saw that the lump under the blanket covered the length of the sofa. She struggled for a plan, but stress clogged her mind, and she wondered if she had it in her to pull the trigger. She took five more slow steps and pulled the blanket back. Unfolded men's clothes covered the sofa. Becky assumed Jessie left them there when he fled. Still, she kept the gun in front of her.

She wanted to check the hall and back bedrooms next, but they were completely dark. She kicked herself again for not bringing a flashlight then turned and noted three small windows on the front door. Only the fireplace and chair stood between her and that door. She saw nowhere Jessie could've concealed himself to take the sheriff by surprise that morning. If Jessie had been lying in wait, why didn't Pete see him through the windows? Becky asked herself this question just before she heard Wendy scream.

Sounds of a short struggle preceded a "Get your ass in there," yell. Wendy stumbled through the door followed by the figure of a thick man with a long gun. Lights came on. The man removed his hand from the switch and placed it back on his double-barreled shotgun. The half-buttoned jumpsuit and untied boots he wore were evidence he'd been stirred from bed.

The fact that the old house had electricity surprised Becky briefly. She then hurried toward Wendy and shouted, "Leave her alone."

The man shouldered his gun and aimed at Becky. "Drop the gun! Drop the damned gun or I'll kill you."

She placed her revolver on the floor before putting an arm around Wendy, and receiving a tight, trembling hug.

The man kept the shotgun and his eyes on them while he picked up Becky's revolver. His big hands worked double-duty while holding the shotgun and spilling the bullets from the revolver into his pocket. The revolver followed. "I want you both to get on your knees." His voice was tense. "Put your hands on top of your heads."

Becky heard Wendy's teeth chatter while they followed the instructions.

The man stepped closer with the gunstock shouldered and the barrels staring at them. His fat face bore patches of spider veins. His red hair was uncombed and oily. It extended into unkept sideburns then deteriorated into curly hairs, not quite thick enough to be a full beard, on the cheeks. Becky was familiar with the term "country strong." It referred to a thick-boned man with natural strength, and a diet that had added more than a little weight over the muscles. The man holding the shotgun appeared country strong. "Tell me just what you're doing here," he said.

A squeak came from Becky's throat. She tried again. "I heard Jessie Settle used to stay here. I just wanted to see the place. I'm Ed Hawk's wife."

"I've seen you. Who's she?" He waved the shotgun at Wendy.

Becky heard Wendy crying. "She's a friend of mine. You don't have to point the gun."

"Shut up." The man's eyes squinted. He intently studied Wendy's face. "Look up at me," he demanded. "What's your name?"

Wendy did and managed to speak it.

"I had her bring me here," Becky said. "She has nothing to do with it."

"She's here. So, like hell she doesn't have nothing to do with it."

"Are you Mr. Underwood?" Becky asked.

"How do you know me?"

The squinty eyes told Becky that Max Underwood could be dangerous. "Your name is on the mailbox. I'm sorry we trespassed. We were just out driving. I wanted to see where the man who killed my husband stayed."

"Yeah, I'm sure you were just out driving at midnight," Underwood said. "I saw your brake lights at the end of the drive when the dogs woke me. You hid your car down there and walked up. You're doing a hell of lot more than just out driving. The sheriff is on his way." He leveled the shotgun at Becky's face. "So, before he gets here, I believe you'd better tell me exactly why you slipped up here with a gun and broke into this house before I decide on putting a slug between your eyes."

A rattle came to Wendy's breaths.

Becky realized Underwood enjoyed scaring people as much as his nephew. She snuck a look at his boots. Size twelve she guessed. "I thought Jessie Settle may be here," she said. "I wanted to find him then call the sheriff."

Underwood howled. "Simple as that, huh? I wonder how that would've went? I'll tell you. He'd have cut out your heart and shoved it down your throat."

Becky saw the back door opening.

Underwood pointed the shotgun at Wendy with a grin. "And do you know what he'd have done to you, hot stuff?"

Wendy sobbed at the floor. Her mouth moved but no words came.

Becky watched Jessie Settle step through the door with a large hunting knife. A rough, black beard covered his face now, but the eyes peering through the stringy hair strands would always be a dead giveaway for her. She watched while Jessie crept up and realized the knife was meant for Underwood. She did her best to not let her face reflect what she saw.

"Do you have any idea?" Underwood asked Wendy. "You come here in that fancy dress and high heels and makeup. Pretty thing, you'd have been his breakfast, lunch, supper and dessert." Underwood laughed once more before Jessie's knife sank into his shoulder. Then he screamed.

Jessie jerked the bloodied blade out and swung it toward Underwood's neck. Underwood, his face contorted with pain and terror, managed to raise the shotgun and block it. He stumbled backward and attempted to point the gun at Jessie. Jessie grabbed the barrel and pushed it up. The gun and both men fell to the floor with Jessie on top, moving like a wild animal attacking its prey.

"You and Phyllis have been in on this shit," Jessie said. He was trying to raise the knife, but Underwood had a grip on his arm. "I'm not dumb. I'm killing your fat ass then that bitch."

"No, Jessie!" Underwood's voice was shrill. His arm was jerked around while he tried keeping his grip. His strength was losing to Jessie's viciousness, and his eyes showed he knew it.

Becky stood and took Wendy's arm. "Let's go," she said. She heard Underwood scream again while they ran across the room. They were at the door when Pete stepped in with his Colt drawn. He shoved them aside then took a shooting stance.

"Jessie!" he yelled.

Astride Underwood with his knife up, Jessie turned his head and took a bullet to his face. He fell backward in slow motion.

For several moments, Becky heard ringing only. She then heard Underwood groaning. Wendy fell to her knees and wept into her hands. Becky knelt and put her arms around her. "I'm so sorry I made you bring me here," she said. It was the sincerest apology she'd ever made.

Wendy blubbered something indiscernible while holding her hands over her eyes. She then hugged Becky while she cried.

Becky saw Pete knelt with two fingers against Jessie's throat. Underwood sat on the floor. He winced while holding his blood dripping arm. "I'll be right back," she told Wendy. She stood and quickly found the first bullet hole above the back door. It took her six steps toward the hallway to find the second in the wall, about eye-level to her. She then went to the sofa, picked up the blanket, and held it out. She saw Pete looking at her. "Is he dead?" she asked.

"Yes. What are you doing?"

"Getting Wendy, a blanket. She's cold."

Pete walked over. "Don't put that dirty thing on her. Take her to my car and turn on the heater. Both of you stay there until you're told to leave." He handed her his keys and snatched the blanket. But not before Becky saw what she wanted to know.

7

The three on-duty Bolton County deputies arrived within ten minutes. Five off-duty ones made it soon after. The men from Lewis-Sealy Funeral and Ambulance Services declared Jessie DOA with little more than a glance before administering aid to Underwood. Rescue squad and volunteer fire department members set up emergency scene lights around the house. Two deputies began rolling out yellow tape.

Becky and Wendy watched it all from Pete's car while listening to excited voices crackle on the radio. They'd said little since the shooting. Becky held Wendy's hand. Its trembling was slowing.

Wendy broke the silence. "May I ask when we're having a relaxing evening? One without shooting?"

"Maybe you should stop hanging around me," Becky said. "I would if I were you."

"Kiss my traumatized ass," Wendy replied.

Laughing felt horrible but necessary to Becky, so she did. "Looks like our friend there doesn't mind sharing the story."

Underwood sat on the tailgate of a rescue squad member's truck. His left shoulder and right hand were heavily gauzed, and he puffed a cigarette while engaging in animated conversation with the group around him.

"I'm sure he's laying it on thick," Wendy said. "Bet he's not telling them about that baby squeal he let out."

"Did you notice the way he looked at you when he asked your name?" Becky asked.

"Are you making a sick joke?"

"No. I believe he may have thought you were somebody else." Becky wished she had Candy Fritz' mugshot to show. "You sort of resemble that girl who's missing. Jessie's girlfriend."

"The one they're looking for in the creek?"

"You're not twins, but the resemblance is there. I'm wondering if that could've had something to do with our being shot at the other night?"

"Getting shot because Jessie Settle mistakes you for his girlfriend," Wendy said. "There's the ultimate insult."

Becky watched Pete receive handshakes and backslaps when he joined the group around Underwood. "There's a whole lot I'm not sure about right now," she said. "But I can just about guarantee it wasn't Jessie who took that shot."

Underwood appeared to get off a particularly good quip, and the crowd broke into belly laughs.

"You think it was Jethro there?"

Becky nodded.

"Well, I can't deny thinking the same thing when that two-barrel shotgun was pointed at my face."

"Double-barreled," Becky corrected.

"Whatever. I know nothing about guns but tend to remember what they look like when they're pointed at me. But why in the world would Underwood have come to your house and done that?"

"I'm just wondering if the sheriff has been keeping an eye on me for more than just my protection. I have a feeling there are people he may not want me speaking to. And, after the lie he told about Jessie threatening to kill me, I'm also getting the feeling he wants me scared. I just don't know why."

"In college," Wendy said, "we once had to write an essay on a famous quote. Mine was from Edmund Burke: 'No passion so effectually robs the mind of all its powers of acting and reasoning as fear.' Didn't get a good grade, but the quote stuck with me."

Becky saw Aaron walking toward them. "I doubt the sheriff can quote Burke, but I'd say there's a good chance he'd agree with him. We'll talk more about this later. We've got company now."

Wendy rolled down her window. "Good morning, Aaron."

He wore his uniform neatly, but still had the look of a man who'd been woken early. "You ladies alright? I hear you had quite a night."

"Sorry we keep stirring up so much trouble for you," Wendy said.

"Don't be sorry. Not sure what you were doing here, but it sounds like Max waking up and calling the sheriff probably saved his and his wife's lives. Looks like Jessie meant business. Glad neither of you were hurt."

"Any idea why Jessie wanted to kill them?" Becky asked.

"No. We knew Jessie was getting pretty desperate. Maybe he thought they were giving information to us. But, for now, I need one of you to sit in my car while we wait for the SBI to show up. It's best to separate witnesses until they're interviewed."

"We're waiting for who?" Wendy asked.

"State Bureau of Investigation. They investigate all police shootings. They have two agents on the way from Raleigh."

"Sounds like this could really be a long night," Wendy told Becky. "I volunteer to wait in Aaron's car."

The agents arrived an hour and a half later. Becky watched them speak to Pete briefly before they entered the house. Jessie's blanket-covered body was rolled out and loaded into the ambulance soon after. The older of the two agents then walked to Pete's car, introduced himself as Marty Feezor, and invited Becky to his car for an interview.

"These are the kind I like," Feezor said inside the car. He fetched a clipboard and notebook from the backseat. "Nice and clearcut. No sense in wasting everybody's time here if all the statements are consistent. If my partner processes the scene fast enough, I may have my report ready for the DA's review before noon." He removed a pen from his coat pocket and asked Becky for her full name, address, and phone number. Becky noticed a slight hesitation from him when she gave her name, but it was his only hesitation. In less than ten minutes he had her statement on paper, signed and dated.

"You must do this a lot," Becky said.

"More than I care to. Been doing police involved shootings for ten years, but homicides in general are what I do." He scribbled his signature beneath Becky's.

Becky began to speak but was too slow.

"But six more months. Six more months, then it's goodbye to the late-night phone calls and hello Key West and retirement. Don't mind telling you, I'm ready."

"Congratulations," said Becky. "I..."

"So, I see by your statement that you were Chief Hawk's wife."

"Still am," Becky replied.

"Sorry about the past tense. You have my condolences. I read about it in the paper. Nothing sadder for me than an officer coming out on the bad end of one of these. I'd say Mr. Settle got what he deserved tonight. Maybe he's someplace worse now. Don't blame you for wanting to find him yourself as dangerous as it was." He offered Becky a stick of gum then took one for himself when she declined. He looked out his window. "May I ask you something, Mrs. Hawk? Was your husband investigating anything particular you know of before he died?"

Becky stayed silent.

Feezor looked out the window, waiting for an answer.

"Agent Feezor, please look at me." Becky looked into his eyes. "Did the sheriff tell you to ask me that?"

"No. Why?"

Becky was satisfied. "Never mind. All I know for sure was that he'd been working an armed robbery."

"Did he make an arrest?"

Becky decided to be sparing with the details for now. "No," she answered. "Why are you asking?"

"Just because he left a message at our office the day before he died. He wanted to speak with an agent who handled homicides. I was busy on a double murder in Fayetteville. The message was on my desk when I got back. Sorry I didn't get it in time."

Becky felt a chill crawl through her. "I never heard him speak of a homicide," she said. "There hasn't been one around here I know of–except for his."

"Yeah, that's what the sheriff told me. Just checking to see what you know. We do a lot of training for small town police departments. I imagine he called to get in on a class, or maybe just some advice in case something big ever happened."

"You told the sheriff about the call?"

"Yeah. Thought he might know what it was about."

Despite the early hour, news of the shooting had spread in the community. A few neighbors and Phyllis Underwood now joined the deputies and rescue workers outside the old house. Pete demonstrated one reason he'd won the past four sheriff's elections in Bolton County. All eyes were on him while he talked and made jokes. His voice and the laughs from the crowd carried into Agent Feezor's car.

Becky watched Pete absorbed in the attention. "I'd like to tell you something, Mr. Feezor. But please keep it between us."

Feezor turned toward her a little and leaned back in his seat. He gave Becky a slight nod.

"I think there was more to my husband's murder than what's been told. There are some things not adding up." She looked at Feezor and found it impossible to read his face.

"What's not adding up?"

"Ed received a call from someone at a phone booth just down the road from here before he was killed. He was shot in the back of his head while outside his jurisdiction. The place he was killed at is about two minutes from here. I can show it to you if you'd like. It's an open area where nobody could've been behind him without his being aware of it."

Feezor's silence told Becky she needed to get to the meat of it. "The sheriff said he recovered the gun that killed Ed in that house after Jessie Settle pulled it on him and dropped it. He says Jessie took him by surprise and got away. His word on that is all there is. There are two bullet holes in the walls, one in the hall about head level and the other over the back door. There's a sofa that had a blanket spread over some old clothes in the living room. When I came here tonight, it looked for all the world like someone lying there in the dark. There's two bullet holes in that blanket."

Feezor shrugged. "Ok." It sounded like half a statement and half a question.

"I think the sheriff intended to kill Jessie that night and plant the gun on him. I think the sheriff wanted to cover something up."

Feezor turned away. "You realize that's a very serious allegation against a well-respected law officer, don't you? You'd damned well better have something to back it up if you go around telling that story."

"I'm just telling you what I've seen with my own eyes, Mr. Feezor. You've worked many crime scenes, so tell me if this could or couldn't have happened: The sheriff came here after my husband was killed. Like I did, he thought the lump under the blanket was Jessie. He fired twice into the blanket. The shots woke Jessie in the bedroom, and he ran out from the hall. The sheriff shot at him but missed and got shoved as Jessie ran past. The sheriff fired again while he fell backwards, and his shot went high while Jessie ran out the door."

Feezor grinned and ran his hand around his jaw. "That's a hell of a theory. And what would his motive had been for doing all that?"

"I don't know. But I do know my husband was acting differently the last few weeks of his life. I think something was going on he didn't tell me. And I don't believe he called you for training."

"I'd have to see the bullet holes to say if your theory is possible," Feezor said. "Yeah, I've worked a lot of crime scenes. It takes years of training and experience to do it right. Evidence gives you an idea about what happened, but there can be lots of variables to consider. Things aren't always as they seem. I looked like a fool more than once before I learned that lesson."

"Will you at least look at the bullet holes in there?"

"Yes."

"My husband's badge was torn from his uniform when he was murdered. Would you and your partner mind searching that house and Jessie's car for them?

"Absolutely."

"And can you check to see if fingerprints were found on the gun the sheriff said Jessie had, and if there were, whose?"

Feezor made a barely detectible sigh. "I'll look into it, Mrs. Hawk. I understand your wanting answers, but keep in mind that we must be extremely careful before we investigate anybody, especially elected officials, of serious crimes."

"I know," Becky said. "I'm also keeping in mind that elected officials sometimes commit serious crimes."

Becky replaced Wendy in Aaron's car and took a short nap with the heat cranked up while the investigation concluded. When she woke, her watch showed four forty-five. She saw that Wendy was still being interviewed in Feezor's car. She again felt blame for putting her friend through so much.

Someone brought coffee to the crowd outside the house. They appeared a little more subdued as they waited for things to wrap up. The agent from inside the house soon stepped out with a deputy. He spoke briefly to Pete, apparently telling him and the crowd what they wanted to know. Whoops and shouts rose as they dispersed and began filling the cars in the drive. Becky watched Pete walk directly toward her. She rolled down the window when he stepped up.

"Come to my car," he said. "I need to speak to you."

Becky realized this conversation was going to happen sometime or another. Better to have it with plenty of witnesses around, she decided.

Car engines started all around when Becky sat down beside Pete. The smile on his face surprised her. "Long damned night, huh?" he said.

Becky watched Pete's hands as he leaned back and removed her revolver from his pants pocket. He handed it to her. Becky saw the rounds were still removed. She put it inside her coat.

"I talked Max into not pressing breaking and entering charges against you and your friend. I believe he realizes how lucky he was that his dogs barked and woke him up. All's well that ends well, right?" Pete smiled at Becky and twisted his mustache.

Becky nodded. "Yes. Thank you, Sheriff. Sorry I'm not very talkative now. I'm very tired."

The cars in the drive began leaving. Pete turned the key and checked his rearview mirror. The tires turned and shoved gravel.

Becky fell against the door. "What are you doing?" she shouted.

"Taking you to the Jessie's dead celebration."

"I'm with Wendy. I need to stay with her. My pocketbook is still in her car."

The car bounced on the uneven drive behind a line of taillights. Pete grabbed the radio mic. "Powers, stay on the scene. When the Martin girl is through with her interview, tell her Mrs. Hawk is going with us. Grab her pocketbook from the car and hold on to it also."

"Yes, sir," came Aaron's reply.

"Where are we going?" Becky asked. The thought of opening the door and jumping out crossed her mind.

"Grady's Country Kitchen. Best breakfast in the county." Pete made a hard turn from the driveway and gunned the car up Highway 9 until he caught up with the caravan.

"I'm just ready to go home. Take me back."

Pete grinned. "I'll take you home. What's wrong with me buying you some ham and grits first? You can at least let me repay you for helping me find Jessie." He turned into the left lane, passed three cars, then cut back into a small break when headlights appeared down the road. "You know, I never thought much of the Furies until the sixty-one models came out." He drove with one hand and an arm flung over the top of the seat. "I like the body style. This one will move too. Watch this." He made another whiplashing cut into the left lane.

Becky felt her back press into the seat and tingles sweep over her while the engine roared. She placed both hands on the dashboard and squeezed it. White lines in the headlights became one continuous blur.

Pete put both hands on the wheel and passed the rest of the vehicles before cutting back into the right lane before a sharp curve. He braked just enough to keep control while the tires squealed. "Hell of car ain't it?" he yelled with a laugh. "Nobody gets away from me in this." He slung the car through two more curves then opened it up on a straightaway while keeping an eye on the speedometer. "Let's see if we can top this baby out."

Becky's every muscle tightened. The tingles now pushed toward panic. "Slow down," she begged.

Pete let out a gleeful yell instead.

The car kept accelerating until it reached a speed that seemed impossible for a two-lane country road. The white line blur disappeared altogether. Becky knew any mistake by Pete would only give her a split second to know it. "Please stop," she yelled.

"What's wrong?" Pete asked. "Ain't getting carsick, are you?" He checked the speedometer then let up on the gas. "There it was. A tick over my best. Didn't mean to make you queasy."

The car coasted to a normal speed. Becky looked back to a dark road. Her knees trembled. "Let me out," she stammered. "I'll find a way home."

Pete returned to one-handed driving. "Sorry. Just blowing off some stress." He checked the rearview mirror and slowed more until the other cars caught up. "And, who's going to write me a ticket?" He looked at Becky and laughed.

Pete dropped his smile when he spoke again. "I never follow—always lead. Some people say that's an arrogant attitude, but I don't really give a damn. Can't afford to care what people think. Nobody has more power than the high sheriff. If you're not willing to use that power, you won't stay sheriff long. There's always somebody wanting to take you down. Always somebody wanting to take away what you worked so damned hard for. Next year, I will have served sixteen years in this county. And you can count on another four after that. Hell, Kennedy didn't make it through his first term, and he had secret service and police protection every time he stepped out. I know how to survive, Becky girl. And to survive in my position, you'd better be ready to fight like a mad dog if it calls for it. People who cross me learn that." He led the caravan into the restaurant lot and parked. "You might think I'm a bastard for being that way. But I'm the bastard the people of Bolton County want protecting them. And I'm the bastard who killed the man who murdered your husband. I don't know what you were doing at that old house last night, or why you were asking Whitey those questions the other day. I'm not asking. Our slate is clean for now. But I wouldn't dare mark it up if I were you."

Becky immediately found a phone inside the restaurant and called Wendy's apartment with only a slim hope she would've returned by then. As expected, there was no answer. She didn't know how she'd get home, but she knew she'd never place herself alone with Pete again. She hung up the phone and walked into the dining area.

It surprised her that the news of Jessie's death and its celebration at Grady's had spread so quickly. All seats of the dining room were filled with more people coming through the door. A line waited at Pete's booth to shake his hand.

"Right here, Becky," Pete said when she walked by. He grabbed her hand and pulled her toward a space beside him. "Clear back, folks.

This is Chief Hawk's wife. She was in on it too." Becky found herself pressed against Pete in the booth.

Max Underwood laughed at her from across the table. "Yeah, she was there. Bet she'd have killed Jessie if the sheriff didn't." He laughed again and toasted her with a flask before taking a long drink and then pouring some into his coffee.

"You need to get to the doctor and get sewn up, Max," Pete said. "Blood's showing through your bandages."

"I'm going," Max said, interrupting a bite of a sausage biscuit and littering the front of his jumpsuit with crumbs. "Just getting myself a little sedated first." He waved the flask and brought a few laughs from the crowd.

"What are you having this morning, sweetie," a waitress with a trace of anxiety in her voice asked.

"Just black coffee," Becky said.

"I'm buying," Pete said. "You gotta be hungry."

"Just coffee," Becky said again. She saw Sam Roberts pushing through with a camera and one of his young reporters in tow.

"Hi, Sam," Pete said. "Better charge more for advertising this week. I have a feeling you're going to sell a lot of copies."

"I imagine we will, Sheriff," Sam said. "There's my front-page picture. He aimed his camera. Pete put his arm around Becky's shoulder and pulled her close just before the flash. "That's a keeper," Sam said.

The reporter leaned toward Becky with a notepad. "Are you relieved that Jessie Settle is dead, Mrs. Hawk?"

Pete pulled Becky tight against him. "Of course, she is. Settle killed her husband. He was a dangerous man. We're all relieved."

"Anything you'd like to say, Mrs. Hawk?"

Becky looked up at Pete. "Just a thank you to Sheriff Scotland and the sheriff's department for their hard work."

"That's good enough for me," Pete said with a smile. He squeezed her against him again.

"Here ya go, sweetie." The waitress placed a coffee mug down.

The reporter didn't appear satisfied. "I hear you were at the scene when this happened. Can you tell me why?"

"She was looking for Settle the same as me," Pete said. "She helped me find him."

"But how?"

"That's enough for now, Nick," Sam said. "We can talk to the sheriff more later. We're interrupting their breakfast. Thanks, Pete."

"Anytime, Sam."

"Hey, son! Hey, son!" The calls came from Underwood and were loud enough to quieten the restaurant. His reddened eyes looked past Becky. "Hey, son!"

Becky turned. Will Bailey stood at the cash register with two take-out boxes. He looked back without expression.

"Things ain't changed that much," Underwood yelled. "You still have your food brought to you at the backdoor. You understand me?"

Will turned his eyes away and pulled out his billfold.

"I asked you a question," Underwood said. "Don't you turn your back on me..."

"That's enough, Max," Pete said. "We don't want a scene here."

Becky stood and walked to register. "Hello, Will. Can you please give me a ride home?"

"No problem."

Pete stretched across the booth. "Where are you going?"

Becky stepped back to the dining room. It remained quiet. All eyes were on her. She glanced at Underwood pulling a Camel cigarette from its pack then looked at Pete. "I don't really care for the company, Sheriff," she said loudly enough for everyone to hear. "And it has a lot more to do than with skin color." She turned and walked out.

Will smirked while driving his truck from the lot. "I'd die to know what they're saying about you in there now."

"I couldn't care less," Becky said.

"Seems like high excitement. You should've stayed and listened to Pete and Max brag."

"No thank you. I was about to begin walking home if you hadn't showed up. What brings you out so early?"

"It's Lily's birthday. I told her to sleep in and I'd serve her breakfast in bed. I just didn't tell her it would be Grady's Big Breakfast Special."

Becky grinned. "Tell her happy birthday for me. And thank her for having it today so you'd show up and rescue me."

"You looked like you needed saving," Will said. The truck wound its way into gear. "Come on Betsie. You can do it." Will slapped the dashboard. "About two minutes of Max's company is what the average person can stand." He shook his head. "Damn, Jessie, Pete, and Max all going at it together. I bet that was a sight. Too bad two of them walked out."

"Who is he—Max?" Becky asked.

Will shook his head and snorted. "Who is Max? Well, that's a tough question. If you ask him, he's Pete's righthand man, political advisor, and head jailer. If you ask me, he's a big chunk of ignorant, loud-mouthed, white trash."

"I agree with your assessment. He's really the head jailer?"

"That's his title, but only because he's the sheriff's old buddy. Head Goon would be better. He handles Pete's dirty work."

"What do you mean?"

Will shrugged. "Oh, hell, where do I start? It can be anything from getting information from prisoners to intimidating political enemies to probably a hell of lot worse. Max is—was—Jessie Settle's mother's brother. But I'm guessing you already knew that since you were out there last night."

"I had no idea I'd run into all that."

"Damn. You need to be careful, girl."

"Tell me about it. I mean tell me why."

"Well, I don't know anything more than most people who've lived here all their lives know. Max's daddy was a bootlegger. Pete and Max made the deliveries for him and made collections. Kind of like a half-assed, backwoods Mafia. Max took over the business when Old Man Underwood died. Pig farming is just a sideline. The joke is Max raises pigs to cover up the smell of liquor cooking. Jessie wasn't really raised by anybody. I've seen alley cats that had a better upbringing than him. Max put him to work making deliveries when Jessie was barely old enough to see over the dashboard. Pete tries pretending he doesn't, but I have no doubt he still has a hand in the operation."

"Do you know Phyllis Underwood?"

"Just that she's Max's second wife. The first one fell down the basement stairs and broke her neck." Will rolled his eyes.

"When Jessie was trying to cut Max, he said something about Max and Phyllis being in on something. He said he was going to kill them both. Do you think that could've had anything to do with Ed?"

Will frowned. "I wish I could tell you. It's hard to say with that bunch. I doubt there ever has been a day when they weren't doing something crooked. The only reason I reported it when I saw Jessie that day is because I thought he *might have* killed Ed. I instinctively question any story Pete tells. But let me tell you what I do know. There ain't nothing more dangerous than a man without a conscience in power. Do you know how many people have died in Pete's jail since he was first elected? Four. One had a heart attack while fighting with deputies. Three hung themselves. Three jail hangings in this little hick county, and all since Pete took office."

Becky's heart pattered as she felt her suspicions moving closer toward reality. "Were they investigated?"

Will laughed. "You're smart, Becky, but you still have a lot to learn about this place. I only know the details of one—Mackie Phelps. He was a tree faller for the plant. Big guy. Way over six feet, and strong as a bear. I used to fish and hunt with him. He wasn't a saint, but he had a lot of influence in the lumber town. Pete paid him a fair amount to drum up votes for him there every four years. That's what the bastard does. He buys votes from factory workers in Cypress Cove and Black Lake, gives some of the big influencers a jug of Max's best, then squeezes out just enough votes in Deaton to win. Anyway, Mackie hacks himself in the leg one day with an ax and goes home early after getting it sewed up. He finds his wife on the couch providing certain favors to Pete. Pete gets his pants up and runs out the backdoor before Mackie can catch him. So, by coincidence, Mackie gets stopped on suspicion of drunk driving just as he leaves his house that night. He's still pissed as hell and that didn't make the situation better. It took four deputies to get him down and cuffed, and they barely got the job done. Of course, he gets a pile of charges and high bail after that, and he's found swinging by a bedsheet the next morning."

"Are you saying Pete may have killed a man because he got caught cheating with his wife?"

"I'm not saying anything, because I don't know. I do know that Mackie would've killed Pete that day if he'd have caught him. Mackie grew up with Pete. He used to tell me about all the shit they did when they were young. I'm sure he had a ton he was going to spread around."

The Black Lake town limit sign passed.

"I guess Mackie might've hung himself because he was torn up over his wife cheating on him. And maybe I'll be driving a Cadillac next time I give you a ride."

"Was Underwood working in the jail when it happened?" Becky asked.

"Maybe. Probably," Will said. "But I can tell you Underwood wouldn't have been enough to get that job done. It would've taken a truckload of men. You can be sure Pete and Max aren't the only crooked ones in this county."

Will turned onto Dalton Street. "You need to be very careful what you say and do in this town," he said. "Pete has a way of finding out things you wouldn't think he could. He has plenty of eyes and ears around. I don't want anything happening to you too."

"Did you talk to Ed before he died, Will?"

"Yeah. Just a week or so before it happened."

"What about?"

"The same thing you and I just did."

8

"Thank the Lord you're all right," Cynthia shouted. She rushed from the porch to Will's truck. "Wendy called and told me what happened. We only get a recording when we call, saying your number is not in service."

Becky remembered her late bills and hoped the phone wasn't the only utility cut off.

"See you ladies later," Will said with a wave. "I need to get back to the birthday girl."

"Thanks so much for the ride, Will," Becky said. "Tell her happy birthday for me." She turned to Cynthia. "Sorry I worried you. I didn't have time to tell Wendy anything. It's a long story."

"Is it true Pete killed Jessie Settle?"

"Yes."

"And you were there when it happened? My goodness, Becky."

They walked inside. Becky felt relief when she flicked the switch and lights came on. Exhaustion hit her suddenly and made answering the questions Cynthia threw at her toilsome. "I know I shouldn't have gone there," she replied to Cynthia's extended rebuke. "It was a dumb thing to do."

"Well, I'm glad you agree with me on that. Neither me nor Bobby could take it if something happened to you."

"How did Mr. Billings' surgery go?" Becky felt terrible she hadn't thought to ask yet. She dropped onto the sofa and motioned for Cynthia to take a seat.

"I don't have time to stay," said Cynthia. "Got to get back to Bobby. I don't want to leave him alone for long. The surgery went bad. They found more. They're giving him three weeks."

"I'm so sorry." Becky wanted to give Cynthia a hug but didn't think she could get up again.

"I really didn't expect good news," Cynthia said. "I just hope he goes peacefully."

"How's Bobby taking it?"

Cynthia shrugged. "It's hard to say. His moods change so quickly. Some are good. Some are terrible. Quincy is coming in today. We're planning to take the houseboat out this afternoon to cheer Bobby up. Bud's joining us. There's a little island with beautiful white pines on it. We cut a tree for the house there every year. It's a family holiday tradition. I'd love for you to go with us after you rest."

"Yes. I'd love to tag along." Becky felt sleep gripping her. "Would you please call Wendy when you get back? Tell her I'm fine and ask her to hold on to my pocketbook. I'll call her tomorrow."

"Yes. Why is your phone out?"

"Probably disconnected. I haven't paid the bills for the last two months."

"Poor dear. Why didn't you tell me you were behind? We'll take care of that first thing Monday. I'll lock the door for you. Rest now."

Becky was asleep before Cynthia stepped out.

She would've loved nothing more than an evening of television with a frozen dinner, followed by a hot bath and early bed. Bobby was the only reason she joined in the trip. Late that afternoon, she sat with Cynthia inside the houseboat cabin and watched the lake expand from the window. They enjoyed cookies and punch with their conversation. Bobby helped Quincy and Bud Sweeny at the helm above.

"Thank you all for not bringing up what happened last night," Becky said. "I know everyone is curious. I'm just not in the mood to talk about it now."

"Put it out of your head," Cynthia said. "It wouldn't be appropriate to talk about it today anyway. Jimmy started taking Bobby to get a tree on this island when he was very young. Bobby looks forward to it all year. He calls it Christmas Island. So, lets all try to get in the spirit for his sake." She tuned a radio to holiday music.

The ride took fifteen minutes before the hatch above opened. "Land ho" Quincy shouted. "Christmas Island dead ahead."

They anchored, then Quincy, Bud, and Bobby untied a johnboat and motored away while Cynthia taught Becky to play rummy. The boat returned shortly with two white pines hung over the gunwales. Cynthia and Becky went outside to help hoist them aboard.

"We got one for your house too, Becky," Bobby said from the boat.

"Thank you. It's beautiful."

"Wouldn't seem right if the old house didn't have a Christmas tree," Quincy said.

They then took advantage of the few hours of remaining sunlight to cruise the secluded back section of the lake. Deer drinking water looked up and watched them pass. A raccoon was seen washing his meal. An osprey swept its talons into the water near the boat and flapped away with an impressive fish.

"Those are bald cypresses," Quincy yelled. He slowed the houseboat and guided it as close as possible to a group of large, Spanish moss cloaked trees in the shallows. A multitude of wooden projections around the thick buttresses of the trees reminded Becky of stalagmites from a cave.

She walked to the rail for a closer look. "Are those stumps in the water?"

"They call them knees," Bud said. "They're part of the cypress' root system. It's believed they stabilize the trees and keep them standing in soft ground."

They approached a cove, and Quincy let the boat drift. "Look at this one coming up," he called. "It's said to be one of the oldest trees in the world."

The water-floored woods within the cove appeared. The tree stood out from the others around it. It seemed an atavism from a prehistoric forest. Becky estimated the gnarled buttress to be at least twenty feet wide. A hurricane, it appeared, had once broken off a quarter of the top. New branches sprouted from it.

"It's estimated to be over twenty-five hundred years old," said Quincy.

"Amazing," Cynthia said. "It was growing over five hundred years before the birth of Jesus. Think of all the events that have passed on this earth in its lifetime."

Bobby leaned against the rail beside Becky. "I think I can feel its spirit," he said.

"Me too, Bobby," she replied.

A portly man wearing a wide-brimmed hat and heavy clothing paddled a canoe from behind the trees. A long lens camera was slung around his neck. He waved and guided toward them.

"Shouldn't you be wearing a life preserver?" Cynthia called.

He smiled through a chest-length, graying beard. "Believe I'd just rather drown if I were to tip over with this camera." He spoke in a jovial German accent. "It appears we have this part of the lake to ourselves."

"Great place to take pictures," Quincy said.

The man drifted to the houseboat and placed a hand on the side to steady his canoe. "Very much. Beautiful, lovely place here. I got some shots of a bald eagle in that tree earlier. An old bald eagle on an old bald cypress." His hearty laugh made everyone smile. "Those trees are a treasure. Very durable wood too. I've heard stories that Noah's ark was made of cypress. Gopherwood it's called in the bible. I recently sold a picture of that one to a magazine."

"Are you a professional photographer?" Bud asked.

"Not enough of one to make a living. Just a retiree who found his true love late in life. That would be nature photography."

"What did you retire from?" Quincy asked.

The man shrugged. "Just work," he said. "I moved here about a year ago and bought me a little lake house. It's not much but suits me perfectly. I don't usually get out much this time of year but needed a cure from cabin fever today. Probably my last paddle until spring. Finn Franks is the name." He took a moment to wipe spray from his horn-rimmed glasses. "But I won't keep you good people any longer. There may be just enough daylight left to make a pass down that shore and get a few more shots. There's rumors an albino deer has been seen there."

"We'll be glad to haul your canoe aboard and give you a ride if you'd like," Bud offered.

"No. I can use the exercise." He patted his belly and laughed again. "Have a nice evening all." He gave them a smile and a wave.

They all bid Finn Franks adieu then watched him paddle away.

"Would anyone object if Bud and I made one more stop while we're out?" Quincy asked. "I found some Japanese buyers who are interested in cottonwood trees. It's become a popular lumber over there for furniture. I invited them to stay in the lodge when they visit to discuss business. Just want to see if everything is in order there. Shouldn't take long."

Cynthia looked at Becky.

"Not at all," Becky said.

A large sign atop a cliff made the warning clear: "No Trespassing! Members of Boar Island Hunting Club Only!" Behind the sign, parts of an enormous slate roof and fieldstone chimney showed, bespeaking the size and style of the lodge.

"There's a channel running between here and the bank," Quincy said after he dropped anchor. He and Bud carried flashlights and boarded the johnboat. "Lots of nice sized catfish are down there if you want to try your luck while we're gone." He and Bud motored toward the low-lying side of the island. The reflection of an orange-pink sunset rolled in their wake.

"Have you ever been up there?" Becky asked.

"Goodness, no," Cynthia replied. "That sign means it when it says members only. The only others allowed are potential business clients. A woman would have a better chance of getting into Augusta Country Club than onto that Island. Not that I'd care to, though. The place isn't named Boar Island for nothing. Some genius once thought it would be a good idea to populate the island with them for hunting. I hear the place is overran with them now. They're mean and dangerous."

"Any other game there?"

"Of course. The members capture and release young deer, rabbit, and quail there often. That's why the boars are such a problem. They multiply quickly and destroy the habitats."

"It doesn't sound very sporting."

"I agree. But the members don't want their clients to work very hard at bagging game."

Becky knew what her ancestors would've thought of the practice.

"But I think the men mainly go there to drink scotch and tell off-color jokes," Cynthia continued. "Sure, there's been more than one important business deal hammered out there, but it's very much like one of those clubhouses you see little boys build from scrap wood with a 'No girls allowed' sign hanging on it–just a lot bigger and fancier. You and Bobby see if you can catch our supper. I'll go to the galley and make us hot cocoa."

Bobby had a hook and doughball in the water before Becky could rig up. The rod bent, and the reel whirled.

"Let him run, Bobby," Becky said. "Don't reel against the drag." She found the net and dropped a few more instructions before he fought a five-pound flathead within her reach.

Bobby whooped.

"Good job." Becky removed the hook and let the fish flop on the deck. "Put him in the cooler while I give it a try. Don't let him barb you."

The last vestiges of daylight dwindled when Cynthia turned on the boat lights and brought mugs of cocoa. Bobby and Becky took a quick break. Thumps and jerks from the last few fish caught shook the cooler.

"We're just fishing for fun now," Becky said. "There's plenty for a fry."

"Already?" Cynthia asked. "Good gracious. You've only been fishing for half an hour."

"This channel we're over must be a catfish highway," Becky said.

"They're really in here," Bobby said. He tossed his line back in. Almost immediately the reel squealed. "I need your help, Becky," he said, holding the rod with both hands. "This one's a monster."

"I believe you can do it on your own," Becky said. She drunk her cocoa and watched Bobby fight his fish.

The cooler was full of filets when Quincy and Bud motored back and climbed aboard with muddied clothes.

"Well, you two have been gone long enough," Cynthia said. "What did you get into? You're both filthy."

"Sorry," Bud said. "We surprised a sow with her babies when we went ashore. She chased us." He and Quincy laughed.

"We had to slide down a muddy bank and wait for her to leave," said Quincy. "It's funny now but wouldn't have been if she'd have gotten us with her tusks."

"I told you those horrible creatures are dangerous," Cynthia told Becky. "Whose bright idea was it to stock the island with them to begin with?"

"I don't know," Quincy replied. "They've been there for as long as I can remember. The place is overrun with them now. We need to get up a hunting party soon and thin them out."

"Well, I hope your adventure made you both hungry, because Becky and Bobby caught and cleaned our supper while you were away. We'll be eating late now thanks to you two and the sow."

A cast iron skillet crackled and spat hot oil on a grate over Bobby's fire pit. The filets, dipped in batter and coated with cornmeal, were turning brown with a crunchy crust. Leftover cornmeal and batter were mixed with chopped onion, rolled into hushpuppies, and tossed into the oil. Cynthia brought slaw and a pitcher of tea from the kitchen. Once the fish were cooked, wood was piled on the fire to cut through an icy chill blowing from the lake. Everyone sat around the pit and ate from paper plates. The hot catfish warmed their bellies amid a happy conversation.

"Now that you have a new fishing buddy, we'll do this more often," Cynthia told Bobby.

Becky smiled and watched him eat. It occurred to her that he hadn't stuttered all evening.

She returned home just before midnight and propped her tree in the corner. It gave the living room a woodsy, Christmas scent. She fetched two armloads of firewood then made a pallet of blankets and pillows on the floor. The fire she built was the first in the hearth since the previous winter. The burning hardwood smell enhanced her memories of Christmases in the mountains. She watched the flames while sipping muscadine wine until a peaceful, happy sleep fell over her.

9

She heard the knock at the door the next morning while pulling a pan of cookies from the stove. She smiled, discarded her cooking mitts, and picked up two oatmeal and raisins.

"You don't have to knock, Bobby. Just come on in. Sorry. I thought you were someone else." The young man's smiling face was familiar, but it took her a few moments to recollect how.

"Remember me?" He wore a hat and brown suit and cradled a bible. "Grady's Country Kitchen? Bolton Record?"

"You're the reporter who was with Sam Roberts."

"Right," he sang. "Sorry we weren't properly introduced yesterday. "I'm Nicholas Hughes–Nick for short."

"Have a cookie, Nick." Becky handed him one. "My hands are too doughy to shake."

Nick smiled before taking a bite. He then looked to the heavens with an exhale of delight. "Amazing. Wonderfully amazing." He finished the cookie and licked his fingers. "I just wanted to apologize if I seemed pushy yesterday morning. I recently started writing for Mr. Roberts. It's my first job and I am anxious to do well. Sometimes I let my eagerness get in the way of my manners. Let me also say that I heard of your recent loss and am very sorry." He removed his hat and bowed his head. "You have my deepest sympathy."

He reminded Becky of a funeral director. She stepped onto the porch and glanced around. "Thank you. Where's your car?"

"Don't have one. I'm renting a little apartment downtown. I can walk just about everywhere I need to go. I'm new here. Just recently graduated from the UNC School of Journalism. I did my internship with the Record, and Mr. Roberts was kind enough to take me on. I love the town. So quaint. Lovely people too. Still trying to meet everybody. Anyhow, I was on my way to worship, and thought I'd drop by and introduce myself. I recently began going to Creek Fork Primitive Church. Ever been there?"

"No," Becky said. She was tiring quickly of the young man's friendly act but was curious about what he wanted. "What can I do for you?"

"We would be delighted if you came. There's a wonderful pastor there. His sermons never fail to stir the soul." He looked at his watch. "But since I have some time, I just wonder if I could get more information to beef up my article. Grady's wasn't the ideal place for an interview." He removed his hat and stepped toward the door. "Have a minute?"

"What do you want to know?" Becky asked. She ate the cookie while studying Nick's face.

Nick turned his eyes to his shoes until his smile returned. "Just wanting to know the circumstances that led to your being there when Mr. Settle was shot? Were you really helping to hunt him down? That would be a wonderful addition to the story. I would love to talk about it over more of those delicious cookies."

"I'm expecting company," Becky said. "The shooting is still under investigation, so it wouldn't be appropriate for me to say anything else. I recommend you call Agent Feezor with the State Bureau of Investigation if you want to know more."

Nick grinned. "I sensed tension between you and Sheriff Scotland. May I ask what brought that on? Off the record, of course."

"There's no tension between me and the sheriff."

"But you said that you didn't care for the company. You made that very clear. Something was wrong. As I said, we're off the record."

"It had just been a long night. I was ready to go home."

"Yes, but..."

"As *I* said, I have company coming, Mr. Hughes. I really need to get back to my baking as well."

Nick put his hat back on. He nodded and glanced down the street before turning his eyes back to Becky's. "Just two quick yes or no questions, Mrs. Hawk. Do you think Jessie Settle really killed your husband?"

She wondered if Nick had come on his own or been sent. In any case, she knew nothing she'd say to him would be off the record. "Yes," she said.

"Do the names Helen and Shannon Monet mean anything to you?"

"No."

Nick tipped his hat. "Have a nice Sunday, Mrs. Hawk." He turned and made a slow walk across the yard.

Becky knew he expected her to call him back. She waited until he reached the street before deciding to or not. "Nick," she called.

The smile returned when he looked back. "Yes?"

"Creek Fork Church is the other way."

"So it is," he said with an awkward chuckle and turn.

Becky watched him walk away. It was after he'd turned the corner when she remembered a name Bobby had screamed in despair at the firepit–"Shannon."

"So basically, he held you against your will and terrorized you." Wendy returned Becky's pocketbook shortly after Nick Hughes left. Her expression changed from terror to anger while she listened to Becky describe her early morning ride with Pete. They sat at the table while another batch of cookies baked. "That man is crazy. Wait until I tell everyone about what a creep he is. Hell, I'll write a letter to the editor. Bet he won't win the next election."

"Don't you dare. You're right, he is crazy–crazy enough to hurt anybody who crosses him. I don't want you getting involved in this any more than you've already been. I'm still feeling guilty about dragging you to that old house."

"Come on, Becky. I've already told you I don't blame you for that. And you don't have to protect me. I'm a big girl. Something *is* going on here. I kind 'a doubted it at first, but not now."

"I know that too. But we have to be quiet about it. Don't say a word to anyone."

"So, what are we going to do? Just let this jackass get away with it because he acts tough?"

"No. We're going to let things take their course. When you're hunting deer, you don't go rushing up to them. You sit back in cover and wait for your shot. Going around making a lot of noise won't get us anywhere. I told Agent Feezor about my suspicions. He's an experienced investigator. Something will shake loose eventually."

Wendy frowned. "I don't know if I'd be holding my breath on that."

"Why?"

Wendy looked away. "He was asking me questions about your mental state since Ed's death. He told me about how it's not unusual for people to come up with wild theories when a loved one dies that way. I told him that he really needs to look into this. He said he would but didn't sound very convincing."

"So, he thinks I'm crazy."

"I told him you are as sane as me. Doubt that helped."

"Did he go back into the house and check the bullet holes?"

"What bullet holes?"

"The ones I saw in the wall and blanket after Pete got there. Did he go back into the house?"

"You really noticed something like that? Even with Mr. Neanderthal doing show and tell with his popgun? That's amazing. All I remember is wondering if the pee in my panties would soak through to my dress."

"I bet he didn't check," Becky said. "Sounds like he didn't take me very seriously." The disappointment she felt was in herself from believing it would all be that easy.

"I can't say if he did or not," Wendy said. "I was too busy asking Aaron where the sheriff had taken you."

"I bet that's not all you talked about. He told me he wanted to take you out."

Wendy's eyes gleamed. "He did. We went to a very nice French restaurant in Holland last night. I wanted to call and tell you all about it. Good grief, we had a great time."

Becky clapped her hands. "Yay! Tell me all about it."

"I smell smoke," Wendy said.

"Bet you do. I can tell there's chemistry between you two."

"It's coming from your stove."

Becky cursed while fumbling with her cooking mitts then pulled a ruined batch of cookies from the stove while Wendy cackled.

The Hudson cruised the narrow backstreets of the oldest section of town. It passed well-kept homes spaced between oaks and gardens. Becky had never been there but decided a trip back when the flowers were in bloom would be worth it. "Thanks again for the ride," she said. "I promise this afternoon will be calmer than the other two nights you were with me. It could be pretty boring, in fact. I'll try keeping it short, just don't count on it."

"Baby, I'm ready for boring," Wendy said. "Don't think you have to rush things on my account. Whatever the conversation may be sure beats a Sunday alone at home."

"You don't have another date with Aaron?"

"He's working tonight. We're set up for Thursday. He said something about The Dragon's Wok."

They looked at one another then broke into a fit of laughter that nearly caused Wendy to run a stop sign. She hit the brakes hard. A green pickup behind them tooted its horn.

Wendy gave an apologetic wave. "Which way, Beck?"

"Right, I think."

Only the mailbox and red driveway reflectors of Pearl Wilson's home were visible from the street. Evergreen trees surrounded the rest of the property. An ivy-covered archway stretched over the drive. It led into the small world of gardens, hedges, and walkways that surrounded Pearl's redbrick cottage. Birds and squirrels burst away from feeders all around the lot when the Hudson entered.

Wendy whistled. "Peachy. Did this old lady do all this herself?"

"I bet she did," said Becky. "This must be her life's work." She stepped from the car with a tin in her hands and looked over the lot. The weathered statues and fountains gave it all a rustic beauty. She noticed some neglect in the outer lying parts of the yard, probably evidence of Pearl's age, but realized the spring blooms would cover it. "No wonder she's so concerned about kids trampling over this."

"The sign says no solicitation," Pearl said when she came to the door. Loose strands of hair floated around a white bun. Wide glasses magnified annoyed green eyes. But the eyes softened then moistened when Becky introduced herself and presented the tin of cookies. Pearl's wrinkled hand took Becky's with a surprisingly strong grip. "Well, I'll declare," Pearl said. "It sure is you. Please come in and sit down. Your friend too. I was at the visitation and funeral but didn't think you'd ever remember me."

A caustic smell met them when they walked in. The source was easy to find. Glass oil lamps of bright reds, greens, and blues sat on the mantle and tables of the living room. A grandfather clock's pendulum swung with ticks. A very old photograph of a man with greased, parted black hair and a mustache extending past the width of his face hung behind thick glass in an oval frame over the mantle.

"Your place is beautiful," Becky said.

"Thank you," Pearl said with delight. "Please have a seat. Both of you."

Becky sat down on the couch and smelled Vitalis and Old Spice. She sometimes still detected it on Ed's side of the bed and the headrest of the recliner. She knew she wasn't mistaken in believing that end of Pearl's sofa was where Ed had sat on his visits. "I'm sorry," she told Pearl. "There were so many people at the funeral home and church. All the faces just blend together."

"I understand," Pearl said. She switched a blaring television evangelist off and sat down while allowing a large, yellow cat to hop into her lap. She held the tin high when the cat pawed it. "These aren't for you, Yeller. I've told you, you're on a diet." She handed Becky the tin. "Please, hide these under a cushion. He'll pester me to death for one if you don't." Then to Wendy: "Another chair please. That one is old and fragile." She smiled to Becky. "How are you getting along now?"

"Good days and bad days," Becky said.

Pearl patted her hand. "Of course. Edward was a very special young man. His death shook me to the core. I think about him every day and miss him horribly. You have no idea what it means to me that you're here. He must've told you about me."

Becky felt warmth toward the lady. "Actually, I'm the one who..."

A whistling sounded.

Pearl shooed Yeller to the floor. "Perfect timing. Hold that thought. I was about to have my tea. There's plenty of hot water for us all. Do you ladies take yours with sugar and cream?"

The teapot was nearly empty an hour later. Yeller had moved from Pearl to Becky, and now seemed very comfortable curled on Wendy's lap and receiving a bite of cookie when Pearl wasn't looking.

Pearl had talked steadily the entire time, randomly changing subjects in a way that made it difficult to follow her.

Becky made a waving hand-signal and shook her head when Wendy slipped the cat another bite. Wendy made a face and stuck out her tongue. She gave Yeller more then pointed to her watch.

"And you're the one I've spoken to all those times on the police department line." Pearl brought up the subject again with the same level of astonishment as before. She shook her head. "I wish you'd told me before. I had no idea."

"I just didn't realize you and he were such good friends. Your place here is so beautiful." Becky blushed some when she realized she'd already said it.

"I know it's small, but thank you," said Pearl. "This lot is just part of the property my father once owned. Thomas Jefferson Wilson. Our old house stood in the lot beside here. Dad was a blacksmith and Black Lake's first postmaster. His shop used to be right here where my house is now. He and Collin Billings founded this town."

"I never heard that," said Becky, taking interest.

"Oh, yes. They were extraordinary men. Between them, they owned most of the land around here. Dad donated a big chunk of his to the town. The school and town hall stand on land he owned. Collin wasn't as generous, but his lumber company, of course, was what the town grew around. Edward told me you and he rented Collin's son's, Jimmy's, old house. I suppose you're still living there?"

Becky nodded and began to speak.

"Well, I'm glad Jimmy became a wealthy man. What he started with was handed to him, but he did work hard all his life. He's not like his father, though. Collin selectively harvested. He didn't cut down every tree standing like they do now. That outfit has gotten too big for good if you ask me. They strip the land bare. Then, instead of reseeding it, sell the lakefront property to developers. I'm sure there's a pretty penny to be made that way, but it's destroying the esthetic traits of the land. That's why I had the Leylands planted around the house. I used to have a beautiful view of the lake. The hills on the other side would be just glorious with dogwood blooms in the spring. Now they're just bare mounds of stumps and red dirt. I suppose it's only a matter of time before houses begin going up on them. It's just too depressing for me to look at."

Becky noticed a small basket containing magazines and newspapers beside the sofa. Lying atop them was the small, weathered book– *Poems of a Southern Belle*, by Pearl Wilson.

Becky took it and, on the back, found a grainy photograph of a young Pearl with dark hair put up in a voluminous Edwardian style. She posed on a garden bench with a cat in her arms that looked eerily like Yeller.

"Oh, dear me, you found it," Pearl said with a chuckle.

"I didn't know you are a poet," Becky said. She carefully leafed through the book and read a few lines. Wendy leaned over for a look.

"Used to be. Just something I dabbled at when I was young and had a deeper and sharper mind. Dad knew a publisher in Winston Salem. Edward used to read at least one when he visited. I don't know why. They're not especially good. But he seemed to enjoy them."

"He read poetry?"

"Yes. He'd read a poem then we'd talk about what inspired me to write it. I enjoyed that the most, because it brought so much of my youth back to me. I remembered so many wonderful things. But he told me stories about himself too. The one of his anniversary dance with you was my favorite."

Becky's heart fluttered. "He told you about that?"

Pearl nodded. "It was special to him. I could tell by the way he recounted it. He remembered how awkward it was at first but then how comfortable and in love with you he felt when he held you. He told me he didn't believe there was another woman in the world who could've made him feel that way."

Despite her efforts, Becky couldn't stop the sob that broke from her. She clutched her hand over her mouth. Tears streamed as she looked at Wendy, who patted her heart while making an open-mouthed gesture.

"Oh goodness, I didn't mean to make you cry," Pearl said. "I should've known your heart wasn't ready for that yet."

"No," Becky blurted out. "Thank you. Thank you for telling me."

"Let me get you a tissue." Pearl rose and walked toward the kitchen. She paused at the back window and let out a shrill cry.

Becky rushed to her with Wendy behind her. "What is it, Miss Wilson?" Pearl's face made Becky worry she was suffering a stroke.

"There they are! There are the scamps who've been destroying my yard. The red-headed one is the one who kicked my angel into the fishpond." Pearl rushed to the back door and began fumbling with the lock.

Wendy took a peek. "Oh, I'll handle this," she said. She unlocked the window, shoved it up, and placed her face against the screen. "Jerry and Joseph."

The two boys, bent down tilting a big rock toward the fishpond, looked up. Their mischievous smiles left.

"Miss Martin?"

"You bet your tooshie it is. What do you two think you're doing? No, never mind. How would you both like to spend your Christmas vacations doing homework?"

The boys gawked a moment more before they eased the rock down.

"I wouldn't like that," the redhead said. "What are you doing here?"

"You never know where I might be, Joseph," Wendy yelled. "I keep up with you. It's my job. And, if I ever hear of you stepping foot on this property again, you'll find out how mean a teacher I can be. So, I suggest you get that angel out of the pond, put it back where it was, and never think about coming here again."

"But the water's cold."

"Tough. You've got ten minutes to do it or I'm calling your parents."

"Yes, ma'am," came from both. The boys began removing their shoes.

"Does she really watch us?" Jerry asked. "That's scary."

Wendy slammed the window down for effect. "Call me at the school if they ever bother you again," she told the smiling Pearl.

For the next hour, Wendy took center stage in Pearl's living room and answered questions that delved into every aspect of her life. Becky sat and learned that Wendy had been engaged to a doctor when she was twenty, enjoyed opera, and became a teacher because her high school best friend had. Pearl was still going strong with her questions when Becky saw the look in Wendy's eyes that said, *Get me out of here.* Becky gave her a nod. She felt apprehensive, knowing it was time for the main reason of the visit.

"Miss Wilson?" Becky said it three times before Pearl heard her and paused.

"Yes, dear?" She looked at Becky with a smile.

"I was just wondering. I know my husband stopped by here often, and you and he chatted a lot." Becky struggled for the words. "Was there—was there any certain things he asked you about or told you about?"

"Oh, we talked about many things." Pearl's magnified eyes stayed happy.

"Did he ask you about anyone or anything in particular? Anything that may have related to his job? I'm just trying..."

"No." Pearl's attention now switched between looking out the window and petting Yeller on her lap.

The grandfather clock made a scratching sound then began bonging.

"I've enjoyed your visit Becky and Wendy," Pearl said with her fingers combing Yeller. "But it's time for my afternoon nap now. You need them when you reach my age."

"We've enjoyed it too," Wendy said, hopping up with car keys in hand. "Let's go, Beck."

Becky stayed seated. She tried remembering the last name Nick had used but her memory failed. "You've lived here all your life, Miss Wilson. Do you know anything about a Helen and Shannon?"

The hand stroking Yellar stopped. There came a hard swallow. Then silence.

Wendy and Becky exchanged quizzical glances. Becky stood and walked over, wondering if Pearl was still with them. A blink and a sniff indicated she was.

"Miss Wilson, are you alright?" Becky asked. "I'm sorry if I upset you. I didn't mean to."

"I'm fine," the response came in a low whisper devoid of emotion. "I just need my nap."

"What was that all about?" Wendy asked, backing her car from Pearl's driveway. "Who are Helen and Shannon, and what is it about them that makes even Pearl clam up?"

"How long have you lived here?" Becky asked.

"I moved to Deaton in fifty-nine, when I took my job at Black Lake Elementary."

"And you've never heard those names mentioned?" Becky saw the green pickup from earlier parked a street down.

"Never," said Wendy. "Who are they?"

The driver of the truck shielded his face with his hand and made a U-turn from the curb before driving away.

"I don't know," Becky said. "But don't dare ask anyone."

10

Snow flurries were in the forecast when Bobby arrived at the door with an envelope of money and note from Cynthia the next morning. "This is for your bills," it read. "Please take Bobby with you. Jimmy is coming home. I would rather Bobby not be here until ambulance leaves."

"I enjoyed fishing," Bobby said when they walked into town. His breath steamed in the air. "Want to decorate your tree when we get b-back?" He became silent and moved close to Becky when they passed crowds on the sidewalk.

"Sure," Becky said. "But don't you think you should spend some time with Uncle Jimmy."

"Aunt Cynthia's going to b-be with him."

"Shouldn't you too?"

They walked half a block before Bobby tried answering. "It's just that…It's just…"

They stopped at a corner and waited for the light to change. "It's just that you hate seeing him sick," Becky said.

Bobby nodded. "Yeah."

The barge blew its horn. Becky and Bobby waited for the workers leaving the grill to clear a way.

"Want some breakfast?" Becky asked.

Bobby shook his head. "Aunt Cynthia fixed something. Look, it's s-snowing."

A light flurry fell.

"Just tell him you love him," said Becky. "I know he knows it, but it will make him feel good." She received a few sideways gawks from the crowd. A newspaper rack stood ahead. "The gentleman always walks on the outside of the sidewalk." She moved between Bobby and the rack, blocking his view of it. The Monday morning paper was out with the headline "Chief Hawk's Widow Present at Shooting of Killer." Enough of the photograph beneath it was visible to show Becky's awkward expression while Pete smiled, gripping her.

Cynthia smoked a cigarette in the snow when they returned. "He's inside," she said. "The ambulance just left."

Becky saw the worry. "What can I do?"

"Go inside, Bobby," Cynthia said. She waited until he did. "You're doing it already. This is going to be the hardest part for us yet. I'm very thankful you're here to help us through it. It's a deathwatch now, and Bobby is going to need time away from it or he'll break under the strain. I hope you don't mind if he visits you a little more."

"You know I don't. May I see him?"

"Jimmy will enjoy that," Cynthia said. "Keep it short, though. He's very weak."

Lumbering since his youth built James Billings' body stout. Long hours in the sun tanned his skin deeply enough to keep his face and arms brown throughout the year. He laughed often, and his voice boomed when he told his stories and jokes. Becky hoped some traces of these things were left when she knocked on the bedroom door. What she saw instantly caused her to better understand Bobby's aversions. She felt relieved the drawn curtains and low lighting from a small lamp hid some details as she approached. The man on the bed looked skeletal. He managed a tired smile.

"Hello, Becky," came the whisper.

Enough of the old Mr. Billings' spirit remained to flash in the eyes and inspire Becky to kiss his head. "I'm glad you're home," was all she knew to say.

"Me too."

Little else was spoken. More was said with the eyes than by mouth. *I'll miss you* was felt rather than spoken. Mr. Billings gave her a look that told Becky he was ready.

Becky took his hand. It felt so frail she didn't apply a grip. She saw him trying to inhale enough breath to speak, and she leaned to him.

"Look after Bobby." It rattled in his throat. "Protect him. Please. Watch out for yourself too."

She removed the banded stack of paid phone bills from Ed's desk to add the last two months to it. She took a moment to thumb through them for any recent long-distance calls, and found one made to Savannah on the twenty-first of October. She checked the stack and found the same number on the September bill. Both calls lasted over twenty minutes. She dialed the number. A recording began telling her the number was no longer in service when the doorbell rang.

Pearl Wilson stood on the porch. Snowflakes melted on her black coat and the scarf tied over her head. She didn't smile. A woman maybe ten years younger than Pearl waited in a running car. "I just wanted to return your tin. The cookies were delicious. Thank you." She handed Becky the tin and turned before speaking all the words.

"You're very welcome, Miss Wilson. Won't you come in?"

Pearl didn't look back. "I must go. My neighbor was good enough to give me a ride. We need to get back before the streets turn slick. I didn't get a chance to wash the tin. You'll need to."

Becky watched the car leave before going to the kitchen and placing the tin on the counter. Helen and Shannon. The mention of those names had changed Pearl into another person. Becky felt guilty for it, but also had to know who they were. She returned to the den, dialed the Billings' number, and hung up before it rang. Now wasn't the time to ask Cynthia, she felt. She checked the directory and reluctantly dialed another number.

"Bolton County Record. Sam Roberts, editor speaking."

It was the last person Becky wanted to answer. "Nick Hughes please." She heard a tremor in her voice.

Sam paused. "Who's calling?"

"Janet. I went to school with him."

"Janet who?"

Becky almost hung up. "Smith."

"What school did you attend with him?"

"The University of North Carolina. I'll call back if he's busy."

"Well, he never showed up for work this morning and hasn't answered his phone. Give me your number. I'll have him call you when I hear from him."

Becky hung up.

The vote at the town council meeting that night officially dissolved the Black Lake Police Department and Becky's job. Marge Bowers was assigned the duty of informing Becky the next morning. The vote had been three to two. It surprised Becky that two board members hadn't caved to Frank and Sam's pressure.

"I was surprised too," Marge said. "It was Sonny Johnson and Mark Clayton who voted to keep you. Looks like the old guard's influence is slipping some. I'm just sorry it wasn't enough."

"Change takes time," Becky said. "Thank you, Marge. It's probably for the best anyway."

Soon after the call, Becky felt mental exhaustion settling on her. There were headaches and cold sweats that night. It horrified her to think she may be returning to her dark place. She decided a mental vacation from burdening thoughts was necessary. She spent the next two days fishing by the firepit with Bobby and chatting with Wendy on the phone in the evenings. Muscadine wine by the fireplace provided the perfect nightcap. On Wednesday night she treated herself to a good book and bubble bath. The sensation of her body and mind uncoiling felt wonderful as she soaked. She had no doubt her sleep would be pleasant when she pulled back her covers and went to the window to close the blind. It was then she saw the headlights of a passing car glint off the windshield of one concealed in the woods near the boat access. She conned herself into believing it meant nothing and went to bed.

"Agent Feezor please," Becky said. It was nine-thirty the following morning. She still wore her gown while sipping coffee and keeping an eye on the window. Bobby was coming to help decorate the tree, and she wanted to complete the call before he arrived.

She waited five minutes then, "Marty Feezor here."

"Agent Feezor, this is Becky Hawk."

"Good morning, Mrs. Hawk. Nice hearing from you."

"Good morning. I just wanted to follow up on what we discussed at the shooting. Did you find out anything about prints on the gun?"

"Gun? Oh, you mean the gun used in your husband's murder."

"Yes."

"Yes, ma'am, I did check on that. There were no usable prints found, only smudges. That's nothing unusual though. More times than not we fail to lift matchable latents from evidence. I also checked on the class and individual characteristic comparisons of the bullets retrieved with the suspect's revolver. One was too fragmented for a good comparison but the other matched up without a doubt."

Becky waited for more, but Feezor said nothing else. "I already knew that. Did the revolver appear to be wiped down?"

"The report didn't indicate that, Mrs. Hawk, but that can be difficult to determine."

"I understand the serial number was scratched off the gun. Did anyone there try to bring it out? I hear there are ways that can be done."

"I didn't see any serial number restoration request in our file."

"The sheriff never requested it? Why wouldn't that have been done?" She stood and began pacing.

"I don't know Mrs. Hawk. That's a question you should ask Sheriff Scotland."

"That would get me nowhere." Becky heard the frustration rise in her voice and tried calming herself. "Agent Feezor, I want you to understand that I'm not crazy. I believe my husband may have tried contacting you because he was on to something he didn't want the sheriff to know. The names Helen and Shannon have come up. You need to do some checking on them. I don't know who they are, but I think there could be a link between them and Ed's murder. Also, I'm being watched and followed. I don't know by who, but I know I am." She realized how much this sounded like paranoia and changed the subject. "Did you check for the bullet holes in the house, like I asked you?"

"Yes, Mrs. Hawk. I found two bullet holes in the wall of the house. The sheriff says they got there when he was trying to apprehend Jessie Settle after your husband's murder. That does make sense."

Becky guessed the soft deliberateness of Feezor's tone was his way of dealing with hysterical people. "What about the blanket on the sofa?"

"There were no bullet holes in that, Mrs. Hawk."

"But I saw them. There were two in it."

"The lighting in that old house wasn't very good. I checked it thoroughly with a flashlight. There were no holes of any type."

Becky now found his measured tone enraging. "What color was the blanket?"

"White if my memory serves me correctly. Yes, it was white."

"No, it was blue. Did you even look at it, Agent Feezor?"

"Of course, Mrs. Hawk. I wouldn't lie to you."

Something occurred to her. "They switched them," she said. "Jessie had a blue blanket over him when they rolled him out. Pete must've known I saw the bullet holes and used the blanket on the sofa to cover him." She now sounded crazy even to herself. Feezor's silence told her he agreed. "Did you inspect the sofa for bullet holes too?"

"No. When there were none in the blanket I..."

"Mr. Feezor," Becky said in a calmer tone, "I don't claim to have all the answers, but Ed was on to something that I believe got him killed. If you want to think I'm nuts then fine, but please respect my husband enough as a fellow law officer to have an open mind about his death."

"I don't believe you're nuts, Mrs. Hawk. That's the truth. But I believe your mind may be clouded some now because of the trauma you've been through. I think you may be reading more into some things than are there. However, I will admit it's unusual for the sheriff to not have requested the murder weapon to be processed more thoroughly. Our folks in the lab should've questioned that. Give me a little time so I can go over things with my supervisor. Just keep in mind, our opening an investigation into your husband's murder after it's been closed by local law enforcement would require a lot. But we will review what we have here."

"Thank you," said Becky. "And you will contact me back?"

"Yes, ma'am. Sure will."

"I'm going to hold you to that. Please call me soon. Those six months to retirement will pass fast." Becky said her goodbye and hung up with a glint of hope.

She had time to dress and build a fire before Bobby arrived carrying a large box of Christmas decorations. Becky had the tree waiting in a stand in the living room.

"These are some Aunt Cynthia said I could bring," Bobby said. "They're old decorations but still pretty."

Two-inch colored lights were strung on first then a star attached to the top of the tree. The lights lit and the star flashed when Becky plugged them into the wall.

Becky stepped back and looked at the tree. "Well, that sure makes the house look like it's Christmas. I believe we did a fine job stringing them. I heard you're partial to peanut butter cookies."

Bobby dug balls and tinsel from the box. "Sure am."

"I have the dough made. You hang the decorations while I bake. Just be careful of the lights. They get hot." She walked to the kitchen and put on her apron, feeling delighted that Bobby was so happy and at ease.

"I found a wreath to hang on your front door," Bobby said. He walked past with it. "Is the nail we used to use still there?"

"Yes." Becky removed the dough from the refrigerator and placed it on the counter. She then found her rolling pin, wax paper, and baking sheet. The cookie tin Pearl had returned still lay on the counter. Becky put it in the sink and took a wash cloth. She opened the lid.

"Where is..." the headline of a yellowing newspaper article inside began. Becky unfolded it. "...Shannon Monet?" She looked at a photograph of a smiling young girl in pleated skirt and buttoned sweater. She wore white ribbons in her hair and held a lunchbox. A woman stood behind her. She also smiled with her arms wrapped around the girl's shoulders. A scrap of paper was also in the tin with a phone number and the words "Don't visit. Call," scribbled on it.

"Now you have a wreath too," Bobby said when he reopened the door.

Becky shoved the article back inside the tin and closed the lid.

11

Bobby didn't want to go home after he decorated the tree. He didn't say it, but Becky saw it. She understood the gut-wrenching feelings accompanying the look in his eyes. She promised him she would visit shortly, after she took care of some things around the house. Becky watched through the kitchen window while he walked up the hill. She felt terrible for more than less running him off. When he was out of sight, she locked the doors and removed the tin from under the sink.

The article took up a full page of the July 2nd, 1950, Sunday edition of the Charlotte Chronicle. The author's name, Hudson Perry, seemed familiar to Becky. She took another look at the smiling girl's face before reading:

"Two years ago, this Independence Day, a young couple rode home from a fireworks show in the small community of Cypress Cove. They'd chosen a scenic lake route to enjoy a few last rocket explosions in the sky. But at 681 Pelican Drive, their attention turned to the broken-down front door of one lakefront home. Something lay inside. They stopped to shine a light then sped away, horrified and in search of a phone. Within minutes, the distant sound of sirens broke the night silence.

"It was 35-year-old Helen Monet who lay supine inside the door, her neck gashed to the jugular, blood splattered on the wall and floor behind her. Bolton County deputies secured the scene then began a desperate search for Shannon Monet, Helen's fifteen-year-old daughter and the only other member of the household. Bloody footprints left by an unknown person were found throughout the house, along with evidence of a struggle in Shannon's upstairs bedroom. Blood matching Shannon's type was found inside and outside the house and on a pier in the back. Despite a massive search, which included the dragging of a large section of property adjoining Black Lake, Shannon remains missing to this day. No arrests have been made.

"Located in Bolton County, Cypress Cove is an unincorporated, textile plant town, incised with tributary streams and creeks of the sprawling lake. The Monets moved there from the neighboring town of Black Lake when Helen took a fabric cutter's job a month before the murder. Shannon remained enrolled in Black Lake High School. She was a rising sophomore."

The middle part of the article covered highlights of interviews with the principal of Black Lake High, a few of Helen's co-workers, and two neighbors still living near the murder scene. Both neighbors recalled hearing firework explosions and shouts carrying across the lake until late into the night. "Nothing unusual for the Fourth of July," one said.

The article concluded with: "First-term Bolton County Sheriff Pete Scotland said that the investigation is inactive at this time but will never be closed. 'This is the only unsolved murder in Bolton County,' Scotland said. 'I hope to one day make an arrest. Information often comes quickly, but sometimes it's slow and requires patience. I will never stop looking into leads as they come forward.' While Scotland would not confirm or deny the existence of suspects or known motive in the case, it is certain that somewhere in Bolton County someone knows who killed Helen Monet and what happened to Shannon. The clock of justice is ticking toward the truth."

Becky dialed the phone. It took five rings for Pearl to answer.

"Miss Wilson?"

"Just a moment." Pearl's voice was jagged. She coughed. "Are you alone?"

"Yes."

"Do you have a party line?"

"No. Private."

"Just a second." Away from the receiver came another cough and "Move Yellar. Give me room." Becky heard chair springs squeak. "I wondered if you'd call," Pearl said, short of breath.

"I just opened the tin. Was this what Ed asked you about?"

"Yes." Pearl took a drink of something. "But first, are you aware that Sheriff Scotland is watching you? Maybe not now, of course."

"How do you know that?"

"He visited me just after you and your friend —Wendy was her name?— left. He pretended to be following up on the children's trespassing, but the conversation quickly turned to you and the purpose of your visit. He asked in a roundabout way, but there's no doubt he knew of your visit here beforehand. I know he believes I'm a feeble-minded old woman, so I just played along."

"What did you tell him?"

"I told him that you are a friend of mine. That I know you through our conversations on the police line. That you and Wendy brought me some cookies for Christmas. And that Wendy solved the trespassing problem very nicely. He asked about my conversations with Edward too. I didn't tell him anything. Now, don't take me wrong, Becky. I very much enjoyed your visit the other day, but I believe you had an ulterior motive as well."

"I'm sorry if I seemed underhanded," Becky said. "I enjoyed the visit too. I just have questions about Ed's death and knew he visited you often. I wanted to know what he talked about."

"Most nights I sit up and think about it too. I can only wonder if our conversations put him in danger. You'll have to forgive me for my silence and lie Sunday. Your questions took me by surprise. I didn't know how to respond. I've prayed over whether I should tell you or not."

"I need to know, Miss Wilson."

"Yes, you do. You're his wife. But I expect this to stay between us."

"It will."

"Fine then." Drinking sounds preceded the clink of a cup returning to a saucer. Then, in a heavy, throaty voice: "The little girl in that article had a special connection to my heart. I doubt she ever knew how much. I called her my 'Grocery store girl' before she finally told me her name. That's because Parker's Grocery is the only place I ever saw her and her mother. She must've been six or seven when I first met her. She was slipping a Baby Ruth into her Little Lulu toy purse." Pearl made a soft chuckle with a sigh in it.

"'Good little girls don't steal,' I said. She looked up at me with the loveliest, big blue eyes. She looked so sorry and scared that it broke my heart. 'Don't tell Mommy,' she said. I gave her a nickel. Her mother walked down the aisle with her cart, and I told her I was buying her daughter a candy bar for being so pretty.

"So, that's how it started. It was a while afterwards when I saw her there again. She ran up to me with her arms out and gave me a big hug. That's when we told each other our names. I bought her another Baby Ruth that day and every other day I saw her there. Sometimes

142

that would be months or even a year. Each time Shannon was a little bigger, of course, but there was always a smile and hug. She must've been a teenager the last time I saw her, and she told me, 'You don't have to buy me candy today, Pearl. I'm too big for that now.' She hugged me once more and said, 'Thank you for always being so nice to me.' Then she kissed my cheek."

Pearl swallowed hard. Becky detected weeping. "I'd always noticed that Shannon and her mother wore rather plain clothes, sometimes worn. Her mother only bought discounted groceries. So, one day I gave Alvin Parker a ten and told him to take it out of their groceries for as long as it lasted and let me know when it ran out. But, I never saw nor heard from them again. It was only when I read that article did I learn what happened."

"This article was written two years after, Miss Wilson. You never heard about this before then?"

"I'm a recluse," Pearl said. "My life mainly revolves around my little tract and gardens. I still wouldn't know about it if I didn't subscribe to the Sunday edition of the Chronicle."

"Why did Ed ask you about this?" Becky asked.

"He didn't ask me particularly about it, just if I knew of any tragedies or major crimes in Black Lake before 1950. This was the only thing I knew of."

"Why only before then?"

"Edward told me nothing about his reasons. But I believe this was the story he was after, because he asked me every detail of what I knew, which is very little other than what's printed in that paper."

"They never found her?"

"No. I did learn that Helen Monet is buried in the old Shiloh Church cemetery in Cypress Cove. My neighbor drove me there once.

It sits on a little hill overlooking the lake. I put some flowers on the grave then walked to the water and tossed a few in, because that would be my guess where Shannon is. I began writing a poem there called 'Shannon's Silent Song,' but never finished it. No matter how I tried, it always sounded too macabre. I didn't want that for the sweet girl, so I gave up."

Becky tugged her ponytail. "Why didn't Ed tell me about this? Why did he keep all this a secret from me?"

"Quite possibly to keep you safe."

"Safe from what? What's so dangerous in this town, Pearl—Miss Wilson? You've lived here all your life. Is it a crooked sheriff or is there more?"

"There's more. And I believe it *is* dangerous. Knowing of it could be why Edward is dead. Please don't blame me for telling him, Becky. He asked me about it. Somehow, he already knew part of it."

"I don't blame you. Please, just tell me." Becky waited several moments before Pearl spoke again.

"It started in the early nineties. I was young, not yet in my teens. As I told you during your visit, my father and Collin Billings were founders of Black Lake. My family was one of the first to live in this area. Collin came here later with lots of money and purchased huge amounts of land. Dad sold him much of what he owned, and the two of them became friends. I remember Collin and Dad having discussions in our den and at the shop about forming a town here. Collin had already begun cutting and selling lumber to the local farmers, but he wanted to expand and hire more workers and bring people and business here. But they needed a fast way to transport large amounts of lumber to Wilmington. Wagons were too slow. They considered barges, but the creeks trailing from the lake are too swampy and shallow for large boats to make it to the Cape Fear River.

144

A railroad was the only answer. Industry and efficient transportation of goods are most important to a town. Dad used to talk to me and Amelia and Rose about things like that. They were my older sisters. He wanted us educated beyond just the three R's."

Becky wanted to be certain Pearl wasn't settling into one of her monologues, in which the point of her initial conversation is lost. "This is what you and Ed talked about that's dangerous?" she asked.

"You need to let me finish, dear." Pearl's tone sharpened. She went through another coughing fit before her voice returned. "Dad and Collin worked hard preparing a proposal that our timber would be profitable for a rail line. They left out one day for Richmond to meet with some men from the railroad. They stayed gone for nearly a month and returned happy and excited. Dad brought us all gifts back. Mine was a porcelain doll. I still have it. They told us the railroad agreed to build a branch line through here and that in a few years we might have a nice town. Dad told me and my sisters that we might even live long enough to see it become a big city." Pearl sniggered. "He was a smart man, but I think he missed that prediction.

"A while later, the railroad company wrote to let them know they were sending some men to scout the area, determine the best route, and purchase land. Well, Dad and Collin planned this big welcome party at our house. They really wanted to put their best foot forward. Mother and a few other women cooked the day these men were to arrive. We children helped clean and fix up the dining room. Dad and Collin practiced their speeches in the parlor. Amelia, my oldest sister, did my hair and Rose's. No detail was overlooked.

"So, there we all were, dressed to the nines with a spread of food fit for a king on the table, when a wagon pulled in with the dirtiest and vilest men we'd ever encountered. There were three of them, and they walked into our house as if they owned it. They all sat down at the table with hardly any introductions and filled their plates. There were no manners about them. None of them even removed their hats or wiped their scraggly beards while they ate. And, oh, how they cursed. It was bad enough that Dad sent all the women and children out of the room."

Becky found the story interesting but wondered about its point. Then Pearl told the rest.

"Before I left the room, I noticed that each of these men wore a badge somewhere on them. The man closest to me had his pinned to the brim of his hat. I found it curious and took special note. It was bronze and seven-sided with an engraving of a manticore in the middle. There were also some words there, but I wasn't brave enough to lean in and read it. Do you know what a manticore is, Becky?"

"No," Becky said. But the thought of Frank Frye's tie tack hit her between the eyes.

"It's a winged creature from Persian mythology with the body of a lion, face of a man, and tail of a scorpion. It sings softly in a human voice while it devours its prey and never leaves behind a trace of its victims." Pearl let out a mirthless chuckle.

"Was this some kind of group?"

"Yes. Dad did research on them later. So did I when I got older. There's little about them recorded. Dad learned what he did through correspondence with sources he trusted. It seems the Manticores were some sort of small, secretive club that formed during The War Between the States. They practiced espionage for the Confederacy. It seems they plotted the assassination of Union leaders and planted boobytraps in front of Yankee troop movements among other things. But I've been told also they were nothing but profiteers who worked for either side when there was pay to it. The group survived after the war and became little more than outlaws. Now, why the railroad sent an outfit such as that here I have no idea. Or maybe they wanted them in case it was necessary to deal with problems such as the O'Haras."

"Who were they?"

"A farm family who lived near us. Mr. And Mrs. O'Hara were friends of my parents. My sisters and I used to go over and play with their children. There were five of them close to our age and two younger children, one an infant. Mr. O'Hara's mother lived there too. Their farm covered over a hundred acres and sat right smack where the railroad wanted to lay the branch line. Mr. O'Hara refused to sell, even though he was offered a very pretty penny for it. I don't believe he ever really liked Collin much and didn't want to see the land around here ravaged by a big timbering operation.

"Anyway, this group–these Manticores–had grown here by then. I'd guess there were twenty or twenty-five of them. They set up a camp close enough to our house that my sisters and I could sit on the balcony at night and watch their fires. We could hear them whooping and cursing. They'd help themselves to our garden and fruit trees. Others had hogs and cows taken. I swear they reminded me of a group of marauding pirates. They wore knives and guns on their sides. Some even had swords. Dad told us to avoid them, but he didn't have to. We were terrified of them. One morning my sisters and I walked to the O'Hara's to play. The front door stood open, and the dogs ran out. But nobody else was there. Everything they owned remained– clothes, furniture, food. The only evidence of anything were sets of wagon tracks in the front yard. We ran back and told Dad. He and a group of men conducted a search, but nothing was ever found. It's as if ten people just disappeared from the earth.

"Of course, everybody suspected those horrible men. I heard when Dad and the others confronted them about it at their camp a gunfight nearly broke out. Turns out these men had Mr. O'Hara's signature on the paperwork. Dad told me later that he saw it, and best he could tell it was no forgery. He believed Mr. O'Hara signed it under duress before something terrible became of him and his family. I still wonder."

Becky caught herself scanning the windows. "I never heard a word of this," she said.

"There's much you won't hear of in this town," Pearl said. "Anyway, the railroad came through. The lumber company prospered. Black Lake was established. It was all just as Dad and Collin had planned, except for the Manticores. Their camp grew, and so did the problems they caused. I heard enough of Dad and Collin's conversations from the parlor to know that those scallywags were claiming responsibility for the railroad and demanding to have a cut of the lumber profits. Nobody was going to allow that, but Dad knew big trouble was coming, and it did. One night we saw this enormous glow in the sky, nothing like I'd ever seen. It was the lumber company. They'd set it afire and bent the track railings. That was enough for everyone around here. Most of the men were in favor of attacking the camp at night and shooting every last one. Dad and Collin, praise the lord, were more level-headed. They wired the governor, and he sent down a National Guard unit and the railroad sent detectives. They arrested many on outstanding warrants. The detectives tried figuring out what happened to the O'Haras also. Unfortunately, they were unable to pin that or the fire on that bunch, but that was all right for us, because the crowd of them pulled out after that. Or so we thought."

"They came back?" Becky asked.

"Yes. Not as many as before, but we began seeing strangers who wore the symbol again. It was just after I'd begun high school. Rose was a senior. Amelia was away at college. There weren't problems at first. Most of them took regular jobs and raised families. Everyone was still leery of them, though. Dad and some of the others tried finding out why they were back. He considered calling on the governor again. Then, five of them showed up on our front porch one evening. Dad went out and talked with them. I don't know what was said, but I remember hearing voices raised. It was the only time I ever heard Dad utter a curse word, and he did it several times. It was also the first time I saw him scared, because his face was white as a sheet when he came back in. He told Rose and me to avoid those men at all costs and never speak of them. And he never uttered a word about the Manticores again. Not to me anyhow."

"What is their purpose here?" Becky asked.

"That's a question Edward asked. I don't know. Maybe it's only a silly club now. But I'm afraid there's more to it than that. Even today I see the symbol on occasion, not on the gaudy badges anymore, but sometimes on tie tacks and pins."

"Who wears it?"

Pearl took a few moments. "Some I don't know. A few are men of prominence. I won't go into names. I see no need to. Just know they are here. I keep to myself because I think it's best in this town. If I were young like you, I'd move and start over. I told Edward the same thing. I'm sure it's against his wishes that I've told you this. But perhaps it's safer for you if you know of them. But do not repeat any of this. Do not pursue it in any way. Swear on Edward's grave you won't."

Becky remembered Ed's unusual silence near the end of his life. He'd been different, and it was from the stress of not knowing what to do. She understood that now because she felt the same.

"Becky?" Pearl shouted.

"I swear. Do you want your paper clipping back?"

"No. Burn it now."

A few minutes later, Becky knelt at the fireplace. She watched the paper blaze, and asked Ed for forgiveness.

12

She attempted two phone calls after speaking with Pearl. The first, she left a message with the SBI receptionist, asking Agent Feezor to call her. The second resulted in the out of service recording again when she tried the Savannah number. She banged the receiver down then dropped onto the sofa, repeatedly wrapping her ponytail around her hand. The anniversary picture now sat on the mantle over the hearth.

"You should've told me," she told Ed. "Tell me what to do now. Find a way." She realized just how overwhelmingly alone she felt. This time Ed's smiling at her in his tight tuxedo made her angry. She remembered her promise to visit Bobby and went to the closet for her coat and toboggan.

Halfway up the Billings' driveway, shouts brought her out of deep thought. The blast from a siren made her turn and jump aside to allow Lewis and Sealy's ambulance to pass. She ran up the driveway behind it while more shouting came from the house.

"I tried calling you four times. Is your phone still out?" Cynthia looked at Becky with a stress cringed face while holding the door open for a stretcher.

Becky huffed from her run. "I'm so sorry. I had a phone call. Is he gone?"

"I don't think. Not yet. Please help me with Bobby. I can't control him."

"Where is he?" an ambulance man asked.

"Follow me." Cynthia trotted down the hall toward screaming. Becky followed with a fluttering stomach.

"Wake up. Wake up." Bobby shouted. He knelt on the bed with his hands on James' shoulders, shaking the frail body.

"Stop, Bobby," Cynthia cried. "You'll hurt him."

"Step back, son," one of the men said. He placed his hand on Bobby's arm.

Bobby jerked away. "No. He-he's just asleep. He's as-sleep."

"We need to check him."

Becky moved around the stretcher. She pulled Bobby back. "Step back. They're here to help your Uncle Jimmy."

Bobby jerked away and turned. Becky saw his fist swing but was unable to dodge. It struck her jaw. White light flashed. She fell on her rump in a daze.

Then the ambulance men battled with Bobby. One took his arms and the other his legs while he thrashed and kicked. "Don't take him!" Bobby squealed. All three crashed to the floor beside Becky. One man held Bobby down while the other went to James.

Becky felt Cynthia's arms under hers, dragging her back. Cynthia let go then appeared in Becky's blurred vision.

"Are you Ok?"

Becky held her chin and nodded.

The man checking James removed his stethoscope from his ears and said, "Not much pulse and breathing shallow. We need get him there quick."

"Better call the sheriff's department," the other shouted. "This boy ain't quitting and he's strong."

Becky crawled over. "Wait a minute." She put her hands on Bobby's cheeks and her face directly in front of his. "Bobby. Bobby, snap out of it," she shouted. "Uncle Jimmy needs help. Let them."

The last screech became a sob. The resistance stopped.

"Let them help him."

Bobby's tear-filled eyes came back from some other place then focused on Becky. His lips moved before he spoke. "Osiyo," he whispered.

"Osiyo," Becky said back.

"Need some room," the ambulance driver said. "Your chin alright ma'am?"

"Yes," Becky said. She helped Bobby to his feet then guided him aside.

"He's in God's hands," Cynthia told Bobby. "Can you stay with him while I follow the ambulance to the hospital?" she asked Becky.

"Yes. We'll go to my house. Do you need me to call anyone?"

"No, I'll call Quincy from the hospital." Her voice broke. "He'll contact everyone else who needs to know. I'm sorry you got hurt. Thank you for your help. I don't know what we'd have done if you weren't here." She wiped her eyes with her dress sleeve. "What was that you and Bobby said to each other? O say O?"

"Osiyo," Becky said. "It means hello. But I think Bobby meant he's ready to be brave by it."

"I'm sorry I hit you." They sat on the sofa. Bobby stared at the lit Christmas tree. Becky let him talk when he wished.

"It's fine. You didn't mean to. Do you even remember doing it?"

"Not much. Some-sometimes I just–I just. I forget what I'm doing."

Becky felt his hands squeeze hers. The grip continued until it caused her pain.

"It just happens." He hissed the words.

"It's going to be all right." Becky said. She pushed a thought from her head–because it was unthinkable.

Wendy called that afternoon with an invitation to the school Christmas assembly the next day.

"I don't know if I can make it," Becky said. "I doubt Mr. Billings will make it through the night. Mrs. Billings is going to need help, especially with Bobby. He's here with me now." She looked up the stairs to check the bedroom where he napped.

"Bring him with you," Wendy said. "Listen, I know what's going on is a real drag, but the kids have got something for you. I wasn't supposed to tell you, but you must be here. It's only an hour."

"Why are you having the assembly now? There's still a week of school before Christmas break."

"Just shut up and be in the auditorium at nine-thirty, Little Miss Nothing Gets Past Me. What'cha doing tonight?"

"I told you. I'm keeping Bobby."

"Want some company? Aaron broke our dates for tonight and tomorrow."

"Why? I thought you and he were getting along great."

"We are. He says there's some special duty the sheriff called him about. Geez, I wish he didn't work for that jerk."

"What kind of special duty?"

"He didn't tell me. Whatever it is, he didn't sound excited about it. Who knows, maybe he's finally beginning to like me more than police work. I swear I believe the guy gets an erection when he hears a siren. So, can I come over? Maybe I can get you guys to laugh. You probably need it."

"This really wouldn't be a good night," Becky said. "I'll see you tomorrow morning."

Ed was a frugal man except when it came to hunting and fishing equipment. The Ross Stepsun binoculars used for spotting game were no exception. Becky rummaged through the gun closet before she found them. Bobby was still sleeping in the room next to hers when she went upstairs and pulled a chair to the foot of her bed. She pulled the blinds up three inches and zeroed the binoculars in on the approximate location she'd seen the car at the boat access the night before. Then she took a nap.

The call came just after Becky set the table and removed a meatloaf from the oven. Cynthia sounded tired and somewhat relieved. "He left us less than a half hour ago. Bud is here, and the pastor is on the way. I've called Quincy. He's taking care of a few matters but should be here in a few hours. You don't have to tell Bobby. Quincy or I will do it later. You don't need another episode like before."

Bobby looked at Becky from the kitchen. He held a spoonful of gravy over his creamed potatoes. His eyes dimmed.

"He's right here and he already knows," Becky said. "He can spend the night with me if you'd like. I know you have a lot to do. I'm so sorry, Cynthia."

"Thank you so much. It may be best if he stays with you for a day or so. I expect there will be a lot of people coming to the house. Crowds are difficult for Bobby, especially at a time like this. But you tell me if it's fine or not." Several voices began speaking around her.

"Of course, it's fine. I've been invited to the school's Christmas assembly tomorrow morning, but I can take him along."

"Just let me know if it becomes an inconvenience," Cynthia said. "Tell him I'll see him tomorrow and to be strong. You're a true blessing."

Perry Mason was on with the television volume turned down. Bobby took a small sip of Ginger Ale on the sofa. His eyes were still red. He wiped them and his nose with a Kleenex. Becky sat near him. Any more comforting words she could say would be repetition. "Are you sure you can't eat some meatloaf?" she asked.

Bobby shook his head. "I know Uncle Jimmy's in heaven," he said. "He has to b-be."

Becky stroked his shoulder. "Of course."

"Do the Cherokee believe in heaven and hell?"

"They believe in an upper world and middle world. They believe in a creator that is everywhere. It's not much different than what you've learned." Becky was reminded of the old belief that evil spirits sometimes rise to the middle world from the lower world through deep springs and lakes.

"They s-say in church that you have to b-believe in hell if you b-believe in heaven. Do you think there's a hell?"

The question made Becky very uncomfortable. "I don't know. I believe in forgiveness," she said.

Bobby watched Della Street silently speaking. "Even for the worst things?"

Becky felt her heart beating. "Yes," she said. Her next question terrified her. "Why do you ask that?"

Bobby pulled in a breath. His lips moved a little before he slipped into thought. "I want to s-sleep. I'm tired," he said.

Bobby's question repeated in Becky's head while she put a plate of barely eaten meatloaf and potatoes in the refrigerator. She flicked off the television and lights then walked upstairs. She turned on a lamp beside her bed before stepping into the shower and letting cold water run over the bruise on her chin. The frozen image of Bobby's face when he'd struck her flashed in her mind. She tried blotting it out, but there was no way around it. His eyes reminded her of Jessie Settles' the night he stabbed Max Underwood.

She turned off the lamp, pulled back the sheets, then sat on the edge of the bed for ten minutes. She wondered if it were not best to follow Pearl's advice: "Do not pursue it in any way." Ed had wanted her to not know what he knew. Why not honor his wish? It seemed best. Still, she slipped to the window and looked through the binoculars. It took her a few moments to find the concealed car. She watched for some time before someone stepped out. It was Aaron.

13

She woke at sun-up the next morning and checked the now empty boat access area. Aaron stayed as late as two. That was when she'd checked after Bobby's last nightmare woke her. It happened twice during the night. Each time a low babbling followed the shrieks. Indiscernible words were said. She looked in and saw him sleeping soundly this time. His pajama top and hair were damp with sweat. She straightened his bed covers without waking him. Part of her wished she knew what the nightmares were about. Part of her didn't.

Downstairs, she rummaged through the cupboard feeling stressed and tired. She'd planned on pancakes and sausage for Bobby, but the flour was low and only one egg was left. Sausage and cereal would have to do. While the sausage fried, she looked to the den and the anniversary picture. *I need an answer*, she thought.

"Black Lake Elementary Christmas Assembly Today 9:30–10:30." It was stenciled on poster board in red and green magic marker with a generous amount of gold and silver glitter and taped to the front entrance of the school. Mr. Gentry met Becky and Bobby there and walked them to center front row seats in the auditorium. Still a half hour before the show, only a handful of parents had shown up.

"Is there something going on I should know about?" Becky asked, taking her seat.

Gentry chuckled. "Nope. Just enjoy the show from your best seats in the house."

The arrival of more parents grew to a steady stream until the back of the auditorium was full and humming just before the show. The music teacher entered and played "Jingle Bells" on the piano while lines of students entered. They stood and waited for the teachers to take their place in the front row. Gentry walked to the stage and signaled for all to sit.

Hazel Robbins sat down beside Becky with a smile and "Good morning."

Wendy took a seat beside Bobby. "Good morning, guys. Glad you made it." Her smile faded a bit when she looked at Becky. "You good, Dolly? Jeepers, what happened to your chin?"

"Just a little accident. I'm fine. Tell me what's going on?"

Wendy put her finger to her mouth. "Shhhh. No speaking during the show."

Gentry welcomed the parents and made a few short opening remarks before nodding to the music teacher.

"Rudolph the Red Noised Reindeer" played. Laughter and clapping scattered through the place while the first graders marched onto stage with red Styrofoam noses and antlers. Each grade performed two songs onstage. Short skits were worked in beginning with the third graders. A few forgotten lines and other miscues brought chuckles and blushes, but every child left the stage smiling to ovation. The fifth graders wrapped it up with a fine performance of The First

Christmas then sang "Away in the Manger." An enthusiastic ovation followed while Gentry stepped onto the stage with his microphone. He glanced at Becky with a grin.

Becky felt her stomach churn. "Whatever you've done, I'll get you for it," She whispered to Wendy.

Hazel chuckled. "Just relax," she said.

"Very nice job students," Gentry said. "Thank you. Thanks so much to all the parents and family who made it. It was a last-minute decision to have our show today instead of a week from now, and I want to give sincere thanks to our music teacher, Mrs. Williams, for putting this all together on short notice."

Mrs. Williams rose to applause from her piano bench. She gave a quick wave and modest smile.

"Now, I think we have someone waiting in the lobby who made his way down from the North Pole today," Gentry said.

Happy, excited sounds came from the children.

"But before we ask him to join us, I would like to invite Mrs. Becky Hawk to the stage."

Becky gave Wendy a quick deadpan stare and blushed as she made her way onstage. A boy and girl followed her. The girl carried a large manila envelope.

"As most of you know," said Gentry, "our mornings at Black Lake Elementary have been a little different for the last bit. A few smiles have been missing. And that's because we are missing this lady at our crossing. I know she's missed, because I'm told so by students and parents every day." Gentry looked at Becky. "And I miss you too. So, at the suggestion of Miss. Martin and the agreement of everyone, we decided to have our Christmas assembly a week ahead this year, because sometimes Christmas just needs to come early. Each student and faculty member pitched in on this gift to show our appreciation for what you've done for our safety, care and overall good spirits so many mornings, rain or shine."

The girl stepped forward and extended the envelope. "Merry Christmas, Mrs. Hawk."

Becky took it and removed a large, glittery Christmas card made of construction paper. She unfolded it to the signatures of every child and faculty member. A check from Black Lake Elementary in the amount of two hundred and fifty dollars was also there. She held her mouth while an ovation washed over her. A handful of parents stood then everyone. Becky looked out to the faces of children and adults while realizing how glowingly good people could be. It made her ashamed of the times she'd felt self-pity recently– the times she'd cursed God. She mouthed a sincere "Thank you" to the parents in the back rows then the children in the front.

But a thought sobered the moment. Once Helen Monet would've attended Christmas shows there and watched Shannon perform. If something horrible hadn't happened fifteen years ago, Shannon very well might've been one of the parents in the back that day. Helen might've been there as a grandmother. Becky looked at the teachers in the front row. They all stood, clapping with wide smiles. Bobby did the same.

Mrs. Williams struck up "Santa Claus Is Coming to Town," and the children squealed in delight.

"Are you keeping any to spend?" Bobby asked. He waited in the teller line with Becky at Bolton Bank and Trust.

"Yes. Ten," she said. "How about buckwheat pancakes with blueberries tomorrow morning?" She wondered if the money was Ed's way of answering her question. Maybe he was telling her to move on. Maybe Bobby was her purpose.

"Never had them but they s-sound good."

The teller took the slip and check. She completed the transaction and slid a ten across the counter. "Do you have a minute, Mrs. Hawk? I think Mr. Potter may need to speak with you." She lifted her phone without waiting for an answer. "Becky Hawk is out here. Do you still need to see her?"

Calvin Potter emerged from his office on the other side of the lobby. He was short and pudgy with a balding head and waddling gait. He buttoned the top of his shirt and slid his tie up while he came over. "Good morning, Becky–Bobby."

"Good morning, Calvin."

Bobby nodded to him.

"Sorry about your uncle, Bobby. He was an outstanding man and a fine mayor. This town will miss him."

Bobby nodded again.

"Is there something you need from me?" Becky asked.

"Yes, ma'am." Calvin took her arm and guided her away from the line. He spoke in a low tone. "I wanted to tell you how horribly sorry I am about Ed. I apologize for not coming by the funeral home, but this job keeps me so darned busy. You have my sincere condolences. Also, I wanted to ask you about your plans for his safety deposit box. Do you wish to continue renting it?" He took a glance around the lobby.

"I didn't know he had... Bobby, would you sit down over there for a minute?" Becky waited. "I didn't know he had a deposit box."

"Yes. He rented it just before he passed away. I checked, and it's in his name only. I was hoping your name would be there too to save us some problems."

"What do you mean?"

"Normally we would need a court order to turn it over to you. That's the rule, anyway. But I don't believe it's always best to follow formalities, especially in this case. I'll simply add your name if you'd like to keep paying rent. Or I can release the contents to you today. If you promise to keep quiet about it. It'll be that simple."

"I won't say a word. May I see what's in it before I decide?"

"Sure. We just need the key your husband was issued."

"I may know where it is," Becky said. "Can you give me half an hour?"

"Yes. The box is rented until the end of this month. Just be sure to ask for me personally when you're ready."

Becky checked her watch when she and Bobby stepped from the bank. "I need to go by townhall," she said. "Want to race me there?"

Bobby looked confused. "I guess. Why?"

"One, two, three, go." Becky trotted ahead. She kept a look over her shoulder and allowed Bobby to stay close and catch up when they crossed intersections. Townhall was four blocks away. They made it just as Marge Bowers walked out.

"Becky, what brings you here?"

"Marge, that keyring I turned in. Where is it? Please still have it." Becky panted while watching Bobby catch up.

"The one with all the alarm keys? In my desk drawer."

"I need to see it now. I left one of Ed's personal keys on it."

"Now? I was just leaving for lunch."

"Yes. It's important."

Becky deflected Marge's questions and attempts at conversation while rummaging through the keys. Nothing she saw looked like the one. She started over, flipping keys after studying them.

"You know I have only an hour for lunch," Marge said. "Why don't you come back?"

"Bolton BT-12." It was stamped on a small key between two large ones. Becky removed it without giving Marge a chance to read the stamp. "Thanks, Marge. Come on, Bobby."

She cringed when they met Frank Frye entering the building. He gave Becky a tip of his hat, but his eyes were cold. Becky knew he would find out about the key from Marge. She hoped suspicions wouldn't be raised but wasn't betting on it. She took Bobby's hand and hurried past Frank without speaking. His overcoat was open. This time he wore a simple tie clip.

She watched over her shoulder while she and Bobby walked to Parker's Grocery to buy buckwheat flour, milk, and eggs. Alvin Parker worked at the cash register while his employee took lunch. His apron and hair were as perfectly white as his ever-present smile. Becky loved the man and his gentle nature. She would always remember his bringing turkey with all the fixings from his store to her on Thanksgiving. He'd talked and prayed with Becky that day and helped ease the pain of her first holiday without Ed. Becky thanked him again.

"You're more than welcome," he said while bagging her groceries. He waved away the bill Becky held out. "Merry Christmas. Let me know if there's anything I can do for you. Sorry about your Uncle Jimmy, Bobby. You can rest easy knowing he's in a much better place now. Tell your Aunt Cynthia I'm praying for her comfort."

"Back at 12:30" read the sign on Calvin Potter's office door. Becky and Bobby took a seat in the lobby. A copy of the Bolton Record lay on a table between their chairs. "Black Lake Mayor, James Billings,

Passes Away." A photograph under the headline showed him smiling, still healthy and strong. Bobby saw it first and picked it up.

"There's not many people who get a front-page story when they pass away," Becky said. "I'd like to read it when you're done."

It took him less than a minute, then he handed her the paper before staring away.

After initial information, the article gave an abridged history of the Billings family, primarily focusing on Collin's role in the founding of the lumber company and town. James' inheritance of the lumber company was detailed next before going into a lengthy section covering his accomplishments as city councilman and mayor. Most of the information Becky already knew. But she learned something from a brief line near the end: "He was a decorated First World War Army veteran who fought gallantly in the Battle of Cantigny and will be buried with full military honors."

"Your groceries would've been safe in the lobby," Calvin told Becky when they entered the vault and walked to box twelve.

"They're not heavy," Becky said.

"Just slip your key in the right keyhole and turn it". Calvin waited for her to do it then completed the unlocking process with a bank key. "Simple as that. I suppose you'd like some privacy while you view the contents."

"Yes, please."

"Just press the button on the wall when you're done,"

Becky laid her purse and grocery bag on a chair then waited for Calvin to leave. She pulled open the drawer. Red tape sealed a plastic bag containing Frank Frye's jewelry. An evidence tag was attached. Becky laid it beside her purse. Two phone numbers in Ed's handwriting on notebook paper came next. Becky recognized one of them as the out of service Savannah number. The other had a different area code. Beneath this lay a sketch done in pencil. Ed had dated and initialed it at the bottom: "10/26/63, 11:45 EH." "Yard" designated the area under a line drawn across the sheet. "House" was written in a square there. Above it, lines with measurements extended from corners of a rectangle designated "Pier" and met. "A" marked the convergence point. Printed at the top of the sheet was "681 Pelican Drive, Cypress Cove." Becky folded it and placed it and the phone numbers in her purse.

A brown paper bag sealed with more red tape lay at the bottom of the drawer. It was marked "Item A" with Ed's initials and the same date written. She knelt and found her fingernail file in her purse. With care, she slit open the seal. Her file hit metal, and she opened the bag. A steel bird's head stared at her. Becky thought of the ornate handle of a walking cane. She reached inside, felt diamond grips, and pulled out a large, rusted knife. She placed the bag of jewelry back into the drawer and the knife into her grocery bag.

14

Cynthia and Quincy sat on the porch swing when Becky and Bobby returned. Becky winced and checked her grocery bag and the Bolton Record spread over the contents before she walked up.

"Well, here they are," Cynthia said. She went to Bobby and gave him a long hug. "It's going to be Ok. Uncle Jimmy isn't suffering now. Just always remember how much he loved you. Now, go up to the house and put on some dress clothes. We have things to do this afternoon."

"See you later, Bobby," Becky said. "I loved having your company this morning. She watched him silently walk away."

"How's he holding up?" Cynthia asked.

"He's struggling. There's good and bad moods. He seems to be having a bad one now."

Quincy stood. "Let me take your groceries."

Becky swung back. "Thanks, but I've got them. You and Cynthia probably have a lot to do anyway. Sorry for taking so long."

"It's all fine," Cynthia said. "All we can do is comfort him now. And hope time heals him quickly. Anyway, Little Brother and I were just chatting while we waited. You'll never guess what he just told me."

"I said not to tell anyone yet," Quincy said,

"No need in keeping it quiet. People should know as soon as possible." Cynthia looked at Becky and announced with a proud smile, "Quincy is running for United States Congress."

"Thinking about it," Quincy said. "The seventh district representative is retiring. He called and suggested I put my hat in the ring."

"He's endorsing you," Cynthia said. "And you should. You're young and smart, in touch with people's needs, and you know how government works. Maybe this will be the start of something big. Maybe one day you'll run for president."

Quincy laughed, but Cynthia's expression said she believed it could happen.

"Best of luck. You have my vote," Becky said. She took a step toward the front door.

"There's two," Cynthia told Quincy. She looked at Becky. "We're going to take Bobby by the funeral home before visitation begins so he can see Jimmy once more without a crowd around. Would you like to join us? It may help things go smoother for him."

Becky felt on the spot. "I'd like to. It's just that I have a few things to do here before I go."

"Perfectly fine. I don't expect you to be his full time guardian. Would you like for us to give you a ride later?"

"I don't know exactly when I'll be ready, and don't want to keep you waiting. I'll walk."

"It begins at six," Cynthia said. "I'd arrive early if I were you. There will be a crowd."

"I will. See you then." Becky stepped inside and watched them leave. She then locked the door and drew the blinds. She carried her grocery bag and purse to Ed's desk, sat down, and turned on the lamp. She spread the newspaper then removed the knife. It felt cold and heavy. Bits of rust and dried gunk fell onto the paper. She tested the edge with her finger and found it still sharp. The bird's head atop stared at her with its big eyes. It seemed to have a story to tell. But Becky felt sure she knew part of it. This was the knife that cut open Helen Monet's throat.

An evidence tag was tied to the handle. "Item A. Possible WWI German trench knife. See diagram for location found." Becky removed it and the phone numbers from her purse. "Measurements approximate," Ed had written on the "Pier" rectangle. One line leading to "A" from a corner of it was marked "20 ft." The other was "30 ft." Becky wondered how Ed had retrieved it, but her main thoughts pondered the significance of the location. Someone could've tossed the knife from the end of the pier. Or, it may have been dropped from the far side of a large boat docked there. A houseboat perhaps.

She unfolded the paper with phone numbers and tried the Savannah again, only to get the recording. She then tried the other number and felt a tug in her stomach when she heard the ring tone. On the tenth ring someone lifted the receiver.

"Hello." The voice was a woman's and sleepy.

"Hello. May I ask who this is?"

There came a sniff and swallow. "Who the hell is this?"

Becky Hawk. My husband is Ed Hawk. I…"

"How did you get this number?" She was awake now and pissed.

"My husband wrote it down. I found it in a locked box. He was murdered. I only want to know how you knew him."

"Get rid of that number and don't ever call me again." There came a click then a dial tone.

Becky hung up and dialed. It rang just once before the receiver was lifted then hung up. There came a busy signal when Becky tried a third time.

She cursed before snatching everything up and going upstairs to the closet. Ed's lockbox was too full to get the knife inside, so she removed the stack of letters from Mike Ledford and placed them in her nightstand drawer. The knife just fit then. She locked it up with the diagram and phone numbers, slid the box to the back of the shelf, then threw a pile of Ed's sweaters over it.

In the five minutes it took to do this, Becky's frustration had turned to an angry determination. She realized it was a hazardous mindset, but it didn't stop her from going downstairs to the gun cabinet and removing a hunting knife and poncho. On the back porch she found some left over twine used for tying pea vines the previous summer. She made sure the boat access area was empty then went there and made a small, low-lying blind with sticks and the poncho. She then covered it with twigs and Spanish moss.

A line of people extended out the front door of Lewis and Sealy Funeral Home at six o'clock. Becky looked at every man's tie tack as she waited. When she entered the parlor, a hunched over man with a cane stood from a chair and worked his way in behind her. Halfway to the casket, she sensed his eyes on her and turned.

"Quite the popular man James Billings was," he said. His smile showed he wished to make conversation.

Becky took a glance at his tie tack then returned the smile. "He was."

"I suppose the lady over there is his wife, but where's his nephew, Bobby?"

Becky looked. "I don't see him. He's not partial to crowds, though."

"I heard he was like a son to James."

"Yes," said Becky. She saw the man wanted to talk more and was grateful that the line moved then. She passed a large display of flower arrangements and noticed the man taking note of the senders' names.

Pictures of James with family and friends preceded the casket. In the first, Bobby, maybe three years old, sat on James' lap while being read a book. The last was of Bobby and James on a pier. James held two fishing rods. Bobby smiled while holding high a stringer of fish. Becky stepped to a half-flag draped coffin. It was then she saw the seven-sided emblem, not on a tie but pinned to James Billings' lapel.

She tried composing herself then looked across the parlor. Cynthia was occupied receiving condolences. Quincy and Bud stood with her. A man with long, silver hair and pointed chin beard sat with proud posture in a wheelchair there too. He looked ancient except for the icy blue eyes he stared at Becky with.

She turned to James' makeup palliated face then let her eyes trail to his lapel again. The pin was large enough to carry a detailed engraving of a crouched manticore, its wings folded, and scorpion tail ready to strike. The humanoid face made a toothy snarl. The words under it were tiny. Becky leaned in to read them.

The man behind her also looked and angled his glasses to magnify the words. "Can you read it?" he asked.

Becky spelled it for him.

"Ah, yes. *Vis unita fortior*–unity makes strength."

Becky wondered who he was and decided to introduce herself just before Sam Roberts strode to the coffin.

170

"What are you doing here?" Sam's voice was low but angry.

For a moment, Becky thought he was addressing her.

"I didn't know an invitation to a viewing was necessary," the man said. "But maybe things are done differently in Black Lake."

Sam took the man's elbow and walked him a few steps from the coffin.

The man jerked his arm away. "Don't put your hand on me."

"You're not welcome here" said Sam.

"Why? Are you afraid of me?"

"You know damned well why, and I think you should leave now, or this is going to get really ugly."

Their voices rose enough that half the people in the parlor dropped their conversations and turned. The man in the wheelchair looked on without emotion and wiped the corners of his mouth with a Kleenex.

Alvin Parker kept his smile while he worked his way through the crowd. "Calm down, gentlemen," he whispered. "Remember where you're at. This isn't the time nor the place for that."

The man with the cane gave a nod. "You're right." He waved his hand. "You have my condolences," he said toward Cynthia before teetering away. "Let me know if you hear from Nick, Sam. His family is worried about him."

Alvin came to Becky and took her by the arm. "So sorry you saw that. Come visit with Cynthia. I know she'd like to see you." He leaned toward Sam and patted his back. "No need in that, sir."

"Who was that?" Becky asked.

"Who knows," said Alvin. "Sam can be so hotheaded. Most likely one of his old business or political competitors."

Cynthia smiled. "Becky dear, you didn't have to wait in line. You're family also. Come join us."

"Glad you made it," said Quincy. He leaned down and gave her a short hug.

Bud smiled and waved.

Becky tried to act at ease.

Cynthia pulled her aside. "You do not look well. Are you all right?"

"Not really. Just the funeral home and Ed, you know."

"I understand completely." Cynthia kissed her head. "By all means, go home." She led her to the man in the wheelchair. "But first, I would like for you to meet my grandfather, Harrison Tolly. I was so excited about Quincy running for congress earlier today that I forgot to tell you Quincy drove him down this morning."

"Becky Hawk. Nice meeting you, Mr. Tolly," She leaned down and extended her hand. Harrison's withered hand touched it. He didn't return her smile.

"Papa Tolly was like a father to me and Quincy after our parents died," Cynthia said. "He stays in a nursing home now in Richmond. That's where my family is from." A glance from her grandfather seemed to unease Cynthia.

Becky made eye contact with the old man again. This time, she didn't offer a smile. "Where's Bobby?" she asked Cynthia.

"Mr. Lewis took him upstairs to watch television. He's not comfortable being here. Would you mind walking him home?"

"Not at all."

"Also, we're going over Jimmy's estate and financial matters later tonight. If it would not be a bother, I think it might be best for him if he spent another night with you. If you don't have plans."

Becky did have plans. "No problem," she said anyway.

She watched Bobby take the last bites of his warmed-over meal. She wanted to ask him questions. The tension in his manner made her reluctant.

"Bobby, are you all right?"

"I'm g-good."

"You must be tired out from everything."

"Yeah. I'm going to bed. Thanks for dinner."

"You're welcome. I'll fix those buckwheat pancakes in the morning."

"Ok." He walked away.

"May I ask you a question, Bobby? How often does Papa Tolly visit?"

"Never s-seen him b-before. Never knew about him until today."

Becky felt a nervous dread. "Would you mind much if I went outside for a while? There's something I need to do. I'll be close. You can flip the lights on and off a few times if you need me."

He walked up the stairs. "Sure."

She turned her bedside lamp on and checked the boat access with the binoculars. It was still empty. She changed into her cold weather hunting clothes, boots, and toboggan. Bobby slept when she looked in on him. She checked for the car once more before walking downstairs to the gun closet and slipping the flashlight into her pocket. She reached for the revolver but decided it wouldn't be needed. She added a few logs to the fireplace, turned off the downstairs lights, and left through the back door.

She walked fast into the woods past the boat access drive. Finding the blind took considerable time. She had to use her flashlight. Twice she flipped it off and crouched when she heard cars approaching on the street. Both passed. She found the blind, slid into it on her belly, then bundled her arms under her. The poncho, at least, blocked the wind from the lake on a night that was turning very cold. She looked at her house through the twigs and felt bad about leaving Bobby there alone. It was eight-forty. She decided she'd wait until nine-thirty then go back inside if Aaron hadn't arrived.

She looked over her roof at the Billings' house. A single light shined in the house. It came from a curtain-drawn upstairs window. This window provided an unobstructed view of the old house. It was the window Bobby saw the man in the backyard from. Becky knew the sheriff and his deputies watched her by night. But who watched her by day? Were there other reasons Cynthia sent Bobby to stay with her? These questions joined her thoughts of the Manticore pin on James' lapel and Papa Tolly's cold stare.

Five cars passed on the street and turned up the Billings' driveway. A few moments later she heard car doors slam and a multitude of voices from the hill. Another vehicle approached. It slowed at the access drive and the headlights went out before it turned in. The car crept past her then turned quickly and backed. Becky crawled backward while bright red taillights and the word "GALAXIE" came toward her. The car stopped ten feet away. Exhaust fumes floated over the blind. The engine stopped and the door opened. Max Underwood got out. He cursed and walked to a tree beside the blind. Becky froze. She heard Max urinate and then mutter, "Where is that son of a bitch?" He walked back to his car, got in, and eased the door shut.

Becky recognized enough about Underwood's car to be confident it was the same the shot at her and Wendy came from. The shotgun would be in the car again tonight, and she wished she'd come armed. She checked her watch. It was ten past nine. Another car entered the access with its lights on. Underwood jumped out and frantically waved his arms. The lights went off. The car backed in beside Underwood. He jerked the passenger door open and hissed: "You must be the biggest dumbass in the word, pulling in here with your shitting lights. Where the hell have you been?" He got into the car and closed the door. Becky could still hear his loud voice over the engine, but the words were indiscernible. He opened the door five minutes later. "I'll have my radio on at home. Call me if you see anything."

"Yes, sir," came the response.

Underwood got in his car, crept to the end of the access and up the street, turning on his lights a block away. Becky saw the house on the hill now well-lit and noticed movement inside the dining room window. She remembered Bobby alone and waited another minute before sliding out of the blind.

The car was a Fury but, unlike Pete's, was unmarked and solid black. The low crackle of a police radio came from inside. Becky slipped to the window and looked in at Aaron resting his head on his fist. She tapped on the window. Aaron let out a startled yelp and turned to her with eyes that remained wide while Becky opened the door, sat down, and leaned toward his face. "Why are you spying on me?" she asked. His chest heaved while she waited for his answer.

"I'm sorry," he managed.

Becky could tell his mind was spinning. "You were here last night too," she said. "I've been followed also. I want to know why. Don't lie to me, Aaron."

"I don't know." His voice was tight. "I'm just doing what they told me."

"Who are they?"

Aaron paused before answering. "The sheriff and Max," he said. "Don't tell them you caught me, please." His Adam's apple quivered.

"I won't say a word if you're honest with me. Why are they watching me?"

Aaron sighed. "The sheriff said you could cause him trouble. He wants to know if you're leaving at night and who comes to see you. Max said there may be someone visiting you tonight. I'm supposed to follow him when he leaves and let Max know where he goes."

"Who's supposed to visit me?"

"I don't know." Aaron's speech regained a bit of composure. "Max said he's old and walks with a cane. Some guy who's supposed to have caused trouble at the funeral home tonight."

"He had to have given you a name or told you something else about him."

"No," Aaron said, looking her in the eye. "Nothing else, other than I damned well better not lose him or get burned. They'll fire me if they know I told you."

"Would it be such a terrible thing if they did? You must know you're working for a crooked man, Aaron. Is this the kind of job you want? Out here spying on me at night because the sheriff thinks I'm going to cause him trouble?"

"You're not going to tell Wendy about this, are you?"

"Answer my question."

"No. Of course I don't like it. But I work at the sheriff's pleasure. Not only will he fire me, but he'll also blackball me from any other law enforcement job if I get on his bad side."

Becky kept him uncomfortable with silence and a stare. "But you know this is wrong. That makes you just as crooked as Pete and Max."

Aaron wiped his hand over his face. "Listen, Becky, all I ever wanted was to be a police officer. It's been my dream since I was a kid. I didn't know what the sheriff was like when I started. But I agreed to work at least two years for him before I move on. I want to do something bigger, maybe state or federal. But I'll kill my chances if I cross Scotland now." He tightened when a car approached then relaxed after it passed.

"So, this is what you do because you have to," Becky said.

"If I want to keep my job." Aaron reached into a small cooler between him and Becky. He removed two RC Colas. "Want one?"

Becky took it and popped the top. She checked her windows for lights.

"I'm sorry, Becky. But all I've done is sit here and tell the sheriff you're staying at home."

"And helped him search the police department and take Ed's address book without a search warrant."

Aaron sighed again. "Yes. I'm sorry about that. Sorry I cracked your picture frame too. It was an accident."

Becky felt there'd be no better time to ask. "I need a favor from you, Aaron."

"Yeah. What?"

"Bring me Ed's murder file. And don't let Pete know you have it."

Aaron swallowed his sip of cola hard. "I can't do that. The sheriff would have my ass if he found out I removed a murder file from the office without telling anybody. Why do you want to see it anyway? You know what happened."

"I don't believe I do. I think there's a lot more to it than I was told."

Aaron looked at her with an expression somewhere between confusion and fear. "You think the sheriff got it wrong?"

"I think the sheriff is lying. I don't think Jessie Settle killed Ed."

"Good grief, Becky. Sheriff Scotland wouldn't cover up a murder. Yeah, I think he's kind of shady, but he wouldn't..."

"Then let's look at the file. There must be crime scene pictures in it."

Aaron shook his head and glanced at the street again. "I can't. It would be too risky. I don't even know where it's at."

Becky took a small sip. "Fine. I can't force you to do anything. But one day you might retire from police work, and you'll look back on your career. You'll either be proud or ashamed of the work you did. I don't think you'll be too proud knowing you got your start being a tool for men like Pete and Max. That's something you'll remember no matter how far you go." She let this sink in for a moment. "All I want is to see the file."

"Why don't you just go to the office and tell the sheriff you want to see it?"

"You know why. I don't trust him. He'd only show me the parts of it he wants to." Another car passed, and she watched Aaron tighten again. "Have you heard the name Nick Hughes?" She asked.

"The missing reporter? Yeah."

"What's the sheriff doing to find him?

"What he can, I guess. There's not much to go on. He just disappeared. The guy wasn't originally from here anyway. Probably just decided to go back to wherever he came from."

"He was here a week ago Sunday," Becky said, then thought of Bobby and worried she was painting herself into a corner.

"Why was he here? Did you let anyone know?"

"He came by asking questions about something Ed may have been looking into. It was just before he went missing. I'm letting you know, but I'm sure it would only stir up trouble if you told Pete."

"What was he asking questions about? What was Ed looking into?"

"You bring me the file first. Then I'll tell you everything. For now, just trust me. You're working for a dangerous man who just happens to know how to win elections so he can wear a badge."

Aaron's face showed he was trying to process it all. He began to speak when a car snuck into the access road. "Shit!" he grunted. "Get down."

Becky slid down and watched the car park just inside the access drive. The door flung open. A cane came out before the old man.

Aaron killed the engine and slid the car out of gear. It rolled backward ten feet before he pressed the emergency brake.

The man disappeared into the woods then emerged, lumbering across Becky's backyard.

"That's the guy I'm supposed to follow," Aaron whispered. "Who is he?"

"I have no idea," Becky answered. "He was behind me in line at the funeral home. Sam Roberts got upset because he was there for some reason."

The man climbed the steps of the back porch and knocked on the door. "Bobby is in there," Becky said. "I better go see what he wants before he wakes him."

Aaron grabbed her arm. "Wait. Let's see what he does." He brought up binoculars and watched.

The man didn't wait long. He knocked once more then slid something into the door before beginning his walk back to his car.

"I'm going to talk to him," Becky said.

"No, don't," said Aaron. "Let me tail him and see where he goes. If the sheriff finds out he was here, he'll want to know why I didn't follow him. He slid something into the door. I expect it has his name on it, probably a phone number too."

They watched the man make his way back to his car and leave the access.

"Ok, get out," Aaron said. "I'll come back later."

Becky stepped out. "Don't tell them anything about him unless you have to. They may kill him." Her head jerked when she heard the back screen door slam. The porch and upstairs lights were on. Aaron's car started gliding away. Becky yelled and waved her arms before running to the house. She threw the back screen door open and turned the doorknob. It was locked.

"What's wrong?" Aaron yelled. He ran toward her from the woods.

"Bobby locked the door," Becky banged on it and shook the doorknob. "Bobby. Open up."

"I'll try the front," Aaron said.

"It's locked too," Becky said. She moved to the window and looked in.

"You don't have a key?" Aaron asked.

Becky beat on the windowpane. "I didn't bring it. I left this door unlocked." She pressed her face against the window. The fireplace glow cast enough light for her to see, and what she saw shocked her into panic. "Break the door down!" she yelled. "Kick it down! The gun cabinet is opened."

Aaron moved to the side of the door. "He's got a gun?"

"Move back," said Becky. She slammed her boot against the door twice with no results.

Aaron stepped up. "I got it." He kicked beside the doorknob repeatedly. Wood cracked then splintered. The door swung open.

"Bobby?" Becky yelled.

"I'll check upstairs," Aaron said. He drew his sidearm.

"For God's sake, don't shoot him, Aaron."

Becky flipped the light switch and saw the empty holster on the floor. "Bobby!" She ran into the kitchen then back. "Is he up there, Aaron?"

"I don't see him yet."

"Check my room and the bathroom too." Her voice quivered. "He has my revolver."

"Son of a bitch," Aaron said.

Becky forced her panic aside and carefully scanned the room again. She then saw him behind the Christmas tree. He was on his knees with eyes closed and the barrel of the revolver pressed tight under his chin. "Bobby. No. Please no." She heard the words, which didn't sound like hers, rattle out. She took two quick steps toward him.

Bobby's eyes fluttered open. They fixed on Becky. The arm holding the gun trembled.

"Bobby, what's wrong? Why are you upset? Put the gun down. Come here and let's talk about what's bothering you. Please, sweetie." In the corner of her vision she, saw Aaron slowly stepping down the stairs. The tree stood between him and Bobby. "Put the gun down. Please," she whispered and took two more steps.

Bobby raised up on his knees. The finger on the trigger moved.

"Bobby, no," Becky stammered. She froze with her hands extended toward him. Her legs had turned to rubber, so she knelt. She looked into his eyes and knew he meant to do it. She heard his short, tight breaths. "Tell me what's wrong," she begged. "I love you. Talk to me." She saw Aaron move down another step.

Bobby's chest heaved and a tear rolled down his cheek. He then spoke in a slow, deep voice. "You- You know. You know, d-don't you."

"Bob-Bobby." She forced a swallow. "I don't know. I don't know anything. But let's talk about it. It can be worked out. Trust me. Remember what we talked about at the firepit. Remember your purpose. Remember your spirit." Aaron entered more of her vision. He inched toward Bobby.

"My s-spirit is b-bad." Bobby sucked in a breath and clamped his eyes.

"Aaron! Stop him now!"

The Christmas tree crashed when Aaron dove. He landed on his belly behind Bobby and bounced up with a hand reaching for the gun. Bobby fell forward. A shot fired just after Aaron's hand gripped the gun.

Bobby lay flat. Becky didn't take time to stand. She lunged forward and slid herself the last few feet. She grabbed his head and pulled his face up. He stared at her vacantly while she wiped her hands under his chin. There was no blood.

"Is he Ok?" Aaron asked. He lay on the floor with the revolver in hand.

"He's not shot," Becky said. She pulled Bobby to her and put her arms around him. She could feel his body heat and sweat. On the floor behind him lay a business card. She lifted it and read it over his shoulder. "Please call me," was scratched at the bottom with a phone number underlined. Above it were the stenciled words: Hudson Perry — Freelance Crime Reporter and Author."

15

The last note of "Taps" settled over Black Lake Town Cemetery just before one o'clock the next day. Cynthia held her gloved hands out, her left for Quincy and right for Becky. Honor guards folded James' flag. Becky took the hand and felt its squeeze while weeping came from behind the black veil. Becky hadn't planned to sit with the family. She felt uncomfortable there. An honor guard stepped forward with the tri-folded flag then knelt before Cynthia. It stirred a foggy memory for Becky.

"On behalf of the President of the United States..."

Becky remembered words spoken when she received Ed's flag. She wanted to listen now and hear what her grief over a month ago muted. But a glance to her left brought her eyes directly into Harrison Tolly's. He wore a black pea coat and fedora. A white scarf curled under his freshly oiled and combed chin beard. His gaze locked Becky's senses for a moment.

"...for your loved one's honorable and faithful service."

Cynthia released Becky's hand and received the flag. Quincy clutched his sister's shoulder. The pastor and others approached to speak condolences.

"Would you wait for me awhile," Cynthia said to Becky. "We need to talk after I'm done here."

"I'll be at Ed's grave," Becky said. She stood and walked away from the crowd. She'd slept no more than three hours. All she'd learned so far that day was Bobby was at home in bed, medicated and watched by a hired nurse. She made the walk to the south side of the cemetery bordering Simpson Park while dreading the conversation to come.

EDWARD W HAWK

CPL

US MARINE CORPS

WORLD WAR II

JUNE 1 1924

OCT 31 1963

BRONZE STAR

A dying red rose lay at the foot of it. Becky guessed Pearl placed it there. She removed the rose and sat down on a marble bench. It was her second visit since the funeral. The first she cried until her insides hurt. Now, she only sat with her eyes on the words and waited for whatever emotions would come.

The memory of when she'd first seen Ed entered. He'd delivered chicken grain from the farmers' grange to her mother's house. She remembered helping him with the bags. He'd smiled at her with an eye twinkle and said only "Thank you" that day. But he made all the deliveries afterwards, and conversations began. Becky knew he wanted to ask her out. Her mother finally took the bull by the horns and invited him to dinner. That was the beginning. After the second dinner, Ed asked Becky for their first real date. Becky fell in love with him long before his awkwardness dissolved. Two years later, he proposed on a walk by a mountain stream. She reminisced it over again, this time remembering forgotten details. She wiped away a single tear and checked her watch before looking back and seeing the last car leave the cemetery. James' casket was in the ground. Cynthia walked toward her, her veil lifted and face bleak.

They walked away from the cemetery on a park trail. A wide creek beside them made its final rush to the deep water of the lake. Cynthia waited to speak until they reached the end of the trail, where the lake lay at its broadest expanse.

"I know the worst is to come," she said. "Isn't it that way, Becky? Everyone pours out their sympathies in the days immediately after. People visit you, call you, tell you what a wonderful man he was. Then it's over, and you're alone. I'll be honest. I'm terrified of that."

A breeze stirred. Becky pulled her toboggan over her ears. "Me too," she said.

Cynthia wiped her eyes with a handkerchief. "I'll need you. Quincy can only visit so often." Her veil waved in the breeze. "All these people here today thought so much of Jimmy. Many loved him. I'm glad about that. But I'm just his wife. They'll smile and speak to me in town, maybe drop by to visit occasionally. But most days it will be just Bobby and me in that big house. I have no idea how I can make him happy."

"I'm so sorry about what happened last night," Becky said.

Cynthia looked across the lake. A tear fell. She took a Pall Mall from her purse. "I don't blame you. I blame myself and Jimmy. There's so much we haven't told you. We both should've known keeping it from you and Ed would only lead to bad things. It's past time you knew."

Becky heard movement in the woods, but her attention stayed on Cynthia.

"When Jimmy and I married, I worked in the office at the lumber plant. We needed someone to watch Bobby during the day. We found a young girl named Shannon. She was Bobby's age but responsible. Bobby couldn't wait to see her each day. She played games with him, cooked his favorite foods, and made him laugh. Bobby fell crazy in love with her. He started calling her his girlfriend and talked about how he wanted to marry her one day. It only seemed cute then." Cynthia turned from the wind and lit her cigarette.

"She'd worked for us a while when one of Jimmy's buyers invited us to an Independence Day party in Southport. It was an overnight stay. We trusted Shannon enough by then to feel comfortable with her spending the night with Bobby. I'll regret that decision forever. I received a call at the hotel that afternoon from Shannon's mother, Helen. She said that Jimmy and I needed to come home right away. Shannon had left him at the house because he'd made sexual advances toward her. I called Bobby and told him to stay there until Jimmy and I could drive back. It was late when we got home. Bobby was gone. We called Shannon's house. Nobody answered." She took a long pull on her cigarette. A stream of smoke curled around her in the breeze. "I think you know what happened."

Becky remained silent.

"We looked for Bobby the rest of the night. We found him wandering five miles from the murder scene. Blood covered his clothes and shoes. He only told us that Shannon's mother was dead. The sheriff's office found his bloody shoeprints all through the house and his bicycle outside. A knife Jimmy brought back from the war was missing from our house. Bobby finally said enough for us to know he did it."

"What happened to Shannon?" Becky asked.

"We never found out. Pete questioned him in length, but Bobby remembers only parts of it. We think he went there after she rejected his advances then flew into one of his rages when Helen told him to leave. Pete believes he killed Helen then went upstairs after Shannon. There was blood on the pier also. The probability is he dragged her there and threw her in the lake. The current would've picked her up. It was also summer, so the alligators were active. Just another detail to make the whole damned thing more terrible."

"Was he arrested?" Becky felt she knew the answer.

Cynthia looked at her. "No. Jimmy used his status to cover the whole thing up. Pete and Jimmy's friends helped him. There's no other way to say it."

"Good lord," said Becky.

"I know it's terrible," Cynthia said. "But I assure you Bobby has paid. He'll pay for it the rest of his life. You know the issues he has. You've seen it yourself. Something snapped in him that night, and he became a different person. Yes, my heart bleeds for that girl and her mother to this day. But nothing we do will bring them back. Bobby was only fifteen. What good would sending him to a prison or an institution have done? He would've never recovered from that. It would've been a tragedy atop a tragedy. Jimmy was able to help him. At least he can have a life."

Sounds from behind made Becky turn. Three men stood side by side fifty yards away on the trail. They wore long coats with collars turned high and hats pushed low. Scarves covered all but their eyes.

"Stay where you are," Cynthia said. "If you run, they'll come after you. There's nothing to fear if you listen to me. You know about them, don't you?"

Becky nodded.

"I won't ask you how but..."

"Are they going to kill me?"

"No. They don't want to harm you. They only want to be sure they're understood."

Becky scanned the woods and detected as many as ten more men, all with obscured faces.

"Black Lake isn't much," said Cynthia, "but it's their town. It has been for years. When you come here you must abide by their rules."

"What do they want from me?" Becky asked

"Under no condition should you talk to this Hudson Perry. He wrote a piece in the Charlotte paper about the incident years ago. It stirred up old rumors. We tried protecting Bobby from it, but he heard of the article and suffered a nervous breakdown. We had to hospitalize him. Now, this man is back, asking questions. I'm worried deeply for Bobby now. Those men helped cover it up before because Jimmy was one of them, and they are loyal. But Bobby being Jimmy's nephew makes this a powder keg. They will not allow it to explode. They're too powerful here for that. Jimmy is gone now, so Bobby will be sacrificed if things are pressed. They want me to tell you that old evidence can surface. The sheriff can publicly reopen the investigation and make an arrest. Whatever it takes to prevent unneeded attention thrown on them."

The face of Nick Hughes smiling on her doorstep flashed in Becky's mind. "And they won't hesitate to kill if it calls for it, will they."

"Please listen to me, Becky. We must forget them. You and I have too much else to contend with. Our husbands are gone. We cannot change the past. But the coming months and years will be hard if we don't have one another's comfort. I watched you and Bobby fishing that night on the houseboat and saw how much he loves you. Come live with me, Becky. Help me give him a good life. Jimmy worked hard so the ones he loved could live comfortably after his death. You are one of us. We need not be widows living alone and growing old before our time. We can have nice things, travel, see and do things we never imagined we would. It can be a wonderful life for us. It won't mean we don't miss our husbands. It will mean we still want to live. That's my invitation. It's from the heart. Please accept it."

"It sounds like an invitation to not die," Becky said.

"I didn't lure you here so they could kill you. I brought you here to warn you of them. They realize you know about them. They're showing patience. But their patience can quickly wear thin. All you need to do is accept my offer and they will go away. We can forget they exist then. What's your answer?"

Becky knew the *only* answer. "Yes," she said.

Cynthia took a final toke and flicked her cigarette away. The men turned and walked. Becky had no doubt what would've happened had Cynthia crushed it underfoot.

"Did they kill my husband?"

"Jessie Settle killed Ed on a personal vendetta. Now is the time to accept that. I only have some influence over them because of Jimmy. But their secrecy and power are things they'll defend fiercely. I understand your wanting answers, Becky, but you must let it go. Nothing good will come of it if you don't. I promise you that." She took Becky's arm, and they walked back toward the cemetery.

Becky felt darkness closing on her again.

16

The phone rang continually the rest of the weekend. She took the receiver off the hook Sunday and sat by the front window, while sleet clattered on the tin roof. Her head felt groggy from lack of sleep. Insomnia had returned.

Ice covered the world outside when she woke on Monday. The house was cold until she built a fire in the hearth. She didn't wish to speak to anyone but called to check on Bobby.

"He's still requiring medication," Cynthia said. "He's sleeping now. This could be a long recovery for him."

"Can I do anything to help?"

"Not now. We have our lawyer and some others here helping settle Jimmy's affairs. Papa Tolly will be going back to Richmond as soon as we're done. We'll get you moved in then." There was a hesitant tone to the voice that made Becky uneasy, if not scared.

She hung up and checked the directory for the local Esso station, where the bus stopped. She called it and asked for a schedule of departures.

That night, she ate a small bowl of cream of wheat with butter by the fireplace. She looked at the anniversary picture and realized the crack had expanded and now ran between her and Ed. The feeling the photograph provided her with then was an understanding of how utterly alone she felt. *I can't live like this*, she thought.

Banging on the door early the next morning woke her. It took her a minute to force her body to move, then she teetered down the stairs with a hand on the banister. The banging continued until she opened the door.

Wendy was dressed for work. Her face showed relief that turned to annoyance.

"So, you are still kicking. You ignoring me these days? I called all weekend and yesterday and got a busy signal every time. Even tried driving here in that ice storm and nearly wrecked. I had to call Mrs. Billings to make sure you were alive. What's up?"

"I'm sorry," Becky said. "It's been a tough few days."

Wendy stepped in and looked into her eyes. "Good grief. Have you taken pills again? I thought you were over that." She took Becky's hand and tried leading her to the sofa.

Becky pulled away and closed the door. She felt desperate to spill all that was inside to Wendy. "No. Just haven't slept much," she said. "Do me a favor. I really need time alone. I appreciate all you've done for me, but I don't want you to come around or call for a while. One day I'll explain it to you but for now, please, don't ask questions. Just do as I say."

"I thought I saw it last Friday at the assembly. You had that look in your eyes. Something has happened, hasn't it? And you sure have underestimated my hardheadedness. I ain't just letting this slide. Come sit down. I'll fix a pot of coffee. I don't care if I'm late for work. We're having a long talk."

"No." Becky's resolve resounded in the word. She locked her eyes on Wendy's and kept them stern despite the crumbling she felt inside. She opened the door and held it. "I want you to leave."

Wendy's face fell. "Are you in danger? Is it the sheriff? Tell me, please. I swear I won't blab."

Becky blinked back the tears and shook her head. "Things will be fine. I just want you to stay away. I have my reasons. I want you to have a merry Christmas, then maybe we can talk."

Wendy shook her head. "No way it's being merry this way. You don't have to protect me from whatever it is. I want to help."

"Please, do as I say."

"We're still friends, aren't we?"

Becky embraced her. "The best. Don't think I'm not grateful for you. You've already done more than you know."

She stood at the window of Bobby's old bedroom with binoculars. She recognized the cars at the Billings'. They were Bud and Quincy's identical, blue Lincolns and Frank Frye's black Cadillac. Ice still on the windshields proved they hadn't been moved. She then looked at the house windows through the bare trees and eventually saw Cynthia wheel Harrison Tolly into the living room. They sat, talking and drinking coffee. Becky honed on Harrison when he began speaking and wished she could read lips. Harrison had much to say. He spoke long, mixing hand jesters with his words and sometimes pounding his fist on the arm of his wheelchair. Cynthia looked down. She was crying. Becky scanned down the hill to the pier. The houseboat was gone.

A venison tenderloin was the only meat in the freezer. She set it out to defrost then found the number from the safety deposit box and called it once more. The female voice answered.

"I promise this is the last time I'll call," Becky said. "Please let me talk. I don't know who you are, and I won't ask. I swear that what you tell me will stay between us. But I need to know why my husband had your number. I don't think I can go on not knowing."

A long pause followed before a click and dial tone.

Quincy took Hudson Perry's card the night Bobby attempted suicide, so Becky obtained the Charlotte Chronicle's number from the operator. Three transfers took her to a gruff crime reporter, who refused to give Hudson's number but promised to pass along a message. Hudson called back less than fifteen minutes later.

"Thanks for returning my call, Mrs. Hawk," he said. "I'd given up on you."

"Sorry I missed you. I'd stepped out the other night."

"No problem. Let me first say I'm very sorry about your husband. After fifty years of crime writing, I have a deep respect for all men who wear the badge."

"Thank you. Why did you want to see me?"

"Well, I was hoping you might have seen a young friend of mine. Nick Hughes. You know him. He's the writer for the Bolton Record who did the article when your sheriff shot Jessie Settle."

Becky didn't know why but felt as if she were stepping off a cliff. "He came by my house the Sunday morning before last."

"I see. Around what time?"

"Somewhere between ten and ten thirty."

"Why was he there? Friendly visit?"

"He said he wanted to follow up on the story he was writing. But before I answer any more questions, you need to tell me what this is about. All of it."

"Yes, you were kind enough to call," Hudson said, "so I'll be straight forward. Nick has been missing since the day he visited you. I'm worried, because I haven't heard from him. You see, Nick was obtaining information for me. I've been a freelancer now for some time. Unsolved murders are my specialty. To this date there have been five arrests because my articles stirred up fresh interest. Your husband called me not long before his death and asked detailed questions about an old piece I wrote concerning a murder in Bolton County. When I heard he'd been killed shortly after, my investigative reporter's blood stirred. Nick took his job at the Bolton Record to work undercover for me."

Becky removed pen and paper from the desk. "What did Ed ask about specifically?"

"Helen and Shannon Monet. Are you familiar with them?"

"Yes. What questions did he ask?"

"Just about all I knew. He was particularly interested in the crime scene. I wish I could've helped him more there, but I didn't originally cover the story. The only things I know are from the sheriff and medical examiner."

"What specifically did he ask about the crime scene?"

Hudson laughed. "Sounds like I'm the one being interviewed here. Tell you what, answer my questions about Nick and then I'll answer yours about your husband."

"He asked if I knew the names Helen and Shannon. I didn't know who they were at the time. I gave him a fresh baked cookie and he left. He said he was headed to Creek Fork Church, but I think that was a lie."

"Yes, I'm afraid Nick was sometimes too quick to use a ruse instead of being straight forward when he wanted information. That was the last time you saw him?"

"Yes."

"I understand that the house you rent is the Billings' and Bobby Billings visits you regularly."

"Yes. Why?"

"Nick picked up some information before he disappeared. Seems there's a rumor that Bobby knew Shannon and was a prime suspect before James Billings got involved. Have you heard that, Mrs. Hawk?"

Becky didn't speak.

"I'll take it you have. There's more I've learned, but you'll have to read my next article to find out the rest."

"There's more I know too," Becky said. "And I don't believe Bobby did it."

"And why is that?"

"Tell me what Ed wanted to know first."

"As I said, he asked about the crime scene. All I know is from what Sheriff Scotland said and the photos he showed me. The door had been broken down. Helen lay inside. She'd been nearly decapitated. Her carotid artery was severed. It was horrific. Blood even splattered the wall eight feet behind her. There were bloody shoe prints, probably from sneakers, around Helen's body that led upstairs to Shannon's bedroom. A chair was knocked over there. The mattress was half off the bed. A blood stain that matched Shannon's type was found on the floor. There was more of it trailing down the stairs and out the back door. Her blood drops were also found in the yard and at the end of the pier. The presumption is she was thrown into the lake."

"Blood drops or blood smears?" Becky asked.

"Your husband asked the same thing. Drops best I remember."

Becky stood and paced with pen in hand. "Were the bloody shoeprints on the pier too?"

"Just smudges," Hudson said. "But I imagine most of the blood was wiped off the shoes during the walk through the grass."

"What about the footprints in the house? What was their relation to Shannon's blood drops?"

"I can't remember, Mrs. Hawk. Maybe never asked. But, from what Nick uncovered, it does appear the Billings boy knew the girl and was at her house that night. My intention with this article is not to dissect the crime scene. It's to shine light on everything else I've learned, including how things seem to happen to people who ask questions about this old murder."

Becky sat down again. "When is this article coming out, Mr. Perry?"

"You can read it in the Saturday Chronicle."

Becky closed her eyes. "Are you including Bobby's name?"

"No. His name won't be in it. Nor will anyone else's. So, you can tell Mrs. Billings she can call her lawyer off if she's not listening on another line. I won't have to name names to put the heat on some people in that little town. I'm seventy-eight years old with diabetes and heart disease, Mrs. Hawk. I don't give a damn about whom I offend. You can tell anyone in your town that."

"I know it must feel good when your stories help solve a murder," Becky said. "And I know you're concerned about Nick. But you should be careful about your facts before you destroy a young man's life. You say you've been reporting crimes for fifty years, so you should know that there's no way Bobby Billings did this. Not on his own, anyway."

"Why?"

"Mainly because I know him. He'd never do a thing like that. Yes, he does have rages sometimes, but..."

"He has rages? Violent ones?"

"They're spontaneous and short. Nowhere near long enough for him to take a knife from his house and ride his bike all the way to Cypress Cove to kill someone." Becky bit her lip the second she said it.

"Wait a minute. I said nothing about that. Just what all do you know?"

"Listen. Bobby's growth was stunted because his mom drank when she carried him. He's smaller than me, and we're talking about when he was fifteen. He wouldn't have physically been able to kick down a door and nearly cut someone's head off. He surely couldn't have carried Shannon down a flight of stairs and across the yard to the end of the pier."

"Nobody said he carried her." The confidence had left Hudson's voice.

"I doubt she let a boy Bobby's size walk her past her dead mother and to the end of a pier, knife or not. She'd have put up a fight like she did in the bedroom. You said there were blood drops leading from the bedroom to the end of the pier. I might could believe it's possible he killed her then drug her there if there were blood smears, but you said there were drops. Shannon was carried from the house to the end of the pier."

"And thrown into the lake?"

"Or put into a boat."

There was a moment of silence. "Let me ask you a question, Mrs. Hawk. Have you heard tales of some secret club in Black Lake?"

"Did you get that from Nick too?"

"Yes. He said he'd heard some whispers of it the last time I spoke to him."

"I'm sorry to say that I believe Nick is dead, Mr. Perry. There's more I can tell you and just may. But publish that article and you'll never hear from me again. Give me a little time. I'll call you, and you may get the biggest story of your life."

The tenderloin wasn't fully defrosted, but she put it in the stove with potatoes and carrots that afternoon and slow cooked it for two hours. Then, she put on her coat, slipped her revolver into the inside pocket, and found her potholders.

"Don't mean to bother you. But I wanted to do something for you. Hope you like venison tenderloin."

Cynthia's eyes were red and teary. "Thank you, Becky. So nice of you. It smells wonderful." She reached out.

"It just came out of the stove and is very hot," Becky said. "Let me carry it in." She stepped inside and saw Cynthia glance toward the hall with a hint of worry. "How's Bobby?" Becky noted large, tape sealed boxes in the hall.

"Still not well. He had another round last night. Thank you very much for the venison."

Becky laid the pot on the kitchen counter. "Maybe I can cheer him up. Mind if I see him?"

Cynthia looked distressed. "He's not here, Becky. Quincy and Bud took him out on the houseboat. They thought a few days on the lake would be good for him."

"Take your deer and mind your own damned business." Harrison Tolly sat in his wheelchair at the hall entrance. A towel was draped over his shoulder. He ran a comb through his long, damp hair. His chin beard gleamed with wax.

"Papa, Becky is only being kind," Cynthia said.

"She's being nosey, and I refuse to eat anything prepared by some half-breed cunt." Harrison said it with casual arrogance. He combed the silver tip back into his beard before wheeling back down the hall and past the boxes.

"I'm so sorry," Cynthia whispered, following Becky to the door. "He's cranky to everyone in his old age. Sometimes I don't think he even knows what he's saying,"

Becky smiled. "Well, I suppose you can bare it until he leaves in a few days."

Cynthia didn't reply.

She took the venison home then hurried to the bank, making it ten minutes before it closed. She put Frank Frye's jewelry into a bag, turned in the safety deposit box key, and withdrew her money. It was dark when she returned home. She ate a cut of venison with loaf bread then packed an Army surplus backpack with the jewelry, German knife, and things valuable to her. She changed into fatigue pants and a sweater. She then braced a chair against her bedroom door and went to bed with the revolver under her pillow. A bus left for Raleigh the next morning at eight.

17

Headlight beams swept through the room and woke her at a four-thirty. Through the window, she saw a patrol car parked at the access. Tapping sounded from the backdoor. She carried her revolver downstairs and flipped on the back porch light.

"Got it," Aaron said. He held up the file.

Becky flicked off the light and opened the door.

"Day shift starts in an hour and a half," he said. "We'll have to hurry. The only other deputy on duty now is asleep in the dispatch office." He followed her in the dark. "Can we have some light?"

"I don't want anyone seeing lights on this early," Becky said. She used the glow of the fireplace to find an oil lamp, lit it, and adjusted the wick just enough to see by. She placed it by the hearth and sat on the floor. "How did you get your hands on it?"

"The sheriff is out of town for a few days on an investigation. I jimmied the lock on his office door. This was inside a desk drawer."

"What kind of investigation?"

"I don't know. Nobody told me."

"You really are taking a risk. Thank you. Let me see so you can take it back."

Aaron sat down in front of her, ignoring her reaching hand. "Let me just tell you what's here," he said. "There's pictures."

Becky kept her hand out. "Let me see." He handed her the file. She adjusted the lamp wick again then glanced over the first page of the report. It provided the general narrative she'd been told. A crime scene log preceded a stack of handwritten reports from on-scene deputies and emergency workers. Becky scanned through them. "Where's the statements from the young couple?" she asked.

"Young couple?"

"The guy and girl who went there to make out. The ones who found him?"

Aaron looked lost. "I never heard who found him."

Becky studied a sketch of the crime scene. The autopsy report and its front and back diagram of an agender human body followed. Two small circles were drawn on the upper back of the head. She read the report best she could by the low light. "I can't understand all this jargon, but are these little circles where he was shot?"

"Yes."

"Aren't they high? I imagined he was shot directly in the back of the head. These are closer to the top."

"The shots came from about a forty-five-degree downward angle," Aaron said. "He was shot execution style, on his knees."

Becky stared at him.

"I'm just telling you what the report says."

"Then the report is wrong. There's no way Ed would've knelt and let that happen to him."

"I thought it was weird too," Aaron said. "No. Don't look at those."

Becky pulled an envelope marked "Photos" from the file then a stack of 8x10 black and whites from the envelope. She turned the lamp wick higher, and her chest heaved. Ed lay on gravel, face down under lights. His right arm extended forward while his left lay against his side. Becky sucked in her breaths. More photos of the body from different angles followed, then wide view shots covering the entire parking lot.

Aaron grabbed the file. "Stop there," he said. "I'll describe the next one for you. The ones after it are autopsy pictures."

Becky flipped the next photo. Ed was turned over. He gave a death stare to the camera through half closed eyes. Grains of gravel stuck to his forehead. Dirt smeared the uniform that Becky pressed for him the night before. His tie lay unclipped from his collar beside him. Becky's face twisted. Her lungs constricted. She held her chest and made whooping sounds.

"You're hyperventilating," Aaron said. He tugged the photos from her hand. "Close your mouth some. Slow your breaths. Are there paper bags in the kitchen?"

"Bring me some water," Becky squeaked. She crawled to the trashcan beside the desk and vomited into it. Aaron brought her water. She sat on the floor and sipped it until her breathing slowed.

"I'm sorry," Aaron said. "I should've known that last one would be too much."

Becky took a longer drink and swished it in her mouth before spitting it in the trashcan. "Not your fault. It just surprised me, seeing his face and..." Her eyes flashed. "Show me that one again." She moved toward the stack of pictures on the floor, but Aaron held her.

"Hell no."

"I just need to see his uniform. Cover his face with your hand."

Aaron placed the lamp in front of her then the picture with his hand over Ed's face.

Becky took a five second glance then looked at Aaron. "Pete lied," she said.

"The sheriff? How?"

"Ed's badge is still on his uniform. Pete said it was torn off. He said Settle wanted it for a trophy."

Aaron pulled the picture to his face. "Why would he make up something like that?"

"I don't know, but I intend on finding out." She went for the file, but Aaron put his hand on it.

"No, Becky. I won't let you see the autopsy ones."

She nodded. "Then tell me about them."

Aaron flipped through them. "There's a closeup of the shot wounds. They're side by side on the upper back of the head, like the diagram showed. Either one could've been fatal, the report says. His hair absorbed some of the powder residue, but they determined the shots came from about twelve inches away. There are some here that I found interesting. Have a look. It's only his hands. They're covered in some kind of black grime."

Becky looked at her husband's hands. Her stomach squeezed again when she saw the clean ring where his wedding band had been removed. She studied them for only a few seconds before handing them back. "It's tire dust," she said. "He was changing a tire when he was shot."

Aaron looked again. "You could be right. That does look like that black stuff you get all over you when you change a tire."

"I know I'm right. There was a lug nut left at the scene."

"Was that in the report?"

"No. Wendy and I went there first that night Jessie was shot. I saw it in the gravel but didn't think anything of it at the time."

"I'll be damned," Aaron said. "Maybe we can go back and find it. Maybe get an idea of what kind of car it was."

Becky laid the photo on the floor. "Do you know if the jack and tire iron were in Ed's vehicle?"

"I wasn't on the scene, but they aren't lying around in any of the pictures."

Becky stared at the glowing lamp wick. "He was shot by someone he trusted. He would've never turned his back if he didn't. He was trying to do them a favor and they killed him."

"Any ideas who?" Aaron asked.

Becky did but wasn't ready to say. "It all started with a double murder fifteen years ago. The Monets in Cypress Cove. Ever heard of it?"

"Heck, yeah. Mom worked with Helen at Mason Fabrics. I used to hear her and Dad talk about it when I was a kid. It gave me nightmares."

"Nick Hughes was here asking me about them the day he disappeared."

"What does it have to do with Ed's murder?"

Becky checked the clock. "I don't know if I should tell you. You see what happened to Ed. And don't you think you should get that file back before day shift comes in?"

Aaron looked at his watch. "Damn. You're right. But I want to know more. When can we talk again?"

"I've talked to Agent Feezor with the SBI about it some, but he thinks I'm crazy. Do you know where the headquarters is in Raleigh?"

"I can find it."

"I know you've worked all night and must be tired."

"Just give me time to go home and change. We'll grab breakfast on the way."

"Think about this first, Aaron. I don't know everything yet, but there are powerful people involved, including the sheriff. Things could easily go bad. It very well may cost you your job or worse. I was planning to take the bus anyway."

Aaron stood with the folder. "Just be ready. I'll drive Dad to work then pick you up a little after eight."

"You don't have your own car? Whose have you been taking Wendy out in?"

Aaron blushed. "My parents'. I still live with them."

"Ok. Meet me down the street at the corner after eight. If there's anyone around to see us, just drive on by." She rolled her eyes and blew a breath when he left. Then the phone rang.

"Hello." The clock showed ten after five.

"There's a bus leaving Black Lake for Asheville at six," the woman's voice said. "It gets here at twelve. If you want to talk, be on it. When you step off, turn left and walk down Coxe Avenue. There's a bench beside a newsstand. Sit on it, and I'll pick you up. If I see a sign of anyone with you, or if I just don't like the way it feels, I'll drive away and forget the whole deal. My number will be changed, so don't bother calling again."

Becky wanted to keep her voice calm but failed. "You can't talk to me on the phone?"

"No. This will be face to face or nothing"

"I'll be wearing a green toboggan."

"I know what you look like."

"Can you give me a name?" Becky asked. "Just something I can call you if there's some confusion."

"If you're on the bench just after noon there will be no confusion. But your husband called me CI one."

18

Becky ran upstairs the second the phone clicked. She put on a coat then emptied a jar full of change into the cargo pocket of her fatigue pants. She added her bills from the bank then slid her revolver into the other pocket. She dumped some extra rounds in with it before slinging the heavy backpack over her shoulders and grabbing a flashlight.

A dog barked somewhere. It was the only sound Becky heard at the foot of the Billings' hill. She looked at her watch, hesitated, then trotted up the drive. At the edge of the yard, she crouched behind a tree and checked the darkened windows. The three cars were still parked in the driveway. She crept up to the door between twin garage bays, turned the doorknob, and smelled gas and oil when she stepped into darkness. She removed her toboggan, stretched it over her flashlight, and flicked the switch. The reduced beam lit Cynthia's rarely driven red Corvair on the left. A black Oldsmobile with Virginia tags was parked beside it. She looked inside the Oldsmobile and saw more packed boxes in the back seat.

A toolbox sat on a worktable at the far wall. She found a large flathead screwdriver in it then placed her backpack down and squatted beside the right front tire of the Corvair. With one hand holding the flashlight, she worked off the hubcap. Each wheel stud had a lug nut attached. She moved to the back right. That hubcap was nearly off when she heard the familiar hum of an engine and turned off her light. She stood to look out the back window of the garage. The hubcap fell. It rolled around the garage before settling with a clatter on the floor. She whispered a curse then slid her backpack back on while moving toward the door.

The houseboat glided with lights off toward the pier. Becky concealed herself behind Frank's Cadillac and watched over the hood. From her elevated position, she saw the entire deck of the boat. The cabin door opened, and two men stepped out. They carried something in a blanket between them and dropped it on the front of the deck. Becky heard the thud and saw the partial shape of a body when the blanket unfolded. Shovels lay on the deck.

"Damn, he smells to high heaven." It was Bud's voice.

"I told you to tie a handkerchief over your nose." That was Frank's.

The houseboat pulled alongside the pier. A third man came out of the cabin while the other two secured ropes to cleats. "Let's move fast," came Quincy's voice. "She sometimes gets up early." Quincy and Bud lifted the blanket and its weight. They carried it down the pier while Frank followed with shovels. "Put one of those in there with him and take the other two back to the garage, Frank," Quincy said. "There's a spade and mattock in the corner beside Cynthia's car that'll work better."

Frank tossed a shovel into the blanket. "Wait for me at the edge of the woods," he said and walked up the hill with the other shovels over his shoulder.

Becky crouched beside the tire. She exchanged her flashlight for the revolver then pressed against the fender and froze when he walked around.

Frank pushed open the garage door, then he looked toward his Cadillac. With the handkerchief over his nose, he reminded Becky of a cowboy movie bandit. "Well, I'll be damned," he said. One of the shovels dropped to the asphalt. He raised the other with both hands.

Becky leveled her revolver at him. "I'll kill you where you stand if you make a sound, Frank. Where is Bobby?" She could see his mind spinning while he stood with the shovel ready to strike.

"Bobby is just fine," Frank said. "But I promise he won't be if you fire that gun. Just who the hell do you think you are, pointing that at me?" He took a step. The shovel went back a foot more.

Becky thumbed the hammer back, freezing him again. She knew she could pull the trigger. "If he's not, I swear I'll make sure you all pay hell. Go inside. Close the door. If you step out before I leave it will be the last step you ever take."

Frank lowered the shovel and walked slowly into the garage. The door closed. Becky jammed the revolver into her pocket and ran. She crossed the street at the bottom of the hill and heard Frank's enraged cry ring out. She ran into a pine covered lot then through a yard and around a fence to another. Two dogs charged bellowing from behind the house, setting off a chain reaction of bark and howls in the neighborhood. Becky heard an engine crank and race from the hill. She entered woods again and found a small foot trail that led her to Main Street and the soft, white-blue glow of streetlights.

She checked her watch before stepping from the woods and saw she had less than ten minutes. She adjusted the straps on her shoulders and heard the dogs bark again. "Shut up," she heard Quincy yell. Frank's Cadillac sped to an intersection on her right and turned right. Brush crashed behind her. She ran as fast as the weight of her backpack would allow and crossed Main Street, headed toward the railroad tracks.

"She's here!" Becky heard. A glance over her shoulder showed her Quincy and Bud running from the woods at a pace she knew she couldn't match. Frank's Cadillac turned left at the next intersection, raced up Railroad Street, and stopped across the tracks from her.

She ran farther down Main Street and paused at a dimly lit spot, where a gravel covered hill led to the tracks. She struggled up it with the backpack pulling against her. Halfway to the top, gravel slid under her feet. She slid back to the bottom and crouched in a ditch when she heard shoes slapping the pavement. Seconds later, Quincy and Bud stopped ten feet from her.

"She's right here somewhere," Quincy huffed. "Dammit, we can't let her get away."

"Looks like she might've gone up the hill," Bud said.

"She's on the tracks. I guarantee it," said Quincy. "Let's get up there. You go left. I'll go right. Frank has the waterfront covered in case she crossed."

Becky made herself keep still for one minute after they left. Just enough light let her see it was three till six. She crawled up the hill, crossed the tracks, then fell and slid headfirst down the other side. Ignoring pain in her hands and knees, she crossed Railroad Street then slipped in and out between buildings and shadows while making her way to the bus stop. Lights were on in the lumber village homes. Breakfast smells came from Jabber's Grill. A check of her watch showed six o'clock, and she made a final dash past the plant and lumber yard. Her legs and lungs burned before she saw "Esso" shining in red lights. A Continental Trailways was there with two passengers stepping back in with sodas from the vending machine. The door closed and the bus pulled out. Becky ran behind it, yelling and waving. It stopped, and Quincy's shout came from the tracks nearby when the door opened.

"Who's that?" a slender, bespectacled driver asked. His large rearview mirror showed Quincy running at full speed from the tracks.

"Leaving my husband. He's beating me again." She stepped in and tossed a ten on the driver's lap. "Going to Asheville. You can write out my ticket at the next stop."

"I don't want trouble on this bus."

"Then close the damned door and drive before he gets here," Becky yelled.

The door closed and the bus lurched forward a few seconds before Quincy, his face reddened and sweaty, appeared beside it. "Open the door," He banged on the thick glass hard enough to shake it. "Open the door, Becky, let me talk to you!" The bus left him.

She walked huffing down the aisle. A woman with sleeping children under each arm smiled nervously. "You're better off, believe me." she said.

A sailor in whites laughed. "You sure had him foaming," he said. He offered her a soda and patted the seat beside him. "Need some company?"

Becky shook her head and found a seat in the back of the bus. She watched the lights of Black Lake disappear then slid off her backpack and watched out the window while the bus drove through the country. It was on a stretch of straight road just before Deaton when the headlights of a speeding car appeared half a mile behind.

"You sure you Ok, lady?" the sailor asked when Becky walked back up the aisle. "I've been talking to you for ten minutes. You act like you don't even hear me."

Becky put her backpack on again.

The driver looked back in the mirror. "No standing while the bus is in motion."

"I need off now," Becky said.

"You said you're going to Asheville."

"Just stop and let me off." She looked back and saw the car had cut its distance in half. Ahead, she saw the first traffic lights of Deaton.

"We'll be at the next bus stop in five minutes," the driver said. "I need to give you change anyway. Sit down."

Becky looked back once more. Her hand was on the door lever before the bus stopped for the light. She stepped into the turn lane while the driver shouted. Light flashed a foot away. She heard tires squall then a crash. She ran behind the bus and down a dark street, glancing back just long enough to see the Cadillac against a pole. Frank stumbled out the driver's door. Quincy helped Bud out through a broken window.

19

She ran five blocks through a residential area then followed the sound of traffic to a business district. A phone booth glowed in florescent light two blocks down. She had a dime in hand when she got to it then dialed.

"Bolton County Sheriff's Office." The voice was Vivian's. Her county radio in the background was busy.

Becky watched the street. "I need to speak to Deputy Powers."

"Is this Becky?"

Five seconds hesitation then: "Yes."

"Becky, we had a call that you broke into the Cynthia Billings' garage then ran from a bus in Deaton. They're looking for you. What for Pete's sake is going on?"

"I don't have time to explain it to you. Is Aaron still working?"

"The sheriff and everyone else tore out of here to find you. Listen, you really need to tell me where you are so you can get this whole thing straightened out. This just doesn't sound like you."

Becky glanced up and down the street. The morning traffic was picking up. A patrol car raced by with lights flashing. Becky crouched. "I thought the sheriff was out of town," she said.

"He was, but he came in early this morning and had a meeting with both shifts about something. Then, we got the call about you. Now, please tell me where you are."

"Vivian, there's a whole lot you don't know."

"Just a second." The call was placed on hold momentarily before Vivian came back. "Becky, stay on the line."

Pete's voice blared over the radio. "If she's calling, she's probably at a payphone. Check all phone booths in Deaton."

"Listen to me," Vivian said.

Becky hung up then used her backpack to smash the lights above her. She dug another dime from her pocket and dialed. Crouching, she watched the street. The phone took an agonizingly long time to ring.

"Hello." The voice was sleepy and alarmed.

"I need your help now."

"What's wrong?"

"The sheriff and everybody are after me. I think they'll kill me if they find me. I'm in Deaton."

"Who will kill you? Where in Deaton?" Wendy yelled both questions.

The morning had lit enough for Becky to read the signs around her. "I'm on Glenn Street across from Roby's Game Room. I need a ride to the next bus stop. I have to be in Asheville by noon. I don't have time to explain anymore. Can you help me?"

"What a stupid question. Be there in a flash."

A patrol car stopped at the phone booth a few minutes after Becky hid between buildings across the street. She knelt behind trashcans and watched the deputy inspect the broken glass then speak into his radio. Two more patrol cars cruised the area a minute later. One of them crept past the ally. Becky huddled behind the trashcans while a spotlight beam waved over her. She waited until the deputies left then moved closer to the street and watched the increasing traffic. Wendy's Hudson soon tore onto the scene. It passed Roby's, then made a squalling U-turn in traffic. A furniture truck's horn blared, and the arm of a pink bathrobe with a middle finger extended flew out the window of the Hudson. Becky checked both ways then ran out and tossed her backpack in.

"Where are we going?" Wendy asked and accelerated before the door was closed. She wore blue, fuzzy slippers with her bathrobe.

Becky fell back before slamming the door shut. "Slow down first," she said. "Deputies are all around here."

Wendy coasted her Hudson behind the furniture truck at a redlight. The driver returned his own gesture. Wendy's hand went to her horn before Becky pulled it away.

"Sorry," Wendy said. "Why don't you tell me what the hell is going on?"

Becky slid down in the seat. "Just drive normal. I mean drive like a normal person and get me to the next bus stop after Deaton."

"You said you're going to Asheville."

"I've got to meet someone there at twelve."

"Must be important. I'll take you." The light turned green. "Just let me go home and change. You can explain it all on the way."

"No. They know we're friends. They're probably checking your apartment. Just get me to a bus stop, fast."

"Listen, I'm taking you to Asheville," Wendy said. "No use arguing. But I cannot drive you there dressed like this. No way I'll ever sweet talk a highway patrolman out of a speeding ticket." She looked in the mirror and made a horrified squeal. "Dammit, I only put mascara on one eye."

Becky checked her watch and gave her ponytail a tug. "Ok," she said. "We'll stop along the way and buy you something to wear. It will have to be fast, though. What are you going to do about school?"

"Don't worry about that, just lay low." They passed two patrol cars parked on either side of the street. "Now, what is all this about? I want the whole story."

Wendy pushed her Hudson fifteen over the speed limit when they crossed the county line bridge. Her effort to digest the whole thing showed on her face. "Are you sure it was a body?" she asked. "It was dark."

Becky checked the rearview mirror once more. "I'm sure. A decomposed one. Quincy and Frank had handkerchiefs over their noses to block the smell. They were moving it from one place to another."

Wendy gasped. "Dear Lord, you don't think it was..."

"No. I don't believe it was Bobby. My guess is Nick Hughes."

"The missing reporter?"

"Yes. He was in town investigating them for Hudson Perry."

Wendy frowned at her unmade eye again in the mirror. "So, Ed was onto them?"

"Enough for them to kill him," Becky said. "Cynthia was just buying time for me when she invited me to live with her. Papa Tolly came packed and ready to move in. I'm sure they were going to kill me too when the time was right."

"Good grief, Becky. This is just too much to take in. We're in over our heads. I say we forget this trip and call Feezor. Let him handle it."

"I've got to have more if I call Feezor. They'd just have an answer for everything and convince him I'm crazier than he already thinks. I need to talk to Ed's informant. I think she knows something important–something that'll get Feezor's attention and force him to take me seriously. I'm just worried to death for Bobby. You and Aaron too. I'm sorry I pulled you into it. I just didn't see another way."

"Can it," Wendy said. "If you say another word about it, I'll rip your tongue out. And did it ever occur to you that they know we talk. Now at least I know what we're dealing with. And Aaron may be wet behind the ears, but he has enough smarts to keep himself safe. I'll call his house when we stop. His mother will be there if he's not."

A road sign indicated Greensboro was twenty miles ahead.

"Great," Wendy said. "There will be a place there where I can buy a dress and shoes. I'll call Aaron and the school while you get them. I promise we'll still have time to make it to Asheville."

"We'd better be fast," said Becky. "I won't get a second chance at this."

"Just hold on, and I'll show you what Marilyn Mae can do." The Hudson surged ahead and passed a semi.

"Your car has a name?"

"Yep, after my two favorite blondes. Classy and sassy is she."

Becky waved away the bills Wendy held out the window. "I'll pay. Just hurry and make the calls. I won't be long."

"Eight dress. Something waist defined," Wendy yelled. "Colors that go with the season. Nothing drab. Seven shoes. Basic black will work."

"Damn, Wendy. Go make the call."

"Red or white preferably for the dress. Green will do in a pinch. Oh, and a pair of hose, natural color."

Becky nearly gave up when she found the door locked, but a smiling saleswoman with a key removed the "Closed" sign.

"Good morning. Welcome to Ivey's"

"Good morning. I need a dress, hose, and shoes." Becky trotted past blinking, artificial Christmas trees while listening to the saleswoman's directions. She grabbed what she saw first and was soon back in the parking lot, looking for the Hudson. Worry covered Wendy's face when she arrived a few minutes later.

Becky got in. "What's wrong?"

"Aaron's mother said he hasn't come home yet. She said he always calls when he's going to be late. She was about to call the sheriff's department. She's worried."

Becky remembered the day Ed didn't return. "The sheriff had a meeting with them this morning," she said. "He probably has them all out looking for me. Aaron probably got caught up in it all and hasn't had a chance to call." She hoped this would ease Wendy's mind. She knew it wouldn't hers.

"Yeah, that has to be it," Wendy said. "I called the school too to let them know my great aunt in Roanoke has fallen deathly ill. It's the third time it's happened to the poor woman in the past year." She took the bag from Becky. "I'll change then we'll be on our way." She pulled the dress out and stared open-mouthed. "This is what you got me? This monstrosity?" She gawked at the bright print with puffed sleeves and ruffled lace neckline.

"Sorry. I don't dress shop much," Becky said. "But you said red, white, or green. That has them all. It's not drab either. Now, hurry up and change. We've got less than four hours."

Wendy opened the box and screeched at black and white saddle shoes. "Becky, have you no sense of fashion? Didn't you ever play dress up when you were a kid?"

"No."

"Exchange everything. We'll have time."

"No. It's either those or your robe and slippers, so get moving fast."

Wendy made frustrated sounds under her breath while driving to a gas station. She removed a hairbrush from the glovebox and her Avon case from the trunk before hurrying to the restroom.

Worrying for Bobby and Aaron tormented Becky while she waited. She got out and paced. Her stomach rolled. "Hurry up!" she yelled with a bang on the restroom door.

"Just a few more minutes," Wendy called.

Becky walked inside the gas station and bought a map of Asheville along with a cola for Wendy and a Ginger Ale for herself. A laugh relieved her stress when she went back to the car.

Wendy stared blank-faced. "Why didn't you get me a straw hat with a tag hanging on it? Just so I could get the Minnie Pearl look down pat."

"Didn't have time," Becky said with a smirk. "Anyway, I think you look great, hotcake. Let's go. I cannot be late." She fell back and her Ginger Ale splashed on her when the car peeled from the lot.

They made it through the Piedmont of the state in good time then entered the Foothills. Becky felt a visceral tug when blue-gray mountains appeared in the distance. Snow covered the highest ridges. Beyond those ridges was the place of her and Ed's life before Black Lake. The temptation to stay entered her.

"We'll be there in an hour," Wendy said. "How are you feeling about this? I'm getting nervous. We don't know who this is you're meeting. It could be a setup, you know."

Becky had already considered it. "I'm not worried," she said. "Ed trusted this person enough to use her as an informant." She unfolded the map and searched for Coxe Avenue. Her ears popped from the higher elevation.

"How do you know that?" Wendy asked. "All you really know is Ed had her number locked up."

"I know Ed had an informant. I won't get this chance again."

"I just don't like it," said Wendy. "The whole thing's giving me a bad feeling. Maybe you should just take the jewelry and knife to Feezor. I'll talk to him with you."

Becky removed a pen from the glovebox and circled Coxe Avenue on the map. "I'm afraid talking to him will only make things worse for Bobby right now. The knife Ed found was from the Billings'. We have nothing solid to prove he wasn't involved."

"I hate to ask," said Wendy, "but what if Bobby really did do it? What if Ed's murder was all about protecting Bobby?"

"I don't believe that, but right now I just want the truth. Whoever this person is knows something important, else Ed wouldn't have had her number locked away. Maybe she can tell me who he was talking to in Savannah also."

A highway patrol car approached. Wendy slowed then smiled and waved when it passed. "I know of one connection between Black Lake and Savannah. Ever heard of Micky Carbo?"

"No."

"I'm surprised. He was before my time but was apparently some kind of legend in town. High school football coach. Won a state championship in the mid-forties."

220

"Tell me what you know about him."

"According to the teachers he was a big-time ladies' man. He got an offer to coach at a bigger school in Savannah four or five years after winning the championship. Met a girl down there and married her. Committed suicide just last year."

"Why did he kill himself?"

"Nobody knows. They all say he was a happy-go-lucky guy when they knew him."

"Do you know his wife's name? Is she still in Savannah?"

Wendy downshifted Marilyn Mae and guided her up a twisting, steep grade. Ice hung from the rock cliffs beside them. "I have no idea, but I'm sure some of the girls at the school could tell me. Think there's a connection there?"

"Yes."

They arrived in Asheville just before noon. Becky navigated Wendy to a street one block away from Coxe Avenue then had her pull to the curb.

"This isn't the street, is it?" Wendy asked.

"Close enough. I'll walk the rest of the way. If she sees you drop me off it's all over. You call and check on Aaron then wait on me here."

"I can't just let you walk into God-knows-what. Let me watch from a distance and tail you like they do in the movies."

"She'll see you for sure. This red car sticks out. Call Aaron then grab some lunch and visit the shops. I don't know how long I'll be." She extended a twenty with a nervous smile. "Find a dress you like."

Wendy waved it away. "My dress doesn't seem like a big deal now. I'll be too worried to feel like eating or shopping. You just get this done and get back here as fast as you can."

Becky crossed between buildings and stopped at the back corner of one across the street from the bus stop. She checked her watch and realized the Trailways was running late. Or, she'd missed it. Ten minutes later, it arrived. She went to it and mixed with the exiting passengers.

"Well, It's you again. The lady who caused all the excitement." It was the sailor holding his duffel bag. "You know your husband and his buddies almost made you spilt paint, right? I almost pissed laughing when they hit that pole. How did you get here?"

"Please leave me alone," Becky said. She walked past him toward the newsstand ahead.

"Buy you lunch?" he asked. "You have to eat."

"Enjoy your leave," she said and walked away.

She sat on the bench beside the newsstand and waited. Her watch showed a quarter past twelve. A morose feeling settled over her and intensified with each minute. At twelve-thirty, she stood, walked to the corner, and waved her toboggan for all to see. Heartsick, she walked in the direction she'd come. A gray, mud-splattered Volkswagen with bad mufflers cranked across the street. It came over and stopped at the curb in front of her. The passenger door opened.

"Get in," the woman said.

Becky did. The car jerked into gear and clattered down the street.

The woman wore big sunglasses and a wool hat pulled low. "If I see I'm being tailed I'll kick your ass out," she said. She handed Becky a pair of blinder sunglasses with lenses painted black. "Put these on. Don't take them off until I tell you."

"Thank you for meeting me," Becky said in darkness.

"I'm deciding if I still want to talk to you," came the reply.

Becky felt more jerks of the Volkswagen stopping and accelerating in traffic. It made at least ten turns before it sped up. The sounds of traffic vanished. She heard only the mufflers' clatter for some time. Another turn brought the sound of gravel beneath the tires. Becky's back pressed against the seat. She felt the car climbing and bouncing. The ascent lasted several minutes before they leveled.

"You can take the glasses off now."

Becky pulled them away to the sight of an old homestead with an above clouds view of the Blue Ridge Mountains. Snow dusted the ground and trees. Kudzu vines wrapped an old barn and chicken coop.

"Let's go to the house," the woman said.

They walked up a short hill to a farmhouse with a tin roof. The woman unlocked and opened the door. The inside was clean and simple.

The woman stoked a woodstove with split logs. She removed her coat and hat before her sunglasses. Her once blonde hair was cut short and dyed black, but the facial features matched Candy Fritz's mugshot perfectly.

20

"Have a seat. I'll be back."

The house was warming. Becky found a chair near the stove.

Candy returned with a whiskey bottle and two glasses. She sat on the sofa and filled one glass. "Need warming up?"

Becky shook her head. "Your place reminds me of where I was raised."

"Yeah, I heard you're a mountain girl," Candy said. "Ed told me." She took a long sip. "I saw you walk up and blend in with the bus riders. How'd you really get here?" Her eyes assured Becky not to lie.

"I had to jump the bus and call a friend. I'm sorry, but they were after me."

"Scotland and his creeps?"

"He's looking for me. But it was the others. I saw something they didn't want me to."

Candy studied the amber liquid in her glass. "Why don't we just have a drink in Ed's memory then I'll take you back. This feels like it's getting out of hand."

"Please," said Becky. "I'll keep it between us."

"Like hell you will. Don't lie to me."

"I swear I won't use your name."

Candy drunk the remainder then poured more. "Ed's murder has been hell for you, hasn't it."

"Hell doesn't fit it. It feels like my soul has been ripped out."

"I can tell," Candy said. She motioned her glass around the room. "This ain't mine, just renting it from my uncle. It was my grandparents'. They raised me here until I was thirteen. They're buried in the family cemetery out back."

"I'm sorry. What brought you to Black Lake?"

"What brings anyone to Black Lake besides timbering? Very shitty luck. My mama died giving birth to me. She's back there where Papaw and Mamaw are now. My old man spent most of his time locked up. One day he learned I was getting social security money. He went to court, put on an act, and convinced the judge he'd reformed. The sheriff showed up and pulled me screaming from Mamaw's arms. I never saw her or Papaw again. The bastard had an old jail buddy named Bill living in a trailer on the lake there. That's how I wound up in that hole. They drank during the day and stole at night. It took 'em about a year to start molesting me. Then I met Jessie. He found out what they were doing and beat them both half to death. He let me move in with him. I was naïve and stupid then and thought I'd found my Prince Charming." She blew a laugh. "That was before he started beating me and pimping me out. All that happened before I turned sixteen. So, my soul has been ripped out too, lady. It just happened over years."

"Why did you stay with him?"

"It's something you wouldn't understand. Damned if I really do myself. I left him time and again, but always returned, except for the times he found me first and drug me back. I don't know. I guess something about his rescuing me from my old man was part of it. He was just stronger and more forceful than anyone I knew. Something about that kept me with him no matter how shitty he treated me. Then I met someone stronger—your husband." She looked at Becky with the hint of a smile. "You don't look worried. Why? Think I was too low life for him?"

"No," Becky said. "I just trust him. I'm guessing he helped you get away."

"You did right to trust him," Candy said. "I can read people. I saw he loved you before he even told me." She kept her eyes on Becky. "Jessie made it a point to keep the upper hand with the cop in town one way or another. My job was to get Ed to bed so he could be blackmailed whenever needed. It didn't work, but I fell for him. He was strong in the opposite way Jessie was, and that attracted the hell out of me. I started giving him information. Just little things, like who sold booze in lumber town. The other stuff came later. I'm sure you hate me, but I wanted him."

"I don't hate you."

"You say that, but I guess you'd say anything to hear what I know. You sounded pretty desperate on the phone."

"I am desperate to know what happened to my husband."

"You shouldn't push it. Those people are more dangerous than you know."

"I need answers," Becky said.

"Well, I can't help with his murder, other than telling you Jessie didn't do it. I'm sure of that. But I'll tell you what I can since you're his wife and you came this far." She topped off her glass. "Sure you don't want none?"

"No."

"I guess you already know Scotland works for them. But Jessie did the dirty work. Frye's Jewelry Store robbery was a sham. Jessie did it with a ski mask and pistol. Frank was to get the insurance money then his shit back, sell it, and make double. Jessie and Scotland would get their usual cut, only this time Jessie wanted more. He hid the jewelry and told Scotland and Frank he'd sell it for himself if they didn't pay him what he thought it was worth. I knew they'd kill him—had no doubt. I thought about telling Ed. He'd park on the waterfront when he wanted information. I'd walk past, wave, and meet him in the lot behind the old cotton mill. We met there a few days after the robbery. He asked about it, but I told him I didn't know anything. Two yahoos on their lunch break from the plant saw us meet. They told Jessie." Candy removed her partial dentures. "It still don't feel right eating solid food."

"Dear Lord," Becky said.

Candy slid them back in. "He told me to meet a john in an ally in Cypress Cove that night, but it was him with a lead pipe who showed up. It was the worst I'd ever got. He wanted to know what I told Ed. I knew I'd die if I didn't say something. So, I told him the one thing I knew of that might save me." She slugged down the rest of her whiskey then placed her forehead in her palm.

"The Monets?" Becky asked.

Candy nodded. "There's been this rumor for years that the Billings kid did it. I told Jessie that. It was enough to make him stop. The asshole thought he was going to be rich and started trying to blackmail Jimmy Billings that night."

"Did you tell Ed?"

"No, but he figured out what happened. He made Jessie his pet project and tailed him whenever he came to town. It didn't take him long to catch Jessie at some shit. I'd have paid to watch that ass beating.

Jessie called me from jail and told me where the jewelry was. He wanted me to sell enough of it to bail him out. During that beating, I promised myself it would be the last I took from him if I lived. I told Ed all about Jessie and the big shots in town. I turned the jewelry over to him too. He wanted me to talk to some agent, but before he could get it set up Jessie somehow raised bail. I knew I had to get out of town then. Ed bought me a bus ticket and gave me two hundred dollars for rent money. He even made some phone calls and got me a job here set up. I just had to promise to talk to the agent."

"Would you have?"

"If Ed hadn't been killed, maybe. Not now. Not for nothing. Tell me how Jessie died. I want the details."

"He was trying to kill Max Underwood. Pete shot him in the face. It was quick. He didn't know what hit him."

"Well, I'm glad—glad he's dead. Do they think I am too?"

"Yes. Did you stage that yourself?"

"Yeah. The job your husband got me was waitressing. A few weeks ago, Scotland calls the restaurant and asks who there knew Ed Hawk. He didn't find out anything, but it scared the piss out of me. Do you know how he found out?"

"Pete searched the police department," Becky said. "He took Ed's address and phone number book from the desk. He was just fishing. Probably called every number in it."

"Well, the number won't do him any good now. I knew it wouldn't be hard for people to believe Jessie killed me, so I quit the job that day and drove to Black Lake. They almost really had a body when I cut myself. I wanted a lot of blood and went too deep on my wrist. But Candy Fritz *did* die that night. I put a rose on Ed's grave in appreciation for that. The name is Dee now. There's a last name too, but don't ask."

Becky glanced at her watch and knew Wendy would be getting worried. "Just wondering, was Jessie a smart man?"

"Street smart. Why?"

"I just find it strange that he thought he could blackmail James Billings with only a rumor that's already been around for years."

Candy looked down. "Well, I might've added something else."

Becky thought of Bobby and wondered if she wanted to push on. "What else, Dee?"

"I told Jessie the only thing I thought might keep me alive in Black Lake. I told him I saw Bobby Billings at Helen and Shannon's house the night they died. The deal I made with Ed was to meet him and the agent away from there and tell the story just once. No testifying."

"The real story?"

Candy nodded with closed eyes and squeezed her mouth. Becky walked over, sat down, and took a shivering hand. It felt clammy. "You were there, weren't you?" she asked softly.

Candy looked away then broke down. Becky held her hand and waited.

"She was the only friend I made there," Candy said in a pained voice. "She sat in front of me in homeroom. I'd flunked a grade and missed a year, so I was a few years older. We got to know each other then started hanging out. Her mom worked nightshifts at the plant, so I spent lots of nights at her house. I even told her about my old man and Bill."

"Shannon?"

"Yeah."

"Tell me, Dee. Take your time. Start from the beginning."

"No. If I tell this, it will be Candy because she promised your husband she'd do it. Dee won't know nothing about it. Do you really want to know? Are you sure? Knowing might be a curse."

Becky thought of the night she and Bobby fished and his smile while he applauded her at the Christmas show. She took the glass brought for her and filled it. She drank some while struggling for an answer. "Yes," she said, and listened. The words came slow at first then sped up as the story was told, but the tremble in the voice stayed.

"Helen called me that afternoon. All she said was Shannon needed company. Could I stay the night? Something happened that day. I could see it in their faces when I got there. Shannon hardly talked. She was scared, really scared. Helen made hotdogs. We ate them on the pier and watched fireworks over the lake. Helen held Shannon while we watched and kept telling her everything was going to be alright. After that, Shannon and I went up to her room. I asked her what was going on, but she only said something had happened at the Billings' house that day. They paid her to look after Bobby. She told me once that he had a thing for her, so I guessed he'd done something to her.

"Shannon had this little jewelry set. It had string and wire and colored beads with letters and designs on them. We sat on the floor in her bedroom, making bracelets and necklaces and listening to *The Adventures of Sam Spade* on the radio. It was a hot night, so I opened the window facing the lake. Shannon started calming down and talking a little. I think she might've been about to tell me what happened. Then we heard the boat pull up to the pier."

Becky took another sip.

"I didn't look out, but Shannon did. Then she yelled, 'They're here, Mama. They've come after me.' Helen ran up the stairs. She turned off the radio then kicked the jewelry set under the bed and shoved us both into the closet. She told us to stay there and be quiet. We heard people beating on the front and back doors then one of them break down. Helen shut the closet and ran downstairs. I held my hand over Shannon's mouth to keep her quiet. We heard Helen yell, 'Go away. I've told the sheriff about you. Shannon's not here.' Then there was this sound like the grunt you make when you're about to puke and a loud wheeze. Son of a bitch, I wish I'd never heard that sound. We heard her fall. I couldn't hold Shannon then and didn't have the guts to go after her. Instead, I pulled the closet door back and pushed myself into the corner. I pulled clothes from the racks and piled them over me, then I sat there and listened to the noise downstairs. There were men's voices. I couldn't understand what they were saying over Shannon's screaming. Then I heard her running up the steps. There was hollering and fighting. All the sudden Shannon was screaming just outside the closet door. I saw her face through the slats. There was this look on it that either said *help me* or *stay quiet*. Ever since, I've wished I knew and was glad I didn't."

Candy looked away for a long time with a trembling lip. "I wanted to help her. I was just scareder than I've ever been in my life. They started asking her who else she'd told. She told them 'Nobody,' but they didn't believe her. They were hitting her. I could hear it."

"How many voices were there?" Becky asked.

"Three. One I recognized because of something he said just before Shannon stopped screaming. There was this thud and crack together. One of the guys said, 'I think I busted her skull.' The one I recognized said, 'Well, that's life in the jungle.' It's something Coach Carbo used to say. If you failed one of his health tests or got tired running in gym, it was just 'Life in the jungle.' His being there made the whole thing even more unreal. Shannon and I both liked him in school. Shannon even bought him a necktie once for his birthday.

"The other voice wanted to leave. He sounded scared. Coach Carbo told them Shannon was still alive—he'd take her to the boat so she would tell them who else knew, whatever that was. He told the other two to check the house and make sure nobody else was there. The closet door opened then. I would've begged for my life if I could've talked. But he only took a quick look then closed the door. The clothes piled over me saved me."

"Did you recognize him?" Becky asked.

"Hell, yeah. He was before my time at the high school, but everybody in town knew Quincy Tolly, the big fucking football hero. I sat there and listened to them moving around the house. Then the lights went out. The boat motor started. I sat there in the dark and listened to it drive away. It must've been way out on the lake when Shannon started screaming again. It's amazing how far sound travels across water. Then there were two bangs, different than the fireworks we'd heard. The screaming stopped then. I don't know how long I sat there. I didn't want to leave that closet. I cried and felt so cold for some reason. And it was quiet, so quiet that I heard a car coming from the main road. It came closer. Then I heard it pull into the drive. A door slammed then someone walked around downstairs. I wanted to know who it was, but still felt paralyzed. The car left and I waited longer. It was like being in a nightmare you can't wake from. Finally, I just had to get the hell out of there. I knew what I'd see would be horrible, I just didn't know how horrible."

"You don't have to describe it," Becky said.

"Words can't describe it anyway. The door was shattered. Helen lay close to it. I was trying to step around the blood when my foot touched another body on the floor. It was Bobby Billings out cold. I thought he was dead too until I heard him breathing. I wanted out of there too much to wonder why he was there. Ever had a dream that you're running away from something at night? The only sound you hear is your own breath, but you know something wicked is there too? That's what I felt that night and lots of other nights since then." Candy stared into nothing. She jerked when wood cracked in the stove.

"Can you drive?" Becky asked when they returned to the Volkswagen.

"If you want to get back. Put the glasses on."

Becky did and pulled her toboggan over her ears. She felt the car moving. "I would like for you to speak to the agent," she said. "You can make them pay for what they did."

"I made that part very clear to you."

Becky heard only sniffling and gear shifting the rest of the ride.

"You can take the glasses off."

Becky did and saw the newsstand again. "Thank you," she said. "You won't hear from me again." A hand grabbed her when she opened the door.

"I wish I could help, but I cannot tell that story again. I can't go back. It would be like opening the lid of hell for me."

"I understand Dee."

"The deck is stacked. They make the laws and the truth there. Your home is less than an hour away–your real home. Go back there, Becky."

Becky stepped from the car. "Not just yet," she said.

21

She spared Wendy the worst details of the story but gained an appreciation of Candy's courage to tell it. The hum of Marilyn Mae's tires on the highway was the only sound heard for a mile afterwards.

"So, Bobby woke up to that," Wendy finally said. "Holy Moses. What did they do, knock him out somehow?"

"Yes, somehow. But worse, he thinks he did it. No wonder he's terrified of Pete Scotland. He must've been interrogated hard and made to believe what they wanted him to."

"You think the whole thing was planned?"

"Of course. Shannon was doomed the day the Billings hired her."

"Why would they do that? Why would they be that cruel?"

Becky saw a truck stop ahead. "There's only one reason I can guess," she said. "Stop here. We've both got phone calls to make."

"Who am I calling?"

"Think your old boyfriend at the register of deeds office can help us?"

"No problem there."

"Agent Feezor isn't available now. May I take a message?" The receptionist said after a ten-minute hold.

Becky slid another dime into the phone. "Yes. Make sure he gets this. Tell him that I have extremely important information about a murder and am on my way to Raleigh. Tell him that I intend to camp out in your office lobby until he speaks with me." She noticed Wendy scribbling on scrap paper in the booth beside her.

"Just a minute," the receptionist said before the click of a transfer.

"What can I do for you Mrs. Hawk?" Feezor failed to hide his irritation.

"You can take me seriously first, Marty. Get a notepad and listen closely." She slid three more dimes into the phone to ensure no interruptions from the operator. Sounds of pen scratching on paper came five minutes into the half hour she spoke.

"Are you sure of all this? No mistakes? No exaggerations?" Feezor asked.

"None."

"You're sure it was a body you saw in the boat? You saw it clearly?"

"I'm sure."

"I need to know the name of this person who told you about the Monets. A phone number at least."

"I told you what I promised. Trust me, she won't talk. But I've told you what I saw. I know you're still wondering if I'm all there or not, but all I'm asking is for you to come to Black Lake and look into this, even if it's a little. Find out for yourself if what I'm saying is true."

"Let me speak to my district supervisor. Give me the number you're calling from."

"I'll call you back in an hour," Becky said. "And just so you know, I have other plans of handling this if you don't." She hung up, motioned to Wendy, and went inside.

Wendy soon joined her at a table with an unreadable expression. "What did Feezor say? Please tell me he believes you."

"I think I finally got his attention," Becky said. "Got to call him back shortly."

Wendy bit a nail. "His mother says they still haven't heard from him. She's worried bad. Something's happened to him. I know it."

Becky felt a surge of guilt from having forgotten Aaron. "Don't assume the worst," she said. "Let's take one thing at a time. It's been a long day. I think it will get longer. How about we relax and eat while we can? Then you can tell me what else you found out." She signaled a waitress.

"Got mustard on your new dress," Becky said when she finished her turkey club.

Wendy shrugged while chewing. "Just another color. This dress has taught me it feels sort of cool not caring what you look like. Are we going back to Bolton County?"

Becky wiped her mouth. "I don't know just yet. Tell me what you found out from Jeremy."

Wendy unfolded her notepaper. "Listen up. Ever heard of Tolly Investments in Wilmington?"

"Yes. It's Quincy's."

"You bet your tooshie it is. Black Lake Lumber Company is also part of it. Jeremy found something called a certificate of assumed business name on file. It lists Quincy Tolly and Bud Sweeney as agents. James Billings' name is nowhere on it."

"When was it filed?" Becky asked.

"July ninth, 1948, five days after the murders. But that wasn't all from that day. He found two quitclaim deeds for land that James signed over to Quincy and Bud, and one to Quincy and Frank Frye. Together the three tracts are over five hundred acres. I told him to check for more when he has time. Want to bet there's a lot?"

"Probably one for each tract James inherited," Becky said. "The Manticores had been after everything he and his father owned for over fifty years. They finally got something to hang over him and got it."

"But why would he have joined them?" Wendy asked. "Was he forced?"

"I doubt he was one of them. Something tells me his marriage to Cynthia was part of their plan. You know, I never heard just how his first wife died. Whatever the case, they got their foot in the door, and he lost everything. Maybe they put that pin on him in his coffin as something symbolic."

Becky thought of Harrison Tolly's cold stare at the funeral home. "No," she said. "Nobody else at the viewing wore that symbol—not Quincy or Bud. They pinned it to James to see my reaction. They wanted to see if I knew about them. It explains Cynthia telling me what she did. She used my friendship with Bobby to keep me quiet about them. At least long enough for them to get a plan. That's why they brought Nick's body back. It's part of their plan, and I believe it means my going to jail."

"For what?"

"Figure it out, Wendy. They're setting me up just like they did Bobby. Cynthia told me herself they can make evidence appear. Hudson Perry has them worried. They set me up with Nick's murder and it solves their problems in one neat package."

"But you'd have to get a lawyer. A good one would blow the lid off the whole thing."

"I won't get a lawyer, and I won't get a trial if they get me in Pete's jail."

"Becky, this all has me terrified. Aaron is missing, now this. You must get Feezor or somebody with authority on this right now."

"I agree. Hand me your notes."

Feezor came on the line almost immediately after Becky spoke to the receptionist. "Where are you?" he asked.

His tone put Becky on the defensive. "That's not important. I have more information. A motive. Something you can verify with one phone call."

"Tell me where you are first."

"I take it you've learned something since we spoke last. What is it?" Becky heard another line open. "Ok fellows, listen," she said. "I plan on being honest with you. You be honest with me. What's up?"

"Mrs. Hawk, Les Sykes, capital district supervisor speaking. Agent Feezor told me about the information you gave him. Normally we require a request from the jurisdictional district attorney to relieve another law enforcement agency of an active investigation. I just spoke on the phone with your DA. He wants to meet with you. He's prosecuting a case in Deaton today but will be in his office after five. When can you get there?"

"Probably seven or eight."

"I'll call and tell him. He'll wait."

"And what happens then?"

"He'll listen to what you have to say and decide if it's enough to request our assistance in an investigation."

Becky pulled hard on her ponytail. "That's ridiculous. I saw three men with a corpse this morning and talked to a person who said they witnessed a double murder. What more do you need to investigate?"

"I think he wants to talk to you more about that body, Becky," Feezor said.

"Be straight with me, guys. What else is going on?"

Sykes blew a breath. "They want to ask you some questions, Mrs. Hawk. The sheriff found the body of a reporter named Nicholas Hughes buried in a crawl space under your home this morning."

Becky clawed her hand over her face. Tears of frustration came. "It's all a setup," she yelled loudly enough to make truckers in the lot turn. "You guys need to wake up to what's going on in that county. You've got organized crime there. People have died, including my husband. More will if you don't stop them."

"Just tell him what you told us," Feezor said. "As soon as he requests an investigation, we'll be down there and go over that place with a fine-toothed comb."

"If Sheriff Scotland gets his hands on me, he'll kill me," Becky said. "If I go to his jail, the headline the next day will be inmate hangs self. You guys remember that."

"If detaining you is necessary," said Sykes, "and the district attorney finds it a safety risk, he can have you housed in another sheriff's jail. I promise we'll follow up after your meeting."

"I have a feeling there's another big story in Black Lake today. What else did the district attorney tell you, Agent Sykes?"

"Normally I wouldn't tell you, but I understand it's already hitting all the news outlets. An arrest has been made in the murder you were discussing with Agent Feezor."

"Bobby Billings?"

"Yes. They have a confession."

"Call the district attorney back and tell him I'm on my way."

Becky bought stationery, an envelope, and a stamp inside before walking back to the table.

"So, what's the plan," Wendy asked. "Are we going back or not?"

Becky handed her a ten. "We're going back. Fill Marlyn Mae up. I've got one thing to do before we leave." She removed one of Ed's old letters from her backpack and used it to address her envelope to Sergeant Mike Ledford of Tahlequah, Oklahoma.

22

They arrived back in Deaton to empty streets and closed businesses. Christmas lights waved over the streets in a rough wind. Both women watched the rearview mirrors. Their conversation had died an hour earlier.

"How far is Courthouse Square?" Becky asked.

Wendy's face looked tense. "About five blocks down. On the left. How you feel about this?"

"Doesn't matter. Turn down the next street on the left and pull over."

"Why?"

"Because you're not going with me."

"Like hell I'm not."

"Turn and pull over, dammit." Becky grabbed the wheel and forced it to the left.

"What are you doing?" Wendy asked. She glided the car to a stop near the curb. "You talked me out of it in Asheville, but no way I'm letting you do this yourself. You have no idea what's going to happen."

"You're right. I don't. That's exactly why we have to separate. You can't show up with me. If they silence us both, then all this has been for nothing. Anyway, there's something important I need you to do."

"Becky, I just can't."

"Listen to me. I want you to get out of this county first. They'll be looking for you too. I'll give you money for gas and a motel room. Get some rest, then tomorrow drive to the Charlotte Chronicle office and ask to speak to Hudson Perry. They'll contact him. Tell him that I sent you. Tell him everything except for Candy's name. Let him know that if he comes here, he should bring others with him and watch his back."

"I can't. I just can't drive away and leave you here. Go with me."

"No. This is my only shot. We don't do Bobby any good if we're caught together. I can't imagine what he's going through in that jail." Becky reached into her backpack and removed the knife and Frank Frye's jewelry. She dug the rest of her money from her pocket and dropped it into the backpack. "Hold on to everything for me," she said. "Spend the money as you need to. Just don't come back here until business is taken care of."

Wendy's bottom lip curled. She held her arms out, and Becky went to them. "I don't want to leave you," Wendy whispered. "There has to be another way."

Becky pulled back and wiped a tear from Wendy's cheek. "Tough bitches don't cry," she said. "I love you." She stuck the knife and jewelry into her coat pocket and walked away. She glanced over her shoulder at Marilyn Mae. A hand waved from the window. It occurred to Becky that she may never see her friend again.

She stayed on dark backstreets until she reached Courthouse Square. The wind gusted against the side of the building where she

242

stood, surveying the area. One light burned in a two-story brick building half a block down. She walked toward it with her hand holding her revolver inside her pocket. A sign on the door of the building confirmed it was the district attorney's office. She knocked and waited until a gray-haired man with neatly trimmed mustache and beard opened the door. He wore his tie loose. The sleeves of his white shirt were rolled to his elbows. His smile was pleasant.

"Becky Hawk I presume. Mack Deacon, district attorney for the thirty-second judicial district. Sorry I don't look more professional. It was a long day in court."

Becky released her revolver to shake his hand. "Anyone else here?"

"Just you and me. I hear you have some interesting information." He held his hand toward the hall. "Let's talk in my office."

The jewelry and knife lay side by side on Deacon's desk. He looked down at them with reading glasses on his nose tip and a hand rubbing his beard. He reclined and read his notes.

"There's probably some details I forgot," Becky said. "But those are the main things."

"Well, I'll be damned," Deacon said, still reading. "I've always suspected a lot of people in this county of some crooked things, including Sheriff Scotland, but I never imagined this. Are you sure you're not mistaken about anything here?"

"No. And I'll testify to what I can."

"I'm glad. But we must get past a few things first. As you know, Nicholas Hughes was found buried in a shallow grave under your house this morning. Obvious blunt force trauma to the head. That could be a reason for you to make a story up."

"You're a seasoned prosecutor. What possible motive would I have had to kill him."

"Well, Hughes came by your home on Sunday the eighth. He was missing the next day. You may have been the last person who saw him alive. That's usually the first suspect. You're close to Bobby Billings. He just confessed to cutting Helen Monet's throat then beating and choking her daughter to death and throwing her in the lake. Hughes was looking into those murders."

"I guarantee that confession has holes all in it," Becky said. "Pete bullied it out of him."

"Maybe. But he's charged. There's enough there to prosecute. You just turned in to me a weapon your husband found in the lake in front of the murder scene. You said yourself it can be tied to the Billings' house."

"Then call the agents and tell them you want them to investigate, for goodness sakes."

"We'll need more. Your word alone is just hearsay. We need the name of the person who said they witnessed this. I'm afraid this won't go too far unless we talk to them."

"I told you I can't tell you that. They won't talk again anyway."

"Do you understand just what's at stake here, Ms. Hawk? You and Bobby Billings are..."

"I understand exactly what's at stake. That's why I want the SBI to investigate this. It seems you should too."

"Ok. Let's just start this way: male or female?"

Becky studied the eyes peering over the glasses. "Male," she said, twisting her toboggan in her hands.

"Does he live in Black Lake?"

"Am I going to be arrested, Mr. Deacon?"

"Maybe. Unless we have more. This is serious stuff. I've been doing this for a long time. I know what it takes to put a case together. I want to be on your side on this, but I must know all the facts. It could mean your life and Bobby's. Think about that young man sitting in jail right now. You have the power to get him out, if you let me prove what you're saying is true. I will need to know that name."

Becky turned away and noticed a picture on the wall. It showed Deacon shaking hands with Dwight Eisenhour. They stood in front of a crowd waving "I Like Ike" signs. Deacon wore a geometrical tie tack.

"You think about that for a minute. I'll get us some coffee. Black or with sugar?"

"Lots of sugar and cream," Becky said, eyeing another door across the office. She waited for Deacon to step out then slid on her toboggan. She ran to the door, through a conference room, and to the hallway. "Exit" she saw, and she did into an alleyway. A Plymouth Fury was parked there. Pete and Max Underwood leaned against it.

"Hello, Becky," Pete said.

Max took a swig from his flask and laughed.

Becky looked the other way. A chain-link fence blocked it. She faced Pete, put her hand in her pocket, and found the grip of her revolver.

Pete stood straight. "If your hand comes out with a gun," he said, "you'll be dead before you hit the ground." He unsnapped his holster and wrapped his hand around the pearl grips.

Becky released it then slowly removed her hand from her pocket. "I know what you're all about," she said. "Even if you kill me, you won't get by with it this time. I promise you that."

Pete shook his head. "I don't know what you're talking about, Becky girl. I just know that I'm going to have to hold you on suspicion of murder. We can talk all about it at the jail."

Becky's hand moved back toward her pocket.

Pete stared at her silently.

"Go on," Max said with a chuckle. "Do it. He ain't really that fast. Let's see your quickdraw." He laughed before turning up his flask again.

A hand grabbed Becky's arm from behind and pushed her to the ground. She fought, and her arm twisted behind her painfully.

"Quit playing games and get her cuffed," Deacon said. "She has to tell us some things."

"Do it, Max," said Pete.

Max removed handcuffs from his pocket. He knelt beside Becky. She felt his hand replace Deacon's on her arm and twist it with force. Cold metal clamped tight on her right wrist then her left arm was jerked back like a ragdoll's and secured.

"Take her gun," Pete said.

Max rolled her to her side and removed her revolver. "You won't be getting it back this time," he said, tossing it to Pete.

Becky saw a car pass at the end of the alley and screamed.

"Shut her up now," Deacon said.

Becky felt her toboggan removed and her ponytail pulled until she was on her feet. She screamed again and thrashed. Max wrapped his arms around her and lifted her high. She saw his face up close and smelled the liquor on his breath. "Shut your bitch mouth," he said. He slammed her against the trunk. She felt the air leave her lungs and crumpled to Max's boots.

"I meant gag her, for the love of Mike," Deacon said. "Use her toboggan and my tie."

Becky rolled on asphalt while fighting for breath. She felt weight on her back.

"Open wide and say ah," Max said. The toboggan was forced into her mouth before Deacon's tie wrapped around her head and tightened.

Pete opened the back door of the car and looked down the alley.

Another hard pull on her ponytail brought Becky to her feet. Max shoved her toward the car. Becky turned and swung her boot upward. The kick would've traveled four feet but stopped at three when it crashed into Max's crotch. Air blasted through his nose and his eyes crossed. He slowly fell to his knees with his hands between his legs.

Becky tried running past Pete. He effortlessly snagged her coat and wrapped an arm around her neck from behind. "Get the shackles from the front seat," he told Deacon. Max still knelt and croaked while Pete pushed Becky past him and into the backseat. He held her on her belly while the shackles clicked onto her feet. Deacon got in the backseat, and both backdoors slammed. Becky felt panic.

Pete took a seat behind the wheel while laughing. "Suck it up, Max," he said.

Max half crawled into the passenger side with a pale face. "I want first at her," he wheezed. "I swear I'll make her beg to tell everything in one minute."

"You'll get your chance at the jail."

"No," said Deacon. "We're going to Cynthia's."

"I can handle this, Mack," Pete said.

"Drive," Deacon replied.

Becky managed to sit up when the car moved. When they turned from the alley, she saw, on the dash-mounted rear-view mirror, the reflection of Marilyn Mae leave a side street and fall in behind.

"Stay down," Deacon said, pushing on her neck.

"You guys don't think I can handle this, Mack?" Pete asked.

"The state boys are already suspicious. I don't want booking records and an autopsy. We do it our way. I'll just tell them she never showed up."

The streetlights lit the interior of the car another few minutes then all darkened except for Wendy's headlights from behind. Becky knew she was too close.

"We're being followed," Max said.

"I know," Pete replied. "Saw it before we left town. It's that old, red Hudson her friend drives."

Becky pushed up against Deacon's hand with all her strength and yelled into the gag. She rose just enough to look back at Wendy and shake her head. She fought against the pull on her hair.

"Do something, Pete," Deacon said. "This could be trouble."

"Relax. This just makes everything easier. I won't have to go looking for her now."

Becky kicked her feet against the door. Deacon pressed more weight on her. He held her tightly while she struggled until her strength left. She felt the car slow and glide through sharp curves. Then it stopped.

Max took Pete's shotgun from the rack and opened his door.

"Sit tight, Max," said Pete. "Let's see what she does."

"What's she doing?" Deacon asked.

Pete looked at the side mirror for a moment. "She don't know what the hell to do. Get out and spook her around us, Max."

Max got out with the shotgun and walked toward the back. Becky heard tires spin and saw lights pass. Max jumped back in and slammed the door. "Get her ass!" he yelled in delight.

The Fury jerked forward then sped. Becky struggled uselessly against Deacon then kicked the back of Pete's seat twice with both shackled feet.

"Make her stop that," Pete said. "Knock her out if you can't."

Tires squalled in a curve. The Fury rocked hard enough for Becky to think they were overturning. Deacon was thrown off her. Becky rose and saw Marilyn Mae feet in front of the Fury. Another sharp curve lay ahead.

"She's done," said Pete with cool deliberation. The Fury screamed and slammed into Marilyn Mae's back bumper just before the curve. Pete braked hard, throwing everyone forward.

Becky made a muffled cry. She watched Marylin Mae spin across the road, flip, and go airborne. It made a metallic exploding sound when it struck a tree then fell in a twisted heap on its side with one headlight shining into woods.

"Go make sure the job's done," Pete told Max.

"You really think there's a doubt?" Max asked. He stepped out with the shotgun and walked through a dust cloud to the wreckage. He bent down and looked through the shattered windshield.

The sound of an approaching car was heard.

"Dammit. Get out of here." Deacon said.

Pete blew the horn. Max ran back and jumped in.

Pete spun out and turned his headlights off until they were a distance from the wreck. "Is she?" he asked.

"As a doornail," Max said.

Becky lay against the seat and bawled into her toboggan. She felt numb and prayed the end would come fast.

23

Five of them stood at Bobby's firepit. They wore black overcoats with their Manticore badges flashing in the flamelight. Pete walked Becky toward them with Deacon and Max following. Becky stared at the ground in a trance state. She looked up when Pete pulled her to a stop. Quincy, Bud, Sam, and Frank were there. The fifth was Alvin Parker. He bore the same gentle expression he'd worn when he brought her Thanksgiving dinner and free groceries.

Harrison Tolly's voice called from the house. "You're in charge of this, Alvin. I'm trusting you to do it right."

Alvin nodded.

Becky turned and saw Cynthia wheel Harrison inside from the house deck.

A siren sounded in the distance.

"Sounds like they found her," Deacon told Pete. "The highway patrol will be investigating. Hide your car and get that dent fixed tomorrow. You can bill me."

Pete handed Deacon a handcuff key. "Make sure you return my hardware when you're done."

Quincy and Bud took each of Becky's arms. They led her to the pier then inside the dark cabin of the houseboat. "Sit down," Quincy said, pushing her to the floor. Outlines of four of them sat down in chairs around her. Deacon lit a pipe. Quincy and Bud climbed to the helm.

"When the time comes, Becky," Alvin said tenderly, "you must be honest. I'd like this to go quickly. You're too fine a young lady to suffer."

The boat began moving. Becky felt dead inside and chose not to think at all. She smelled Deacon's pipe tobacco and waited. No one spoke. The boat rocked and hummed for nearly half an hour, then the engine stopped. A dim light in the cabin turned on. Quincy and Bud climbed down from the helm.

Frank stood with a length of rope. He knelt and wrapped it around Becky's neck. "I haven't forgotten this morning," he said into her ear. He pulled the rope ends, and Becky felt her throat constrict. She fell on her back with Frank over her. He looked into her face with a snarl. The rope cut into her neck and throat with scorching pain. Becky felt her eyes bulge.

"Take that damned rope off her," Deacon said.

"Just giving her a taste of what happens if she doesn't talk," said Frank.

"This isn't about your revenge, Frank," said Alvin. "Don't touch her again without my say-so." He stood with Deacon and Sam. "Get her outside."

Frank loosened the rope. Becky coughed saliva into her toboggan and pulled air through her nose. Quincy took her hands and Bud her feet. They carried her outside and dropped her onto the deck. Sam untied the gag. The toboggan fell from her mouth.

Alvin knelt beside her, stroking her head while she made shivering gasps. "I know you're scared," he said. "Please, please understand that this is very hard for me. I hate that it's come to this, Becky. But I have

252

a job, and I will do it. There's one simple question you must answer to make this end. Now, we only want to know who told you those things about that unfortunate girl and her mother in Cypress Cove. Give us that name."

Becky shook her head. Quincy and Bud lifted her by her feet and dangled her off the side of the boat. "Don't!" she yelled. She went into cold water to her shoulders. She tried holding her breath, but soon heard her gurgling cry. Water pulled into her nose and throat. Her lungs burned. She came out of the water. Her head struck the hull of the boat before she fell onto the deck.

Alvin appeared again. "I don't like this. I don't want this," he said. "But we will get the answer from you. I swear that."

Becky coughed out water. "Just kill me. I won't tell you."

"No, Becky," Alvin said. "You will tell us. I'm afraid we're determined. That was a mere example of what comes next. The second will be much longer. You'll be brought to the verge of drowning before you get another chance to answer. The panic will be severe. If that fails, we have other plans. I'll ask once more before we proceed."

"I can't," Becky said. She screamed when they lifted her again.

"Make it at least one minute this time," Frank said.

"Just make sure she doesn't stop kicking," Sam added.

Clear your head. Clear your head and stay in the fight. It came through her scream. Ed was there. She had no doubt. His spirit felt strong. Her head did clear. And she realized there was a card to play.

"I have something to tell you," she yelled. "Put me down."

Alvin smiled and nodded.

Quincy and Bud lay her against the cabin, and the six men gathered around her.

"Oh, dear. Your head is bleeding," Alvin said. He removed a handkerchief from his coat pocket and wiped her forehead. "Would you like to go inside where it's warm before we talk?"

"No." She looked directly at Quincy while catching her breath. "You should've checked that closet closer," she said and saw the result in his eyes. "But I guess that's life in the jungle, ain't it."

"Cut the bullshit," Sam said.

"Becky, please don't make it this way," said Alvin.

She kept her eyes on Quincy. "There's a letter in the mail. It tells everything, every detail. My husband joined a club too, and their motto is Semper Fi—always faithful. Could throw a wrench in those congressional plans, huh?"

Frank grabbed her hair. "She wants another dip."

"Wait," Quincy said.

Becky could see him thinking and detected fear. She looked at each man. "I *will not* tell you that name. But I will make a deal." She turned her eyes to Deacon. "You need me alive to stop what's coming for you. Have Bobby declared incompetent. Find evidence that contradicts his confession. You guys make the rules. I don't care how it's done, but do it. Find him a good guardian then leave him alone. Do that and you'll never see or hear from me again. And I'll see to it a bunch of pissed off Marines don't pay this town a visit."

"She's playing games with us, boys," said Frank. "We're too smart for this."

"Take her in the cabin," Quincy said. He looked at Alvin and received a nod.

Bud watched her while the others talked on deck. Becky kept a gaze on him while she sat on the floor. She knew he wanted to speak. Finally, he did.

254

"What else did this person tell you?"

Becky had no doubt then who the third person was at the Monets'. "Everything," she said. "I heard you were scared. I heard you didn't want to be there. Did you?"

"Just shut up and sit there," he said.

Voices outside rose and lowered for some time. Deacon led them when they returned. He knelt in front of Becky and looked at her with anger.

"You listen close," he said. "Don't think for a second that you hold the upper hand here. I make many deals. I do it for many reasons. But I never play games. Ask any defense attorney around. He'll tell you I make an offer just once. If it's turned down, I move ahead with everything at my disposal. Here's my one and only offer to you, I will not drop the charges against Bobby Billings, but I'll make sure the court considers his age at the time of the murders and his limited cognitive abilities. He'll get a light sentence. I'll work to get him approved for parole as soon as he's eligible. I'll then see that he gets a responsible guardian. He'll have a life. Take that or leave it."

"He didn't do it, and I want his charges dismissed," Becky said. Deacon slapped her. Her jaw burned while she looked at the other five. Their faces were grim.

Deacon's voice became a hiss. "I don't give a damn what you want. Now, you will go back to wherever you came from. You will see to it we have no problems. In return I will not seek murder charges against you. Lack of evidence will be my reason. But be damned clear, woman—if you ever come here again, if you cause us the smallest whit of trouble, it's all over for you. You'll be found and brought here to stand trial. I'll destroy your story so badly even your husband's Marine buddies will think you're crazy as a bat. And I'll happily be there when they load you into the gas chamber. You can agree to that now or we will resume our interrogation."

Becky nodded.

"Yes, or no?"

"Yes."

"Make her give us the name before we agree to that," Frank said.

"You might as well kill me and deal with the consequences if that's part of the deal," she replied.

Deacon looked back at the others.

"Let's go ashore," Alvin said.

Deacon produced the handcuff key.

"We're making a mistake," Frank said when the houseboat pulled away from an old pier at a desolate part of the lake. "Mark my words. This is a big mistake."

Quincy tossed Becky's toboggan onto the pier. "Be quiet, Frank."

Becky picked it up and walked without looking back. They hadn't told her where she was. She hadn't asked. She crossed over a sandy bank and went into a trot when she reached a dirt road. It was a moonless night. Her wet coat and hair made the air much colder. She glanced back often while running for about a mile. She felt safer and warmer then. But the shock from the events of the night was waning. A dreadful wave of emotion was building.

A quarter mile farther, a dilapidated barn stood off the road. She went to it and squeezed through a half-open door. She waited for her eyes to adjust before seeing a stall with rotting hay mounded inside. She burrowed under it and curled up. The insulation and her body warmth, she decided, would be enough to stave off hypothermia.

Then the wave crashed. She thought it unfair that she must cry that way again.

Her few hours of sleep came hard, and she rose with the first light. Frost lay on the ground when she resumed her walk down the road. Her muscles ached, but she made herself move briskly to stay warm.

The road eventually turned to asphalt and led her past scattered homes and intersections. She approached a gas station, and nearly stopped. However, something seemed to lead her elsewhere. She allowed it without thought. The Cypress Cove town limit sign passed then, two miles more, she turned onto Lakewood Road. Soon, she found her destination: 681 Pelican Drive.

24

She walked into a thicket that once was a yard. Saplings and briars obscured her view of the house. A girls', rusted Schwinn bicycle leaned against a tree. A tire swing, held by a single strand of decayed rope, hung from a dogwood. She saw the peeling paint and boarded windows on the house when she neared. A thick, dead tree limb lay in a break on the roof. The front door was also boarded. Becky thought of what happened just inside that door and felt somewhat relieved when she found the boards over it and the windows securely fastened. A recently hacked trail led her around the house to a dilapidated pier. She sat on the ground there and looked out at an early mist covering the lake. For a moment, she wondered why she was there, then an image of Wendy entered her head and broke her again.

"Hello, young lady."

Becky remembered the accent but not the name. She looked to her left and saw him thirty yards away on the bank. He left his camera and tripod and walked to her.

"Mind if I ask what's wrong?" He sat beside her. "And what brings you here?"

She looked away and wished he'd leave.

"A bevy of Otters play early near the other side. I'd hoped to get some pictures. But don't believe I should waste my time this morning with the fog. What do you think?" He gave her a sympathetic look. "I remember your face. However, I don't believe I learned your name."

"Becky."

"You were on the houseboat with your friends the last day I canoed."

The name came to her. "Only one of them was my friend. Finn Franks, right?"

A big smile came through the beard, "Your memory is excellent. Are you in trouble, Becky?" Then, when she didn't answer: "You look very cold and tired. Would you like to go inside and warm up? Maybe I could fix you some breakfast." He pointed to a small, lake cabin through the trees.

Becky took his hand and stood.

"The backdoor is open. Go in. I'll join you as soon as I recover my camera."

She watched Finn flip sausage links and eggs while she sipped coffee in a warmth that felt delicious. She saw a phone in the den and dreaded the call she had to make. "May I use your phone, Mr. Franks?"

"Call me Finn. Absolutely. The food will be done shortly."

Becky used a directory to look up Lewis-Sealy Ambulance & Funeral Service then dialed.

"Yes. We transported her from a vehicle accident last night," Mr. Lewis said a few minutes later. "Are you a relative?" His voice was subdued.

"Sister. Where did you transport her?" Becky made a steady tug on her ponytail.

"Drake Regional Hospital."

She felt cautious relief. "Not Bolton?"

"No. Drake is better suited to treat the injuries she sustained."

"What's her condition?"

"Serious. I'm sorry, but her injuries are life-threatening. You should call Drake Regional to find out more."

"Thank you very much."

The table was set when she returned. Finn sat at it.

"Finn, I need a big favor from you," Becky said.

He stroked his beard. "I heard. You need a ride to the hospital, correct?"

The food looked too good for Becky not to sit down. "Yes. I have a friend there who was seriously hurt last night."

"I'd be glad to. But first please explain this." He took a Bolton Record from his lap and handed it across the table.

"Fifteen-year-old Murder Solved. Discovered Reporter's Body Possibly Related."

Becky took the paper. The story took up the front page. Her and Ed's anniversary picture was printed there, and she realized it had been removed from her backpack in Wendy's car. This angered her, but it was the photograph of Bobby, terrified and being led toward the jail in handcuffs, that shattered her heart. "This isn't at all what it seems," she said.

"I thought it smelled some like schweinefutter," Finn replied. "No, I'm not calling the sheriff. Eat your breakfast. Then, I think we have a lot to talk about."

Becky sat a short while in the den before Finn entered with a folder. "Something told me you were Becky Hawk when I saw you at the old pier," he said. He took a seat across from her. "I got to meet your husband just before he died. The first time I saw him, he stood exactly where you sat this morning. He was looking through binoculars at the island. What is it named? Bear Island?"

Becky leaned forward. "Boar Island?"

"Yes. Boar Island. The low lying end."

"It's that close to here?"

"Little more than a mile straight out from where you were. He came back three straight days after that and watched it. The last day he arrived early and borrowed my canoe and underwater retriever—simply a magnet tied to a rope. He drug it around that old pier half the day and likely recovered every rusty can and lost fishing lure within a hundred-foot radius before he found what he was after."

"He found the knife that way?"

"Yes. It astounded me. I fought for the other side in the first war and know an officer's trench knife when I see it. I identified it for him and wanted to ask more. But there's an old German saying: 'Sweep only in front of your own door.' He didn't say, so I didn't ask. But I knew of the murder next door and thought it must be related."

"What's in the folder," Becky asked.

Finn removed a small stack of photographs. "When I moved here, I began photographing wildlife and soon became a fanatic. I purchased the best equipment on the market, including a NIKKOR telephoto zoom lens. I refurbished my basement into a darkroom. Nice thing I had a life savings, wouldn't you say?" He handed the photographs to Becky. "Last time I saw him, your husband asked that I record the comings and goings on the island. I can see the dock there very well with the zoom lens, so I simply photographed when I saw activity."

Becky went through the photographs. Handwritten dates showed the first three were taken from October twenty-ninth through the thirty-first. The Billings' houseboat was docked in each. "These were the days just before Ed's murder," she said.

"Yes. The boat left sometime after dark on the thirty-first. Someone stayed in a room at the lodge those nights. I can see the lights on the hill. I read of his murder the day after the boat left. It all made me wonder. I considered calling your local authorities but was torn. I have my reasons to keep a low-profile. So, instead, I just decided to continue watching the island until I heard more."

The next photograph was dated the eighth of December. It was dark, but the Billings' houseboat could be made out at the dock.

"What time did you take this one?"

"It was almost sunset," Finn said. "The boat left about an hour after I took that."

The next two were from the sixteenth and seventeenth. A Bolton County Sheriff's Department boat was docked with the houseboat in each. Becky inspected each picture closely. "Did you get any pictures of the people there then?" she asked.

"No," Finn said. "I thought it interesting a police vessel was there and watched in length. The lodge lights stayed on again until late. Both boats were gone when I checked yesterday morning. However, there is a person in the next one. I saved it for last. Look closely."

Becky flipped to an enlarged and blurred photograph dated the seventh. Streaky foliage framed an immense column and buttress. "There's a person here?" she asked.

"Look at the left of the tree trunk," Finn said. "The dark area."

Becky held the picture under the lamp. "Is he climbing into a tree?"

"Yes. That was taken after I saw you and the others on the lake that day. The two men in your group both climbed into that bald cypress as I canoed past. I thought it was unusual and snapped that picture. Sorry I didn't have time to focus."

"The tree is hollow?"

"Some get heart rot," Finn said. "But the outside wood is sturdy enough to still keep them standing for centuries. Animals make them their homes. Your native peoples sometimes used them for shelter on hunting expeditions."

"Where on the island is this tree?"

Finn looked out the window. "It seems the fog has burned away. Come outside with me. I'll bring my camera."

Becky adjusted the lens to suit her eyes and Boar Island came into sharp focus. She saw the dock extending out from trees in the water. An open beach stretched to the right before trees took over again. "It's amazing how far sound travels across water," she remembered Candy saying.

"There's a cove about one hundred meters to the right of the dock," said Finn. "Several large cypresses grow in the shallows there. The one in the picture is on the bank, about forty-five degrees left from the center of the cove. It's large. You can see it well from the water."

Becky pulled back and looked at the island with her bare eyes.

"What's all this about, Becky?" Finn asked. "Please tell me. What's the secret of that island?"

"Evil," she said. "Pure evil."

Finn stepped beside her. "Was it this evil that killed your husband and the young girl and her mother next door?"

"Yes. And there's others."

"So, what should we do about it?"

"Nothing. There's too much at stake now. I had to compromise with them to save someone I love."

Finn kept silent but seemed to struggle with his thoughts. "I won't contradict you," he finally said. "I'm sure you understand what's best. But, let me just say that I'm very familiar with evil. It's like an invasive vine that keeps growing bigger and stronger until it takes over the forest. It never stops until it's pulled out by the roots. Learning that was a harsh lesson for me. There is a quote from Dietrich Bonhoeffer that will torment me forever: 'Silence in the face of evil is itself evil. God will not hold us guiltless.'"

Becky looked at him and saw the joviality had fallen from his face. "What brought you here, Finn?" she asked. "What did you do in Germany?"

His eyes looked toward the island then at the ground. "If I tell you my secret, will you keep it to yourself?"

"Yes."

"I was an aeronautical engineer. Toward the end of the last war, I spent much time in the Mittelwerk tunnels. I helped with what was believed would give us victory. We used slave labor from the Dora camp. They turned to skeletons from twelve to sixteen hours hours of work daily on the smallest of food rations. It was part of the system. They were intentionally worked to death while giving us the labor we needed. When one died, another was brought. The SS beat or shot them for the slightest infraction. One morning two suspected saboteurs hung for all to see from a crane outside. I saw the agony and despair on the men's faces. I watched them fall and not get up despite the beatings they received. In the end, those tunnels killed more people than the missiles we built in them. I witnessed it and never said a damned word, never lifted a hand.

"When the war ended, the Americans detained me. I was questioned and received a paperclip attached to my file. It meant that I possessed knowledge that could be useful. I thank God the Americans got me before the Soviets. I helped with your space program. I wish I could feel proud of that, but I can never be proud again. I had my chance to do my part, as small as it may have been. Instead, I simply went to work every day and helped build those wretched V-2's. Now, I would much rather have gone to the gallows with Bonhoeffer."

Becky watched him remove his camera from the tripod.

"You're the first here I've told," he said. "Please keep your promise. I would like to live out my days here in privacy. But, if there's anything else I can help you with, I'd be glad to do it."

Becky took a long look at the island. "There is. I Would like for you to go to Drake Regional Hospital. Find out where Wendy Martin is. Tell them she's in danger and under no circumstances should she be allowed visitors. If they ask questions tell them a friend of hers sent you with that message. Stay near her room and stop anyone who isn't hospital staff from seeing her. I'll be there as soon as I can."

"Consider it done."

"Also, I'd like to use your phone again."

Becky made her call and asked Lily Baily to send Will with his boat, a rifle, and shovel.

25

"I got me a feeling we aren't hunting or fishing today," Will said when he steered his inboard to Finn's pier. Two rifles and a shovel lay on the deck. "Seen the paper this morning?"

Becky put her hand on the boat and steadied it against the pier. "Yes. It's all a lie."

"Shit, I know that," Will said. "But that don't mean I won't be in it deep if they catch you with me."

"You don't have to do this," Becky said. "I'll understand if you don't. But it shouldn't take long. All I want is a ride to Boar Island. Drop me off at the dock then go to the other bank and pretend you're fishing. I don't want your boat to draw attention. I'll wave to you when I'm done."

"You'll have to tell me what you're planning to do first."

"I think human remains are buried there. I can save myself and Bobby if I find them. You're the only person I trust who can take me there."

"Lord help," Will said. "Get in. But you'll have to tell me where to dig. I'm going ashore and you're staying on the boat."

Becky shook her head. "No. I'll find another way there if you're planning on that."

"Well, get your stubborn ass in here then."

Will looked in every direction when the boat glided toward the Boar Island dock. "This ain't the place to get caught," he said. "I was throwing my net in the cove once. They blocked me in with their houseboat and held me at gunpoint for half an hour, while all the time making every threat in the book. Lord knows what would've happened if they'd thought I was doing more than catching minnows." He handed over his lever-action 30-30 with sling. "You be damned careful up there and make it quick."

"I may need a flashlight too," Becky said. She slung the rifle and took the flashlight from him. "If anything were to go wrong, contact an Agent Feezor with the SBI, and tell him he needs to speak to that man whose house we just came from. Also tell him our district attorney is one of them."

"I want to hear everything later," said Will. "For now, I'm giving you fifteen minutes. Then I'm coming in there after you. No fussing." He handed her the shovel. "And just because there's no boat at the dock doesn't mean nobody's at the lodge. Watch for the wild pigs too. They're everywhere."

Becky held his hand, stepped out, then trotted past a "No Trespassing" sign and onto a trail at the end of the dock.

"Fifteen minutes," Will shouted while motoring away.

She went into the trees for cover and watched Will cross the lake before she moved farther into the woods. A swampy smell hung there. Nearer the cove, her boots sank into the ground. She heard brush break and knelt behind a tree while shouldering the rifle. A boar walked to the cove for water. Becky thought the creatures were as close to the devil incarnate as an animal could be. She'd hunted them, but this was the biggest she'd seen. She guessed it to be three feet at the shoulder and over six feet long. Its six-inch tusks resembled Arabian daggers. She kept her sights on it until it finished its drink and left the way it came.

The ground became soggier at the cove. Spanish moss waving between the trees blocked her view in most directions. She waded into a foot of water and studied the cove while remembering Finn's description of the tree. She trudged ahead and soon intersected sets of footprints, which she judged were a few days old. They went in and out. She stepped inside them in order to not leave her own. Ten paces farther, she saw the giant tree. Its ten-foot-wide buttress bore a jagged cleft. The footprints led to it. She detected a faint scent of death.

The cleft was just above her head when she stood at the buttress. The stench emanated from inside. Becky thought of Aaron and a terrifying image of what she might see inside flashed in her mind. She slid the shovel in then found a grip on the cleft and pulled herself up. The fall was farther than she anticipated, and the rifle clanked from her shoulder when she landed on her back. She heard scampering then saw a raccoon escape through a small hole at the tree base. Becky removed the flashlight and shined it around the enclosure. It reminded her of a cave. She stood up on a flagstone type floor. Against the wall to her right, the stones were pried loose. Fresh dirt stood around an open grave. She remembered the night she and Bobby fished and Quincy and Bud returning to the houseboat covered in mud. She realized Nick Hughes' grave was dug that night, even as he lived. And she knew where her own eternal resting place most likely would've been if she hadn't escaped the Manticores the night before–and where it certainly would be if they caught her there.

She shined the light to her left. Undisturbed moss covered the stones there. Small ferns grew from the crevices. Years ago, someone took the time to build that floor. Becky felt sure of the reason. She found a crevice in the wall to mount the flashlight in, then began dislodging stones with the shovel. Time and moisture had sunk them firmly into the ground. She made only a two-foot bare spot in ten minutes of work. She hoped Will would be patient as she dug into the soil.

Rocks and roots stopped her progress at three feet, approximately the depth of Nick's grave. She dug toward the wall, dislodging more stones as she went and occasionally lifting the flashlight to inspect the dirt. Near the wall, something dangled out. Becky grabbed the light, knelt, and carefully wiped clay away from material. Cloth fibers broke loose in her hand. She prodded more with the shovel tip. A slight clink made her drop the shovel and dig with her fingers. Then she heard a familiar sound. It was the engine of the houseboat.

The sound stopped in the direction of the dock. She heard voices then another boat motor in the distance, and knew Will was on his way. She turned off the flashlight with her free hand and dug the other deeper, abusing her fingers in frustration. She felt bones.

"These tracks are fresh." It was Quincy's voice.

Becky pulled her hand from the ground and lifted the rifle.

"Big son of a bitch too," Frank Frye said, this time closer.

The sound of Will's engine neared.

Soon, Sam Roberts spoke near the tree. "That smell's just hanging around, Quincy. Think we should fill in the hole in case somebody was to come by?"

"Probably can't make that smell go away, but we should fill it in." Quincy said. "Let's track this hog first. He's close."

As their steps moved away, Becky dug with both hands, slinging dirt aside and bringing blood to her fingertips. She twisted one hand into the ground while digging around it with the other. She felt something again.

"Becky," Will yelled. A shot came immediately after.

Becky gripped what she felt and tugged hard. It broke loose. She crammed it into her pocket and slung the rifle. A commotion in the woods coincided with another call from Will. She jumped for the cleft. Her fingers slipped off the edge and she stumbled backwards. She tried again, this time locking her hands on wood and pulling herself out. The boar, blood streaming from his leg, hobbled past her when she landed. Another rifle crack made him squeal and crash to the ground. Becky jumped over him and ran. She saw Will in the cove. He knelt in the boat with his rifle aimed and waved for her to come.

"I'll be damned!" Frank yelled. "Get down her, boys. I told you we shouldn't have let her go. She was sure enough in the tree!"

Becky dodged behind trees while running. Gunshots erupted with the twang of passing bullets. Will returned fire. Wet ground sucked Becky's boots near the cove. She leapt into three feet of water then was unable to move. Will kept his rifle shouldered while she struggled. Two more shots cracked from the woods.

"Get in here now," Will yelled.

"I'm stuck," Becky said.

Will jumped behind the wheel and puttered toward her. A bullet shattered the console windshield. Will picked his rifle up again and fired another shot. "That's as close as I can get without getting stuck too," he said.

Becky struggled close enough to the boat for Will to take her coat with one hand. "Grab the damned side," he yelled. "Hold tight as you can." He tugged her close enough for her to do it. The boat moved forward while she clamped her hands on the side. She pulled free then rolled in, keeping low as the engine roared and the boat weaved past trees and through Spanish moss. A volley of shots came from the bank. Bullets struck the hull. Will crouched behind the console and drove with one hand up.

A pause in the shooting told Becky they were reloading. She also knew Will would be their target when the boat left the cove. She racked the lever of the 30-30, rose to her knees, and waited for the boat to pass the trees. All three men stood on the bank. The boat left the cove at full throttle. Its movement made sighting impossible, but Becky fired toward the men, working the lever rapidly and expending all five rounds in seconds. Sam and Quincy ran for cover in the woods. Frank knelt on one knee. He shouldered his rifle. Becky tossed the rifle aside and took Will's from the deck. She turned to shoot, and a sledgehammer-like force struck her left bicep, throwing her arm behind her back as she fell. "Keep driving," she yelled.

"How bad is it?" Will asked.

Becky saw blood on her coat. Her arm was numb. "Ain't going to kill me."

Will stayed crouched. "Stay where you are," he said. He drove to the middle of the lake then looked back at the island before throttling down and kneeling over Becky. He pulled her coat off, revealing her blooded sweater sleeve. Worry showed on his face.

"Does it need a tourniquet?" Becky asked. She still felt nothing.

"Don't think so. But I don't like the way it looks. We need to get you to the hospital fast." He looked at the island.

"You can't, Will. They'll come after me."

"Dammit, girl, trust me." He wadded her coat and placed it on her arm. "Keep pressure on it. Drake County is on the other side. We're going there."

Nobody knew the lake or people around it better than Will. He kept full speed while twisting the boat around every sandbar and rock in his way. He watched the bank for help and cursed when he passed bait shops and marinas closed for the season. At Lovette's Bait and Tackle, someone knelt on the pier, replacing boards.

"Clinard!" Will shouted. He docked the boat at the pier.

Pain seeped into Becky's arm. Dizziness hit her when she stood. Will and Clinard caught her and pulled her onto the pier.

"What the hell have you got into, Will?" Clinard asked.

"She's been shot. I have to borrow your car and get her to the hospital."

"You've got to get home," Becky said. "They saw you. Lily's there."

"Shit," Will said. He jumped back into the boat and tossed Clinard a rifle with a box of ammunition. "Take her to the hospital. Drake Regional, you hear? She's bleeding bad."

Clinard looked at the rifle then at Will. "Just one damned minute."

"Do it. And watch her good. There's some real assholes pissed at her." He fired the engine and slung spray. The pier rocked.

Clinard breathed a curse and helped Becky down the pier to a station wagon. "I ain't gonna ask," he said. "Don't you tell. I just came here to fix my pier. Never planned to stick my nose in anyone's business and still don't." He opened the hatch. "Get in and lay down. Hope you don't mind the smell of shad too much."

Becky never noticed the fish smell. The pain in her arm was too great. Thick drops of blood leaking through her coat scared her. She felt agony by the time they reached Drake Regional.

Clinard hurried her into the emergency room and sat her in a chair. "I don't know who you are or what the hell you got into," he said. "But, since you were with Will, I'll guess you're all right. Good luck to you." He made his way toward the door. "That woman needs help now," he yelled back.

An orderly came with a wheelchair. While asking questions, he pulled away Becky's coat and looked at her arm before announcing "Gunshot wound!" Nurses spilled out, calling for security and ordering all doors locked. The orderly wheeled Becky to a room and helped her onto a gurney while the nurses ran in and began a whirlwind of questions and emergency procedures. A young E.R doctor followed. Becky felt needles stick her arms. They cut away her sweater, removed her boots and pants, then inspected her for more wounds before tying a hospital gown to her. Her pain was subsiding, but she felt consciousness slipping while they moved her to X-rays.

She drifted in and out, answering the questions of the voices around her best she could. She wished they'd stop. She felt very weak and wanted to sleep badly. "Looks like the round exited," she heard, "but she's got a closed humerus fracture. The big problem is it's pressing against the brachial artery like a dagger. It's damned near a rupture now. Better get her prepped for O.R."

Minutes later, she wore a hair cover while rolling fast down another hall. A nurse with cat-eye glasses atop her surgical mask spoke soothing words as the gurney pushed through double doors. Only when the anesthesia mask appeared over her face did Becky remember her pants pocket. She tried rising to speak, but hands held her down while the mask went over her nose and mouth.

"Rebecca. Rebecca." The full face of the nurse with cat-eye glasses appeared.

"I'm Becky."

"How do you feel, Becky?"

"Sore some." She felt the weight of a cast on her arm and saw the sling. She moved her feet and felt shackles on them again. A deputy sat in the corner of the room. "What are you doing here?" she slurred. "Take these off me, you bastard."

He stood and walked to the door. "Relax," he said.

The nurse leaned back over her with a smile. "Everything went well. I'm sorry about the cuffs. He insisted on putting them on you."

"Tell him to..." Becky stopped short of another profanity when she saw Aaron and a crewcut man with blue suit enter. She let out a wavering cry and held out her right arm. Aaron came to her, and she gave him a half hug on his neck. "I've never been so happy to see anyone," she said.

"Neither have I," Aaron said. "I was worried about you."

"Just say Wendy is Ok. Say it."

He nodded. "She's hanging in there. But it's bad."

"I want to go see her. Take me now."

Aaron swallowed hard. "You can't. She's in a coma. Her parents are here. Someone told them she could be in danger. They want no visitors but family."

Becky looked up at the still focusing ceiling. "I'm sorry I got her in to this. I'm so sorry, Aaron. I want to die if she does. Call your Mama. She's worried."

"I have," Aaron said. "Nothing is your fault. But listen to me. Sheriff Scotland has a murder warrant on you. He wants to pick you up and take you back to Bolton County when you're released here. When they found the body and arrested Bobby, the only thing I knew to do was to go to my criminal justice instructor. I've told him everything."

Becky laughed out. "A hell of a lot he'll do."

"He's also the sheriff of Drake County. He called the SBI. They're on their way. This is him, David Donaldson."

Donaldson stepped to the bed. "Hello, Becky. They say your surgery went well. I'm glad to hear it. I hear you have a lot to say. Feel like talking to me?"

His easy voice tone won Becky's trust. "Yes, Sheriff."

Donaldson pulled up a chair. "I just want to speak with you briefly, then we'll let the nurse make you comfortable. Aaron is right. You do have a murder warrant from Bolton County against you. You're in my custody now. But I'd like to ask you a few questions if you'll agree to answer them."

"Ask away."

"Who shot you and where?"

"Frank Frye. In the arm. I mean on Boar Island."

Donaldson produced a plastic evidence bag. "Is that where you found this?" He held the bag close to her eyes. A corroded wire precariously held together seven mud-stained beads. Indented letters on them contained only flecks of the remaining white paint. S-H-A-N-N-O-N, they spelled out.

Becky broke through her stupor. "She's buried there in a hollow cypress tree."

Donaldson looked at the deputy. "That's in our jurisdiction. Am I right?"

"Yes, sir."

"I can take you to her," Becky said.

"You're not in condition to. Just tell me where."

"Please let me show you."

"We need to observe you at least twenty-four hours, sweetie" the nurse said.

Becky sat up. "It'll be too late then. They saw me. They'll move her if they haven't already. And Pete will come to pick me up. I'll be killed if I go with him. Just ask Aaron."

Donaldson exchanged looks with the nurse then Aaron.

"I can take you right to her," Becky said. "I'll sign whatever waiver forms you want. Please, Sheriff."

26

Two Drake County patrol and rescue launches cut wakes on sunset reflecting water. Becky stood with Aaron and Sheriff Donaldson in the bow of one. She wore the makeshift attire of a jail jumpsuit and sheriff's department coat zipped over her cast. She pulled her toboggan low and a scarf up against cold air and spray sweeping over her.

Donaldson dug a cigarette pack from his overcoat pocket. "Anybody want a smoke?" He lit one when Becky and Aaron declined. "I was the shift lieutenant the night it happened," he said over the engines. "We offered Pete Scotland our assistance. He refused it. I've wondered why ever since." He looked ahead through binoculars. "I've heard dozens of rumors about this murder, including one about some secret club being involved. But always thought that one of the wilder ones. Until now, I guess. This will be major news tomorrow if we find her."

"You will if they haven't moved her," Becky said.

"It'll be about dark when we get there," said Donaldson. "Just because I took the shackles off you doesn't mean you can go where you want. I want you by my side the whole time. You too, Aaron."

Aaron nodded. He appeared nervous.

Donaldson patted his back. "Don't worry about Scotland. You did right coming to me."

The engines hummed without anyone speaking for some time. Donaldson took another look. He knelt and braced the binoculars against the gunwale. His hand went up, and the engines throttled back.

Becky looked hard into the dusk. Her eyes barely detected the island.

Donaldson watched another minute then removed a walkie from his belt. "People are there. There's a houseboat at the dock, and I can see lights moving on the facing side. Kill the lights. Boat two make a slow and wide circle. Go ashore behind them and set up a perimeter. Let me know when you're in place."

All the lights went out. The second boat glided into darkness.

"Follow me," Donaldson said. He led Aaron and Becky to the stern, where six hand-picked deputies sat with M1 carbines. "Get the rafts ready," he said. "You all will be going ashore." He helped Becky up to the helm with Aaron following.

"The current is picking up here," the driver said. "I think it might carry us right to them." He cut the engine.

Donaldson grinned and tossed his cigarette. "Excellent," he said, taking a seat behind one of two large spotlights. "Crouch down, Becky. Keep covered until I tell you to get up. Aaron, work the other spotlight." He looked through the binoculars. "Another hundred yards and drop anchor. You guys in the back get ready to go."

Becky peeked over. She could see the lights clearly now. They moved in the woods near the cove.

The anchor dropped, and they waited. Voices from the island could be heard. Becky worried that their boat would be spotted. Finally, the radio crackled with the faint transmission of, "In place, Sheriff."

"Go ahead," Donaldson told the deputies in the back. "Be quiet and be careful."

Two rafts slid into the water.

"Let them get close," Donaldson whispered to the driver. "Then pull anchor and drift in as far as you can." Soon, the anchor chain rattled, and the boat moved forward. Voices on the island became clearer. The lights came toward the bank.

"They're coming out of the woods," Donaldson said into the walkie. "You on the island move toward the bank fast. Get ready, Aaron."

Becky bit her lip. She felt pain in her arm but didn't care.

"Now." Light washed over the bank and group of men on it. Shovels and a large bag dropped amongst startled cursing. They ran toward the woods only to be met by deputies with rifles ready. The six deputies wading ashore quickly blocked their next retreat route.

"Put your hands where they can see them, boys," Donaldson's voice echoed over the P.A. "Drop to your knees."

The men hesitated and turned different ways.

"Do what I said!" Donaldson yelled into the mic.

The men on the beach complied.

"Secure them," Donaldson said into his walkie. "Check good for weapons." He handed Becky the binoculars. "Want a look?"

An engine fired and a boat with its lights off shot from the cove. It blew past, rocking Becky and the others. Aaron turned and caught it in the spotlight beam while Becky awkwardly attempted to follow it one-handed with the binoculars. She caught a momentary glimpse of Pete's scowl. A passenger turned his face away.

"It's Pete Scotland and someone else," Becky said.

"Want me to go after it?" the driver asked.

"No," said Donaldson. "We'll deal with him later. Pull up to the dock. When everything's secure, we'll go ashore and see what we got here."

Six knelt with their hands cuffed behind their backs. Only one Becky didn't know, but she knew she'd seen the face before in the paper. Sam and Frank's eyes met her with hatred. Mack Deacon's expression showed defiance. Absent was the casual smile from Alvin Parker's face. Bud stared at the sand and trembled. A tied burlap sack with "Idaho Potatoes" printed on it lay with a pile of shovels, rifles and handguns on the sand in front of them.

"Pretty impressive group we have here this evening," Donaldson said. "Newspaper editor, town councilmen, businessman. A Bolton County commissioner if, I'm not mistaken. And, I'll be damned, our own district attorney. Evening, fellas. Been hunting today?"

Deacon snickered. "Good job on your civic awareness. I guess introductions aren't needed. You and your boys seem to be jumping to the wrong conclusion, David."

"What conclusion is that?" Donaldson asked. "That you bagged more than your limit?" He untied the sack and studied the inside with a flashlight before looking at Becky and Aaron then his deputies. "I'm guessing Shannon Monet has been found," he said.

"She has," Deacon said. "Maybe that explains for you why I'm here. We've done the hard work, so I suggest you take these cuffs off us and do your job while you still have a badge."

Donaldson grinned. "Just wondering why Sheriff Scotland cut a trail. And why you fellows tried to. I have a feeling I'll be wearing this badge a little longer than you'll be called Mr. District Attorney, Mack." He looked over the men and seemed to notice the same thing

Becky had: Bud's fear. "Boat two take all of them except Mr. Sweeny back to the office."

"He has a right to an attorney," Deacon said.

"Don't talk to them, Bud," Frank added. "You hear me?"

Donaldson pulled Bud up. "Get them out of here and keep them separated," he told his men. "Bring the agents here when they arrive."

A fire built on the bank lit Bud's face. He held out his cuffed hands to warm them. One of Donaldson's cigarettes trembled between his fingers. Becky and Aaron watched him while they sat on the sand.

Donaldson watched him a long time before saying, "Here's how this works, Bud. I know what you and your friends did. I just want to know why. You'll get one chance to tell the truth before the state guys get here. That means no tapdancing around. You get no promises from me. But I bet it'll be in your favor if the court hears you were the first to tell the real story. So don't do something stupid like lying now."

Bud took shaky breaths and looked at Becky. "Who else was there?"

"It doesn't matter," she answered. She watched his eyes turn away and waited. Three times he started to speak. Then words trembled out and told a story familiar to her. Only this telling truly defined the calculated, cold-bloodedness of the killings.

Quincy and Bud waited in the woods behind the Billings' house late afternoon that day. They'd known since James and Cynthia's marriage there'd one day be an important job for them, but only the night before had Cynthia told them the details. They were nineteen and anxious to prove their worthiness to the club they knew would give them influence if they were accepted. They were nervous too. The plans had been laid with care. From the beginning, only girls from uninfluential families were considered to avoid too much attention. It was Alvin who'd suggested Shannon. He'd been left in charge of carrying out the final part of the plan in Cynthia's absence. Cynthia had left Shannon instructions to cook dinner at five sharp. She also called just before then and asked Bobby to go get the Fourth of July sale chuck roast she'd forgotten to buy. Parker's was closing, but Alvin had told her he'd wait. A Pepsi laced with choral hydrate and a bottle of chloroform awaited Bobby in the back room of the grocery store.

All seemed to be falling in line when Bobby left on his bike. Bud blocked the outside kitchen door while Quincy entered the front. But Shannon must've seen the look in Quincy's eyes and the knife concealed behind his back when he approached. A pan of hot grease thrown at Bud allowed her to run past him and into the woods. The boys gave chase and desperately looked for her. After doing all they could, they reluctantly went back and called Alvin. But he already knew. He'd just gotten off the phone with Pete and was about to notify Cynthia there'd been a problem. Helen Monet was filing a report. Shannon thought the boys wanted to rape her. Damage control became the utmost priority then. Coach Carbo arrived soon after to make sure there were no more foul-ups.

It was Carbo who gashed Helen Monet's throat at the door that night. Quincy pistol-whipped Shannon in his effort to find out who besides her mother and the sheriff she'd told. The girl pleaded for her life while they took her to the island. Carbo worried her screams would be heard and told Quincy to fire the coup de grace. They then placed Shannon in the cypress to await burial. Quincy made the call to Alvin from a marina.

A tear rolled down Bud's cheek. "I never hurt them. It was Quincy and Coach. I didn't want to be there. I wanted to help the girl, but I knew they'd kill me too."

"And Sheriff Scotland took over then?" Donaldson asked.

"Yeah. Alvin used the stuff on Bobby then took him and his bike there. Scotland said later the poor guy still didn't know where he was when they found him. Scotland liked to brag about how he scared him shitless first then tricked him into thinking he did it. They took him to the lodge after James' funeral and got a detailed confession on paper. Only Scotland made up the details."

"Coerced internalized confession."

"Glad to know you paid attention in class for once, Aaron," Donaldson said.

"I don't know if James was ever convinced," Bud said. "But they all knew he wouldn't gamble on Bobby."

"Whose idea was this?" Donaldson asked.

"Cynthia set it up. But the members who originally came here always called the shots. Papa Tolly is the only surviving one now."

"So, he's been running things from his nursing home in Richmond," Becky said.

Bud blew a defeated laugh. "Nursing home, my ass. He was living in a Greek Revival house when Quincy and I visited him a few years ago."

"Tell me about the other murders," said Donaldson.

"I'm pretty sure they had something to do with the car crash that killed James' first wife, but they never told. Frank and Sam killed the reporter. He'd been asking questions. Sam called him to the newspaper office. He and Frank beat his brains out there with driving clubs. I know because Quincy and I were given the job of disposing of his body."

"You dug his grave the evening we got Christmas trees, didn't you?" Becky asked.

"Yeah. Cynthia also saw him come by your house the next day. They began watching you round the clock after that. They were afraid you knew about them. Papa saw by your look when you saw the pin on James that you did. That was a test. You would've been next if Hudson Perry hadn't shown up. That worried them, and they decided to frame you with the reporter's killing. Papa decided that Bobby would be arrested. He wanted the house and didn't have any use for Bobby after James died."

"Who killed my husband?" Becky asked.

Bud looked her in the eye. "I don't know. They kept very quiet about that. I can tell you that Cynthia found a letter from Coach's wife, Lorraine, to him in your mailbox. I don't know what all Lorraine knew. Maybe Coach wrote something in a suicide note. Or maybe she just sensed he'd done something bad here before she met him. But they saw from her letter she wanted your husband to find out what that was. Coach told us he wanted to start over before he moved away and got married. He never had anything to do with us after that, didn't even come to our ten-year championship anniversary. I heard he had a really hard time. When he hung himself, Quincy and I went down for the funeral. We put a whistle around his neck and the club pin on his lapel. Lorraine must've gotten suspicious about it. The pin was in the letter Cynthia found. It's the same one they put on James."

"But Sheriff Scotland *was involved* in the coverup of Chief Hawk's murder," said Donaldson.

"Yeah. They wanted Jessie dead and blamed for it."

"Anymore?" Donaldson asked.

Bud shook his head. "Just that I never killed anyone. I got pulled into the club when I was only a kid and didn't know better. There was no leaving after that, even though I wanted to. I hope what I told you helps me."

A deputy stepped to the fire. "Hate to interrupt you, Sheriff, but there's something you need to see."

Donaldson, Becky, and Aaron followed the deputy into the woods where the swampy smell was. Their flashlights shined on a narrow, cloven hoofprint covered trail that led to an immense thicket of briars and vines. Inside the thicket stood another giant cypress.

"There's a wild boar den in the bottom of that tree," the deputy said. "A sow ran out and knocked three of us on our asses when we walked past. Given the circumstances, we thought it might be worth a look inside. The sow is gone, but you need to look inside the tree before she gets back."

They knelt and crawled through a tunnel worn in the thicket until they reached a small opening at the bottom of the tree. Donaldson crawled to it with his light and looked inside for a long time before turning. "Take a look," he said.

Becky crawled forward. A strong smell of swine washed over her at the hole. A cluster of eyes shined in her light. Becky flinched then saw piglets inside move away. She turned her light away from their eyes and over deeply burrowed ground. Bones too large to be chewed to dust by the boars lay piled aside with broken human skulls of different sizes.

"This infernal island is a cemetery," Donaldson said. "Now we have to try and figure out who they are."

Becky looked at him. "They were the O'Haras," she said.

27

A command post went up on the lawn of the hunting lodge after Agents Sykes and Feezor arrived with a search warrant. Donaldson stayed busy coordinating the operation. "There's a boat going back soon," he told Becky. "We'll need you on it. You can go too, Aaron."

"I'd like to stay and watch," Aaron said.

"Alright. Just keep out of the way. Becky, you *will* have to go back. I'm sorry, but you'll have to stay in our custody until we sort this all out."

"I'm sorry too," Feezor said, "for not believing you from the beginning."

"All I care about now is getting Bobby out of Pete's jail," said Becky. "Do it right away."

"Agents are there now," Sykes said. "We're just waiting on the court order to move him."

A helicopter flew in and reechoed with a spotlight on the lodge.

Donaldson cursed. "News crew already," he said. "Get out of here, Becky."

On a bulky cot in the Drake County jail's nursing station that night, Becky enjoyed the deepest, longest sleep of her life. A copy of her release order with "Charges dropped" scribbled on it lay beside her when she woke at noon. Her arm throbbed. She took her pain pills with coffee and a bland but nourishing meal, then rode in the jail van to a nearby hotel. New clothes and toiletries lay on the bed of her room compliments of Sheriff Donaldson.

"The state boys are covering the room and your meals," the chubby driver said while escorting her to her room. "There'll be a deputy in the lobby round the clock. He'll take you anywhere you need to go. Wish I could live like this for a while."

"How long am I supposed to stay here?"

"Until they get everybody locked up, I reckon. You're going to be the star of this show. Can't have anything happening to you." He handed her the room key. "No tip necessary," he said with a chuckle.

She rested in the room for the remainder of the day and flicked on the Channel 2 news that evening. Boar Island dominated the coverage. She watched Sykes' interview and learned that "a variety of incriminating records" retained by what he still referred to as a hunting club had been discovered. Sykes refused to say what those records were but did add he anticipated statewide arrests. Donaldson spoke briefly but stayed tight-lipped and offered only basic details. The coverage then switched to the Bolton County sheriff's office and the "possibly related news" of Sheriff Pete Scotland's disappearance. The speculation was, the reporter said, he'd fled to avoid criminal charges that included the false arrest and imprisonment of Robert Anthony Billings. The report featured a brief clip of SBI agents exiting the jail with Bobby, whose terrified expression had changed to a lost stare. The report mentioned only that he'd been placed in protective custody.

She called and spoke to the deputy in the lobby, who had no further information for her. "I'd appreciate your finding out what you can," she said. "Also, I'd like a ride to Drake Regional."

"Her parents are eating supper in the cafeteria," the ICU head nurse said. She walked briskly down the hall with Becky and the deputy beside her. "I'll give you two minutes. It'll be trouble for us all if they come back while you're here."

Becky wasn't prepared for what she saw when she stepped into the soft florescent light of the room. Black and purple bruising blotched the face and intravenous needle bearing arms. The mouth behind an oxygen mask hung open. Once bouncy, blonde hair that had flowed over the shoulders was stringy and pulled behind the ears. Only the wristband assured her that this was Wendy. Becky kissed her cheek. She pulled the blanket up to Wendy's chest then noticed only the bulge of a stump where the right leg should've been. She lifted the blanket and confirmed her fear.

"The doctors did everything they could to save it," the nurse said. "There was just too much tissue and arterial damage. They were lucky to save the other."

At the elevator, a neatly dressed couple exited. The man carried himself with militaristic poise. The woman was an older version of Wendy. They looked lost. Neither appeared to notice Becky nor the deputy when they passed.

The newspaper delivered to Becky's door the next morning reported more arrests with photographs of businessmen from Black Lake and the surrounding area. But the lengthy article didn't answer Becky's main question. She called the sheriff's office and learned Donaldson was back out on the island. The deputy in the lobby knew little, but the captain who called later informed her that Bobby had been transferred to a state hospital in Raleigh for psychiatric treatment. He'd suffered a severe mental breakdown. Becky stayed in the room the remainder of the day, eating little before going to bed early.

The next morning, she placed a call and, for the first time, spoke to Mike Ledford. The call was timely, as Mike had just read her letter and was in the process of contacting some buddies at Camp Lejune to come to Black Lake and "kick some ass." A wonderful, spirit-lifting conversation filled with stories of Ed ensued. Mike's sense of humor kept her laughing and shedding happy tears for two hours. It ended with the assurance from Mike that they would speak again soon. A knock at the door followed.

Aaron held her backpack and a bag of hamburgers.

"Come in," Becky said. "Where did you get my backpack?"

"Feezor and Sykes took it from Wendy's car. They said I could bring it to you. Your revolver is in there too." He sat down at the table. "Rare with mayonnaise and pickles, right?"

"Yes." Becky handed him a cola from the mini refrigerator then got herself one. She swallowed a pain pill then sat beside him.

"I got to see her today," said Aaron. "I heard you were there Friday night."

"Yes. I'm so sorry."

"I feel numb. They're beginning to think she may not come out of it. I don't know what I'll do if she doesn't." He tore open the bag.

"Don't count her out," Becky said. "She's a fighter. She's a tough… She's tough."

They ate in silence until Becky asked, "How's it going out there?"

"Unbelievable. This outfit was organized. They found a locked meeting room in the lodge with records in it going back over fifty years. There are lists of names on the take from all over the state. Some are legislatures, even a congressman and a superior court judge. They were definitely in on lumber bid rigging and zoning ordinance fixing. Probably extortion and bribing too. The state guys have everything from white collar crime specialists to forensic pathologists out there. Oh, they found Ed's badge."

Becky swallowed a bite of half chewed burger. "Where?"

"In a hidden safe in the meeting room. They took it off Ed's uniform after he was shot and mailed it to Lorraine Carbo with a threatening letter. It scared her enough that she moved from Savannah. Savannah police turned the badge and the letter over to Pete. You'll get it back, but it's evidence now."

"Do they know who shot him yet?"

"No. Bud was the only one who talked. Max Underwood probably would've broken. He squalled like a baby when they arrested him at the jail, but his lawyer showed up before they could question him. His wife, Phyllis, did admit to bailing Jessie Settle out so he could be set up. There's a task force looking for Pete and the Tollys now. Unfortunately, a major snowstorm is on the way that'll probably slow things down for a few days."

"Do they think they're together?"

"Yes. Pete's truck was found parked at Cynthia's house with Quincy's and Harrison Tolly's cars. Cynthia's is gone. It looks like they packed quick then took off. There're warrants on them all."

Becky folded up the rest of her burger. "I'm worried that I may never know who really pulled the trigger."

"Maybe not. But at least you have a good idea of what happened now. The hell of it is, Harrison was probably the one who ordered it. He was just smart enough to keep his hands clean of it."

The thought of the old man's soulless stare made Becky wince. She walked to the bed, where her backpack lay and went through it.

She removed the revolver. Her money was still there as well as her anniversary picture. The cracked glass had been replaced. There was also blue matting and a new, cherry wood frame. "Did you do that, Aaron?" she asked.

"Yeah. Dad does some framing in the basement on the side. Sorry I broke it in the first place. It was an accident."

"Thank you." Becky smiled and traced her finger over Ed's face while thinking of their days at the Lumina. She remembered their dance and cradled the picture to her chest. It bothered her that she'd shared that special story with Cynthia. That seemed to defile the memory now. She placed the picture on the nightstand while recollecting that conversation with the woman she had thought was her friend. It had only been a few weeks ago but seemed an eternity. Then, she remembered Cynthia sharing a memory of one of her anniversary trips that night too. One spent on Springer Island. "I doubt there's a more isolated place in the state," she'd said.

"What are you doing for Christmas, Aaron?" Becky asked.

"Nothing. Everyone in the sheriff's office is on leave until the investigation is over. Mom and Dad flew out to Texas yesterday to spend a week with my grandparents. Mom blew a gasket when I told her I wasn't going. But there was no way I was leaving with Wendy in her condition."

"Have you ever been to the Outer Banks?"

28

It was before sunup the next morning, when Becky and Aaron walked past a sleeping deputy in the lobby. Becky tossed her backpack into the backseat of Aaron's parents' car, where a duty belt and an overnight bag also lay.

"The weatherman says this storm is going to hit the whole state," Aaron said on their way to Black Lake. "Nothing short of a blizzard."

Becky looked out the window. "Yeah. I feel it in the air. This probably isn't a good idea. But it's up to you. I'm not forcing you into this."

"I know you're not. As I see it, it'll be to our advantage if we can get there. They'll be hunkered down, not expecting company."

They passed Becky's old house and made a lap around the block to be certain no one was up and about.

"Park near the front door," Becky said.

Aaron drove into the yard and watched the street while Becky got out with her backpack. Her key did not turn the lock. "They've changed the lock," she called.

Aaron joined her on the porch. "Maybe I can jimmy it." He removed his pocketknife, knelt at the door, then looked up wide-eyed when Becky one-armed her backpack through the window.

"Stay here," she said, kicking away the remaining shards then slipping through. "Load the things in the backseat as I hand them to you." She dry swallowed a pain pill before throwing open the gun cabinet. She remembered how disadvantaged she'd felt without a simple flashlight the night at Max Underwood's and packed three of them with extra batteries. She then filled the bag the rest of the way with ammunition, a gunsmithing kit, two hunting knives, and water-proof matches. She handed the pack to Aaron before passing him Ed's duty belt, two shotguns, and a rifle. "There's two five-gallon gas cans in the shed out back," she said. "Go get them while I change." Upstairs, she removed her sling and used scissors to cut off half the left sleeve of her thermal hunting jumpsuit before sliding into it. She also found her snow boots and right-handed glove.

Dawn displayed a menacing gray sky when they pulled out. They stopped in town to fill the gas cans and buy snacks. The first thick snowflakes fell soon after, gradually turning to a steady downfall. Aaron drove at half-speed on whitening roads. He kept the wipers and heater on high while correcting the car when it fishtailed.

"We can stop and stay overnight somewhere if you like," Becky said.

"No. We're getting there today."

Becky liked what she saw in his eyes.

Traveling slowed to a snail's pace, more than doubling the normal four-hour drive to Roanoke Island. By noon, they passed only snowplows and salt brine trucks. Opened gas stations became far between. They stopped just once to fill the tank with their gas cans and take badly needed bathroom breaks behind a closed grocery store. It was midafternoon when they reached the Croatan Sound and made a harrowing crossing through wind gusts on a slippery, nearly three mile long bridge.

"Damn if I want to go through that again," Aaron said, with perspiration on his face.

Becky looked at a state map on her lap. "Looks like there's more bridges ahead," she said. "But it's the stretch between Nags head and Hatteras that worries me."

And that fifty-mile stretch did prove the most treacherous of their journey. The storm became a true blizzard and made Highway 12 disappear on the sandbar between the Pamlico Sound and the Atlantic Ocean. Squalls from the sea pushed the car around, blowing foam and sand onto the windshield. Aaron used dunes to his left as a guiding point through the blowing, white plain. Periodically, gaps between the dunes showed them an angry sea, too close for comfort. Three times Aaron stopped to scrape ice from the windshield then fought with the car in forward and reverse to get them moving again. The hellish ride lasted nearly three hours before the storm eased and they entered Hatteras Village.

"I never thought we'd make it," Aaron said.

Becky flicked on the overhead light and studied the map. "Don't relax just yet. There's still a hell of a long bridge to cross."

"N.C. Ferry System. Hatteras Terminal 1 Mi.," a sign read.

"Better check the map again," said Aaron.

A big "Closed" sign on a blockade met them at the end of the highway. Aaron kept the car rolling to avoid getting stuck again and took the curve past it. "What now?" he asked.

Becky sighed. "Nothing we can do but find somewhere warm to sleep. Maybe we can cross in the morning."

"Don't count on it. After this storm, we'll be lucky if the ferry runs for a week. All I know is we'd better find a place to stay. We're low on gas."

They passed rows of docked boats and dimly lit cottages, many with hand-painted signs advertising shrimp and mullet for sale. Closed seafood restaurants and gift shops indicated the village's dependance on summer vacationers. "Shrimp $1 lb. Ferry to Springer $4," the next painted sign read.

"Stop," yelled Becky.

A long-faced man with black chin whiskers came to the door in thermal underwear and socks. Something steamed in the big mug he held. "What in holy hell brings you two here?" he asked.

Becky cast an engaging smile. "We saw your sign. We need a ferry ride."

It took a moment, but a grin came, then he laughed. "Who's playing the joke on me? Martin Gunter throwing another one of his storm parties tonight and didn't invite me?"

"We're serious," said Aaron. He showed his badge. "We're looking for some people who may be on Springer Island."

The man laughed once more. "No offense, Slick, but you don't look much the law dog to me. And I don't care if you're looking for John Dillinger and Jessie James. Only a stark raving fool would try the crossing tonight. But step in and warm yourselves. Stop letting my heat out and the cold in."

Becky looked around the inside of the cottage. She saw a small room with a fireplace. A woman and three children wrapped in blankets slept on the floor around it. "Thank you for letting us in," she said. "I know we're asking a lot, Mister..."

"Carter Gray. There's no mister attached. Yes, lady, you're asking a sight much. I would offer you some food but can't spare it this time of year. I can offer you a place at the hearth and some spirits, though, if you'd like. But I gotta ask. What happened to your arm?"

"My name's Becky. This is Aaron. It's a long story. My husband was killed– murdered two months ago. I've been trying to find out by who and was shot. We have a friend fighting for her life. Another is in the state hospital. The people responsible for it all are likely on Springer Island."

"You have my sympathy," Carter said. "Sorry I won't be able to help you tonight."

Becky removed her roll of bills, the remainder of her Christmas gift from Black Lake Elementary. She held it out. "It's almost two hundred dollars," she said. "How much shrimp would you need to catch to earn that? Should get you and your family through the winter and more I expect."

Carter looked at the money. "You neither talk nor look like one of the rich northerners that come here in the summer. Getting there must be mighty important."

"It is," said Becky.

He looked out the window. "White-capping out there and blowing. It won't be a fun ride. Did you come about that legal? Swear to it?"

"Yes."

"Well." Carter looked out the window again. "Hell, let me get dressed. The only thing worse than a fool is a poor fool, I reckon. Pull down, careful not to slide into the inlet."

The snow turned to sleet when the little, one-car ferry set out into the rough waves of Hatteras Inlet. Becky and Aaron sat inside the rocking car and listened to the clatter on the windshield.

Aaron kept his eyes closed to avoid sickness. "If they're there," he said, "you know Pete Scotland won't be taken alive."

Becky saw the distant strobes of the Springer Island lighthouse. "I guess not," she said.

29

"The lighthouse stands a mile down," Carter said when they docked. "No use talking to the keeper. He keeps to himself and won't know nothing. Jake Cook's is about another mile past it, then the lifesaving station in another three. Don't think you want to drive all the ways to the village at the other end tonight. I'd try Jake first. Nobody steps on the island without his knowing it in five minutes. He's got decent food and rooms too."

"Thank you very much," Becky said from the car window.

"Here. I think too much of the name Carter Gray for people to think he's a leeching opportunist." He handed Becky her money roll. "I took fifteen out, figuring it's about right for a ride tonight."

Becky handed him back fifty. "You and your family have a merry Christmas."

Carter smiled. "You're good people. Good luck and be damned careful. I'd stay and help, but don't like leaving my family home tonight." He bent down and looked at Aaron. "Take good care of her, law dog. Keep between the trees and you'll keep on the road. Be blasted careful driving off. We're still swaying,"

They drove on straight road between the twisted live oaks of a maritime forest. Columns of ice and snow, resembling passing ghosts, blew in the headlights. When they neared the lighthouse, the strobe hit Aaron's face. Becky saw he was tired and nervous.

"You did good, getting us here," she said. "It was no small task driving through that storm. Wish I could've helped."

"You've done more than you know," he said.

"Are you scared? It's Ok if you are. I am."

He nodded. "Some. But this feels like the right thing to do, a lot righter than when I was spying on you for Pete. Thanks for helping to wake me up to him."

They passed the lighthouse and keeper's quarters.

"I know I've been very obsessed with this whole thing," said Becky. "If I'd have put my head before my emotions more, maybe Wendy wouldn't be in her condition now. When things start happening, tell me when you think I'm making a mistake. If you see things are getting too dangerous, back off. I won't be upset."

"I won't back off," Aaron said. "You're not the only one they took someone special from."

Lights burned in Jake's Tavern and Inn when they arrived. A rush of heat met them when the portly Jake Cook opened the door. "Good land, get in out of the cold," his voice boomed. "Sit down and get warm." They stepped into a room with knotty pine walls and a briny smell. Jake pulled chairs close to a kerosene heater then fetched a bottle of brandy and glasses from behind the bar.

"Thank you," Becky said. She removed her glove with her teeth and sat beside Aaron.

Jake handed them glasses. He passed Aaron the bottle before taking his seat at the heater. "Now, where in thunder did you two come from?"

Aaron poured shots.

"Carter Gray brought us over," Becky said. "We're looking for three men and a woman who may be on the island. One of the men is very old and rides in a wheelchair." She turned back her brandy and delighted in the body warming sensation it gave her. "Have you seen them?"

Jake took his shot then carefully filled his glass again. "Can't say I have. Only a few serious fishermen come here after October. Guess they might've gone to the village on the other end. Did you check with the state ferry?"

"They're closed," said Aaron.

Jake popped himself on his forehead. "Well, of course they are. What am I thinking. I'd make a few calls for you, but the storm's got the phones out."

"You lived her long?" Becky asked.

"All my life, darling."

Becky made her best smile. "Nice place. How long have you had it?"

"Family business for over sixty years," Jake said. "I've ran it myself for twenty. Not much money made of it, but it's something to help when the fishing and crabbing turns bad."

"A James and Cynthia Billings came here once for their honeymoon and another time for their anniversary. They stayed in a house one of James' friends owned. From what I heard, there's woods and marsh around it with a place to fish."

"That fits dang near every house here," Jake said with a subdued laugh. "What few there are."

"Ever met the Billings?" Becky asked.

He looked away while his fingers picked at the course hairs of his cheek. "Billings? Don't believe I have. My memory ain't what it was, though. Those folks friends of yours?"

"No," Aaron said. He reached for his badge but stopped when Becky squeezed his knee.

"We know them," Becky said. "We thought Cynthia may have returned with the others, but Carter said you usually know it when new people arrive. Sounds like we may be on a wild goose chase."

"Carter's right. Most dingbatters stop in for a drink and food after their long drive. Ain't many places where this place ain't a long drive. But I haven't seen anyone in a while. Right now, it looks like I might need to fix you up with some food and a room." He turned his eyes to a banister above the bar. "Nixie."

A woman barely four feet tall with chopped red hair already stood there in a flannel robe.

"We have guests needing food." Jake said. Then to Becky and Aaron: "I guess six dollars would cover it for the both of you. Unless you're planning on staying more than one night or'd you like two rooms."

"One will do," said Becky. She removed her money from her pocket, found a five and a one, and slipped it to Jake.

He removed his wallet and placed the bills in front of tens and twenties. "Thank you much." He walked behind the bar and produced a key. "Number three at the end of the hall. It's my best one. You can fetch your things while I warm up the dining room. Nixie will have you something to eat directly."

Becky waited for him to leave then handed Aaron the room key. "Go get my gun belt and extra rounds," she told him. "Take it to the room. Keep your coat pulled over yours. Make sure the car is locked."

Crab pots and gill nets filled a corner of the two-table dining room. A huge bone, which Aaron and Becky determined was a whale's, hung on the opposite side. Vapors from the kerosene heater Jake lit still hung in the air when Nixie carried in a loaded platter half her size. She refused Aaron's help with a shake of her head before placing cornbread and a mixture of flaked fish, mashed potatoes, boiled eggs, and chopped onion on the table.

"Thank you. Looks good," Aaron said. "Hope you didn't go through the trouble just for us. Are we the only ones staying here?"

Nixie laid plates and silverware down. She nodded and filled their glasses with water before leaving.

Aaron carefully tasted the mixture then salted and peppered it. He looked back. "You think they know something they're not telling?"

"Yes," said Becky. "He was lying about not knowing the Billings. I saw that in his eyes. It also seems odd he would have that much money in his billfold in the off season."

"Then I guess we need to talk to Jake again and tell him to cut the bull."

"He'd probably just lie more. The best thing we can do for now is be quiet. We know they can't leave until the ferry runs again. I don't think either of us is in shape to do much without some rest. We'll take turns keeping watch tonight and decide early in the morning what we want to do. You can sleep first."

They ate while watching the doors.

Becky overestimated her stamina when she allowed Aaron an extra hour of sleep. It was ten past one when knocking on the door woke her. She threw off a blanket with the hand holding her revolver and rose from a rocking chair. She heard Aaron rustle when the knocking came again.

"Where are you at?" Aaron whispered in the dark.

"Right here. Got your gun ready?"

"Yeah. And flashlight."

Becky felt her way around the room. She found the door, holstered her revolver, and stood aside before jerking the door open. Aaron's flashlight beam made Nixie's eyes squint. She held a lit candle. Becky flicked the lamp switch without results.

"The power went out an hour ago," a voice befitting a ten-year-old girl said. "Why are you looking for those people?"

Becky looked down the hallway. "Where is he?"

"Tell me who they are first."

"Aaron there is a deputy sheriff. One of them probably killed my husband."

Nixie squeaked and squeezed her mouth. "I thought they were bad. Especially the old man. He looked almost like the devil. They came a few days ago and paid him to watch. He waited to make sure you were asleep. Now he's gone to tell them you're here."

Aaron threw on his coat.

"Where are they?" Becky asked.

"Just past the lighthouse on the right. Cross Oyster Creek. There's a big house back in the woods, almost to the beach. They'll know you're here before you get there."

"We'd better get moving," said Aaron, tying his boots.

Becky hesitated. "Will you be safe when he comes back?" she asked Nixie.

"Yes. I'll tell him I was asleep when you left. Please don't hurt him. He's not really a bad man, and he's all I have."

"Jake's not the one we're after," Becky said.

The sleet had stopped when they left and followed tire tracks. The headlight beams showed where Jake turned into a narrow opening in the woods. Aaron backed into the small parking lot of the lighthouse and turned off the engine and lights. They cranked down the windows and heard surf crashing.

Becky reached into the backseat and lifted her backpack. "Get you a long gun," she said. "Get me the pump shotgun with the sling." She removed two boxes of double ought buckshot from her pack.

"Can you handle that with one arm?"

"If you load it and rack a shell, yes."

They prepared themselves and waited ten minutes before hearing tires moving in snow.

"What's the plan?" Aaron asked.

"Ain't got one yet."

"I think we'd better take cover while you're working on it." Aaron got out with Becky following. They knelt behind the car.

A few minutes later, Jake Cook's truck turned onto the road and stopped in front of them. Becky pressed off the safety of her shotgun while remaining crouched. A strobe from the lighthouse illuminated Jake's face staring from the window. He shined a flashlight over the car then proceeded down the road, apparently satisfied with upholding his end of the bargain.

"Let's go," Becky said.

Tree branches scraped the sides of the car while they plowed down the drive for a distance before coming to a narrow, wooden bridge. Aaron cautiously drove onto it while Becky looked to her right. Thinning clouds allowed a trace of moonlight to fall over a landscape of white dunes and sea oats. The ocean rolled in the background.

"How are we handling this, Becky?" Aaron asked. "We won't catch them by surprise now."

"Stop on the other side," she said. "Block the bridge and turn off the engine."

"I'm guessing you have a plan now. Want to share it with me?" Aaron stopped at the end of the bridge.

Becky stepped out and slung her shotgun. "Lock the doors and come over to this side." The headlight glow of the approaching car showed when Aaron made it to her. "Walk beside me, straight ahead," Becky told him. "Push down when you step. Make deep tracks."

They walked toward the dunes. Ocean wind threw up blinding clouds of snow and sand. They'd left a fifty-yard trail when they looked back and saw Cynthia's car stop at the bridge. The wind then blocked their view. They heard two car doors slam.

"What are we doing?" Aaron asked.

Becky looked around. "Keep walking."

Fifteen more paces brought them to a dune. A low-lying live oak grew across from it.

"Remember that dune on your left," Becky said. "Walk faster." She looked back while taking another twenty paces then told Aaron to stop. "Make a wide turn to your left and circle back to the dune. Hide behind it and wait for them."

"Are we shooting them?" Aaron asked. His voice was tight.

"Not if we can help it. But you'd better be ready to. Keep in mind that I'll be straight across from you if you do have to fire. Take a deep breath. Try to relax."

She made a circling right turn then hurried to the oak. She knelt and worked her way into the mounded snow under the branches. She saw Aaron take his position behind the dune. Then she watched the tracks they'd made and waited. Between gusts, she saw two approaching figures, one five steps ahead of the other. She pulled off her glove with her teeth and removed her cast from the sling. She leaned back against the branches and propped the barrel of the shotgun on her knee, bracing it with her cast atop the stock. She placed the bead on their tracks.

The figures drew near. Becky determined the taller one in front was Quincy. He carried a rifle and followed the tracks with quick steps. The other moved more cautiously, looking side to side with both hands holding his handgun in front of him. Becky placed the bead on him.

"Slow down," Pete's voice said. "This don't feel right."

Quincy approached close enough for Becky to see his face. He inspected the area around him before taking more steps. "Think they're trying to circle to the house from the beach?" he asked.

Becky took soft, deep breaths through her nose. Her finger flicked off the safety and curled around the trigger when Quincy stepped in front of her.

"Stop! Drop the gun!" came Aaron's shout.

There came sounds of a struggle. Becky saw the second man go into a shooting crouch familiar to her. "Put it down, Pete," she said. His gun moved in her direction.

The wind blew then and created a white-out. Becky remained still while ice and sand pelted her. A shot made a branch above her head splinter. Snow fell over her. She adjusted the bead to where she saw the muzzle flash and made an easy squeeze on the trigger. With the blast came a recoil that sent pain to her arm. She dropped the shotgun, and unholstered her revolver. Her ears rang, and she breathed the sweet-acrid smell of burnt gunpowder. She stepped from behind the trees slowly and heard deep breaths.

Quincy lay face down with his hands cuffed behind him. Aaron knelt over him with his rifle pointed to where Pete last appeared. "You Ok?" he huffed.

Becky nodded. She pointed her revolver at Quincy and mouthed, "Stay." Bending low, she made careful steps. It took her fifteen paces before the snow turned red. Footprints and a blood trail led into the woods. She found Pete's Colt Python in the snow before she found him. He lay on his side, his eyes staring into nothing. His most recognizable feature, the handlebar mustache, had been shaved away. Becky holstered her revolver and checked his neck for a pulse that never came.

Nobody spoke during the walk back to the car. Aaron transferred everything to the trunk while Becky held Quincy at gunpoint. He knelt, trembling in the snow with his eyes down.

"Feel that?" Becky asked. "That's fear. Real fear. Have a taste of what Shannon felt the night you killed her." She cocked her revolver and waited for his eyes to turn up. "Now, who killed my husband?"

Aaron slammed the trunk and ran over. "Don't, Becky."

"Who killed him?" she shouted.

Quincy closed his eyes tight. "Go to hell," he said.

Aaron placed his hand on the revolver. Becky lowered it. "Put him in the backseat," she said. She got into the car and flicked on the overhead light before opening her backpack.

The backdoor slammed then Aaron climbed in. "Were you really going to kill him? No, don't answer that. You've got to hold it together, Becky."

Becky dug through her pack.

"I think we should take him to the lifesaving station," said Aaron. "They'll have a radio to call the county sheriff on. Cynthia and the old man won't be going anywhere."

"That's a good idea," Becky said. "Give me a few minutes then take him there. Bring a few men back with you."

"What are you going to do?"

"I'm going to visit Cynthia and Papa Tolly. Don't dare try to stop me."

The driveway wound through the woods. Becky walked it swiftly. Through the trees, she saw white smoke curling from a brick chimney, then the two-story house. She checked her revolver once more.

A fire blazing in a large hearth cast long shadows across the living room. Harrison Tolly sat by it with a blanket over his lap. Becky watched him and his emotionless face from outside the front porch window. She felt burning hatred toward the man and struggled to suppress it. She wanted her mind razor sharp and clear of emotion. Cynthia walked into the living room and lit a cigarette before pacing the floor. Harrison spoke a few words. Cynthia took a seat across from him and lifted her needlepoint.

Becky holstered her revolver and tested the door. It opened. She walked inside.

A gasp from Cynthia and Harrison's glare met her. Becky walked closer with her eyes on Cynthia only.

Cynthia dropped her needlepoint. "Where's Quincy?"

"It's over, Cynthia. The Manticores are through. You can't run anymore."

"Where's my brother? Is he all right? Please tell me!"

"He's alive," Becky said. "Pete is dead."

Harrison hissed and murmured something under his breath.

"Where is he, Becky?"

"You love your brother very much, don't you, Cynthia."

"You know I do. I want to see him. Take me to him."

"I might. But tell me this: How can a young girl who loved enough to teach her baby brother to walk again allow so much evil into her heart? How could you find it in yourself to let a little girl and her mother die? How could you let Bobby suffer the way he has? How could you take Ed from me? What happened to that young girl?"

Cynthias's eyes moistened. "It's different than you think."

Becky heard a low chuckle from Harrison but ignored it. "How could you tear my soul then have me think you were my friend?"

"I want to see my brother. I want to see him now."

Becky unsnapped her holster and removed the revolver.

"Please, Becky. Don't. Let me talk."

"I'm tired," Becky said. "I'm tired of grieving. I'm tired of wondering why. And I'm just damned tired." She placed the revolver on the floor and slid it between Harrison and Cynthia. "It's up to you how this ends, Cynthia. But I will not leave this house alive until you answer my questions."

"Kill the bitch," Harrison said.

"Papa, please." Cynthia looked at him then back to Becky.

"Do it. Show me your loyalty for once," Harrison demanded.

Cynthia looked at the revolver then shook her head. "I've shown you my loyalty, Papa, many times. But it's, as she said, over. I need to see Quincy."

Becky felt Harrison's eyes on her but refused to look at him.

"You had no problem when things benefited you," said Harrison. "You've sacrificed nothing. It's over when I say it is. I say pick up that gun and kill her."

Cynthia looked out the window. "No, Papa. I won't."

Becky met Harrison's hate-filled eyes. "What's it like having your orders refused?" she asked. "Is it the first time? Bet it hurts coming from your own granddaughter." She watched the eyes burn more. "It must've been a luxury to have people who would kill for you, especially since you never had the guts to do it yourself, you miserable coward."

A terrible rage covered the old man's face. He rolled himself to the revolver and rocked forward until his hand reached it. He sat back, opened the cylinder, and looked at the six brass rounds.

Cynthia stood and went to him. "Papa, don't."

Harrison snapped the cylinder shut and shoved her while struggling for leverage. "Leave me alone! Go away!" he screeched. He pointed the revolver at Cynthia when she tried to take it. "I swear to God, I'll kill you too," he said.

Cynthia's face showed horror as she backed off.

He threw the blanket off, braced his feet on the floor and slowly stood with the revolver pointed at Becky.

"Glad to see you can at least stand on your own two feet that way," Becky said. "Did you threaten to kill your own granddaughter if she refused to shoot Ed too?"

His face cracked a smile that Becky found hard to look at. "I want to thank you and your husband," he said. "I'd begun thinking life was over for me. It's been so sad, seeing my old friends pass. Nobody to talk with about our old adventures anymore. Just an empty house with me and memories. Then, hallelujah, along comes your husband and a reason to live again. One last thrill."

Becky backed up while he approached. She agreed with Nixie. With the fire behind him, he appeared as the devil trudging from the flames of hell. "It's been a long time since the O'Haras, hasn't it?"

A roaring laugh followed. "You know more than I thought. Pretty good for a stinking squaw. Hell, yes. What a grand night on the island that was. Daddy O'Hara couldn't sign his name fast enough. The son of a bitch found out well who he'd crossed. I still dream of his face and his begging while he watched us boys having our way with his wife and daughters." He roared again.

Becky snuck a glance at Cynthia's mortified expression.

"I'd forgotten how glorious it is," Harrison continued. "I'd forgotten how damned sweet it feels." He then made an amazing transformation. His jowls and eyes drooped, deepening his many wrinkles. His mouth hung stupidly. A tremor came to his limbs. He held his hand to his ear as if he were on a phone. "Chief Hawk," a gravelly voice said, "you should be careful in this town. There are evil men here who've done evil things. I regret my family and I were involved. I haven't much time left, sir, and wish to tell you of our sins before I meet my Maker. May we meet somewhere private, sir?" He pressed the barrel to Becky's face. "Oh, dear, Chief, I must've run over a nail. Could you help? I'm too feeble." The hateful face returned with another laugh. "He found out what he wanted to know, just long enough to do a favor for the man who ended his pathetic life." He jerked the revolver twice. "Pow. Pow." He smacked his lips on his fingers. "Mark up another."

Becky listened to a cackle that she was certain could've been heard when Ed fell.

"Now, let me thank you for coming here and making it all complete. Thank you for the pleasure this will be." Harrison gleefully smiled into Becky's eyes like some creature that feeds on human misery.

And, as he spoke, Becky let him feed. She allowed all the darkness from the last two months to enter her again. She felt the agonizing grief and fear tearing her mind and spirit once more while the old man delighted in it. Then, it ended forever with the click of the revolver.

Confusion replaced the smile. Harrison clicked the revolver three more times.

"I removed the firing pin," Becky informed him. She then met his glare with her own.

"Then I'll beat your brains out with it, whore." He swung the revolver toward her head. It struck Becky's injured arm when she dodged.

She yelled out and backed up. In agony, she reached into the back of her waistband and brought Pete's Colt Python to Harrison's nose. She watched him struggle to compose himself. The revolver he held clunked on the floor. She squeezed the trigger.

"Please, Becky," Cynthia cried. She ran over and pulled her grandfather toward his wheelchair.

Becky eased the hammer down and holstered the Python. She found Ed's handcuffs in the back of the belt and followed Cynthia. Harrison screamed curses at them both while they sat him down. Becky clicked one cuff to his wrist and the other the arm of the chair. "I think Ed would want me to tell you you're under arrest," she said.

Three men arrived with Aaron and transported Harrison and Cynthia to the lifesaving station. Becky and Aaron spent the night there. It was the next morning when the county sheriff and deputies arrived. They recovered Pete's body and transported it by ferry to a morgue after their investigation. Late the night, Christmas Eve, Agents Sykes, Feezor, and Sheriff Donaldson arrived. Becky and Aaron watched while Harrison and Quincy were placed into the back of a vehicle. Another waited for Cynthia. She was led out in cuffs by Donaldson.

"Can I speak to her first?" Cynthia asked.

"Make it quick," Donaldson said. "We have a long ride ahead." He stood aside and pretended not to listen.

Hesitantly, Cynthia turned. "When Jimmy and I married," she said, "it was Papa's plan to kill him so I could inherit everything and give it to them. But I'd fallen in love with Jimmy by then and begged Papa to let him live. I convinced him that Jimmy's influence in town would be an asset. I never wanted that little girl and her mother to die. But it was either that or lose the man I loved. You know what that's like Becky. What would you have done to save Ed?"

Becky looked at her without expression.

"I've been trapped in something I never wanted. I was born into it. I know I lied to you many times, but I wasn't lying when I told you I wanted us to be together. The night we had the fish-fry was the most enjoyable for me in a long time. I wanted more of that. I wanted a loving family. I wanted you and Bobby to be that family. Papa just wouldn't allow it."

"You knew what they were," Becky said. "You had a thousand chances to stop them if you wanted."

Cynthia hung her head. "My entire life has been dominated by that man. I've been controlled like a puppet. I'm sorry. I don't expect you to understand it. I don't expect you to forgive me."

"No," Becky said. "I don't understand it. But one day I'll visit you. And I'll decide then if I can forgive the woman I see." She turned and walked toward Aaron's waiting car.

30

Spring came late to Black Lake. But by the third week of April, pink and white dogwood blooms colored the countryside. Warmth and fresh scents invigorated souls. Boats hummed on the lake again. The renovation of the old cotton mill into an apartment building with bright blue paint and white trim transformed the downtown's appearance. The council and new mayor's work toward reopening the lumber plant gave residents and business owners optimism. News crews and reporters no longer held peoples' interest. It was time to move on, time for the town to advance.

Becky helped prepare food in the school cafeteria for the last time on a Friday. She left before the children came to lunch. She hadn't told them it would be her last day, but she knew she would see them again. Being a Friday, it was one of the two days of the week the Black Lake DMV office opened. She went there then stopped for a gallon of milk and buckwheat flour at what once was Parker's Grocery. At the new apartments, she trotted up the old loading ramp in back.

Her and Ed's anniversary picture hung on the wall of her apartment. As was her daily habit, she took time to read the poem beside it– Pearl Wilson's newest work, titled "Our Dance." She checked the clock while putting the groceries away then walked to her room and changed into her new, freshly pressed blue suit. She checked herself in the mirror then knocked on the door across the hall.

"Come on in, cupcake."

Becky stepped in. "What happened to hotcake?" she asked.

"Trying to broaden my vocabulary and sound more worldly." Wendy drew a brush through her hair while sitting on the edge of the bed. She made a few more strokes and held up a mirror before turning to Becky. "Well, I guess it *is* hotcake today. In your case, I'd say the clothes make the woman."

"They feel too starchy."

"I'm sure there's a joke there," Wendy said, "but never mind that. Did you pass?"

Becky sat beside her and produced her North Carolina driver's license.

Wendy squealed a laugh and managed a "Congratulations."

"I know it's terrible," Becky said. "I wasn't ready when he took it."

"Looks like you were trying to hit a high note," Wendy said, still looking and giggling. "It's fine. Goofy pictures are a requirement on licenses."

"We need to get going if you're done laughing."

"Not yet." Wendy pointed to her Avon bag in corner. "Bring it here. You're finally getting made-up today."

"We don't have time."

"Just a little rouge, eyeliner, and lipstick. Don't argue or I'll beat you with my leg. Besides, Aaron is coming to drive us over."

Becky gave in. She sat still and watched Wendy work. She remembered how difficult the first few months were. But, since then, every day brought improvement. Today, more color had returned to Wendy's face. The laughter was more real.

"All done. What'cha think?"

Becky smiled at the face in the mirror Wendy held. "I love it," she said.

"No. Don't cry. You'll make it run." Wendy pecked a tissue on the corner of Becky's eyes. "Now, one more thing." She reached for Becky's ponytail and struggled.

"No."

"Yes." The elastic band came out. Wendy brushed. "Remember, you'll be getting your picture made again. This one needs to be good."

"Anyone home?"

"Back her, handsome," Wendy called.

Aaron stepped in and whistled. "Wow. Who's this?"

"Make her get ready, Aaron," Becky said. "We only have five minutes."

"Fetch hither yon leg so I may travel."

"You're really looking good today," Aaron said, handing Wendy the prosthetic. "How's the walking coming?"

Much practice enabled Wendy to put it on in seconds. "Excellent," she said. Then to Becky: "Did you tell the munchkins they'd better be ready for the wicked witch's return next fall?"

"Yes. They're looking forward to it."

Wendy pulled herself up to her walker. "Such warped kids," she said.

The town council and Mayor Clayton sat in their respective positions in the meeting chamber. Marge Bowers stood at a table facing them.

"Sorry I'm late," Becky said. She stepped beside Marge and watched Aaron help Wendy take a seat amongst a small crowd that included Will and Lily Baily, Pearl Wilson, and Sheriff Donaldson. To the side with a cameraman stood Hudson Perry. Ed's badge lay beside a bible on the table.

"Are we all ready?" Marge asked with a look to the mayor.

"If Mrs. Hawk now meets the last qualification," Clayton said.

Becky held up her driver's license and laughter filled the room.

Clayton nodded with a grin.

"Place your left hand on the bible and raise your right," Marge said.

Yet another tire squall sent Wendy's face near the dashboard. She sat back, tightened her seatbelt, and squinted at the red light thirty feet ahead. "Allow me to repeat, Chief, you persuade the car to stop, not demand it."

"I think I did better with the DMV man beside me," said Becky. She crawled the patrol car forward when the light turned green.

"Sure he didn't just pass you so he wouldn't have to ride with you again?"

Becky looked for a parking place in the crowded Courthouse Square. "Looks like I may have to parallel park like we practiced."

"Absolutely not. Drive down and find a nice, safe parking lot."

"But you'll have to walk a long way if I do that."

"I'll wait in the car," Wendy said. "It'll give my nerves time to settle."

A bailiff directed Becky to courtroom B, where Beverly Graham of Bolton County social services waited in the hall.

"Everything ready?" Becky asked.

"Yes," said Graham. "The judge just needs to sign the order." She smiled when she looked at the badge. "Congratulations. You're the first female officer I've met."

"Thank you. How is he?"

"Much better than when you visited him last. I began seeing a lot of improvement after he adjusted in the group home. He's talking more and doesn't seem as afraid. Yesterday, he even asked for the articles Hudson Perry wrote about you. I was reluctant for him to read them, but he insisted."

"So, he knows everything now?"

"Yes. But I believe it's better than him finding out in pieces at a time. Learning everything seems to have done him good."

"I'm glad," said Becky. "I was worried about having to explain it all to him."

"Before we go in," Graham said, "could you tell me if you've ever heard him talk about spirits? I ask only because of something he said after he read the articles. Something about spirits working as a whole. Just thought it odd."

Becky smiled. "It's a good sign," she said.

A bailiff opened the door. "Judge Queen is ready."

Becky adjusted her tie and followed Graham into the courtroom.

Thoughtful experience showed on Judge Queen's face while he read Graham's report. It took him ten minutes before he looked toward Becky. "Just a few questions, Mrs. Hawk. Excuse me—Chief

Hawk. In my opinion you *will* be able to provide the ward with the compassionate and healthy environment he needs. But I wonder about the size of your apartment. Will there be room for three people if I grant this conservatorship?"

"I have a foldout sofa and two rooms, your Honor. I hope to find us a bigger place soon."

Judge Queen appeared satisfied. "Also, you will be responsible for his legal decisions. Have you spoken to an attorney to help in rectifying the wrongs that have been done against this young man? As I see it, there is a large inheritance that was illegally taken from him, not to mention the possible other personal damages."

"Yes, your honor. I've spoken to many lawyers. Several have agreed to only be paid when a judgement is entered."

"Very well. Conservatorship in this case is granted." Judge Queen signed the order.

"Thank you, your Honor," said Becky, not worrying any longer if her makeup ran. "Where is he?" she asked Graham.

"In the judges' chamber."

Becky followed Graham through a door.

He sat beside another social worker.

"Hello Bobby."

"Osiyo," he said.

ACKNOWLEDGEMENTS

I want to express my gratitude to
Luz, Jeff, Laura, Kelly, Eddie, and Tina.

ABOUT THE AUTHOR

Robbie Lanier is a former law enforcement officer, whose positions over his thirty-year career included patrolman, investigator, police chief, bailiff, and civil process server. He now enjoys spending his retirement traveling to the beaches and mountains of North Carolina with his family.

He gained an interest in Native American history and customs from his father, who was a history and math teacher. In connection with this, he enjoys flint knapping and bow making. He also enjoys fishing and SCUBA diving.

Robbie has written short stories for over twenty years. *Black Lake* is his first novel.

He lives in Lexington, NC with his wife, Sherri , and has a son, Jerry.

TESSELLATA

"The law of evolution is that the strongest survives.
Yes, and the strongest, in the existence of any social
species, are those who are most social. In human terms,
most ethical... There is no strength to be gained from
hurting one another.
Only weakness."

Ursula K. Le Guin

Made in the USA
Monee, IL
05 June 2025